RIPE FRUIT

WELL-SEASONED EROTICA

RIPE FRUIT

Well-Seasoned Erotica

Edited by
Marcy Sheiner

Published in the United States by Cleis Press Inc.,
P.O. Box 14684, San Francisco, California 94114.
Printed in the United States.
Cover design: Scott Idleman
Cover photograph: David Steinberg
Book design: Karen Quigg
Logo art: Juana Alicia
First Edition.
10 9 8 7 6 5 4 3 2 1

"Rome" by Emma Kaufman appeared on the Erotica Readers Association website, July/August, 2001. "Daffodils" by Sally Bellerose was originally published in *Pillow Talk,* edited by Lesléa Newman, Alyson Books 1998. "Looking is Listening...and Shaving" by Rachel Heath was first published in *A Movement of Eros,* edited by Heather Findlay, Masquerade Books, 1996, and again in *On Our Backs* March/April, 1994. "Cotton Gloves" by Joli Agnew was originally published in September 2000 on the KUMA, Black Lesbian Erotica website. "The Erotic Adventures of Jim and Louella Parsons" Bertice Berry was originally published in *Best Black Women's Erotica*, edited by Blanche Richardson, Cleis Press 2001. "Addressing The Intern Situation" by Erin Cressida Wilson was originally published in *The Erotica Project by* Erin Cressida Wilson and Lillian Ann Slugocki, Cleis Press, 2000.

And here's to you, Mrs. Robinson

CONTENTS

MARCY SHEINER

Introduction

Wise. Seductive. Savvy. Willing. Horny. Mrs. Robinson. Dried up. Wrinkly. Pathetic. Predatory. Grateful. Mrs. Robinson.

These are some of the stereotypes used to describe older women's sexuality. While the stories in *Ripe Fruit* prove that there's a grain of truth in each one of them, the women in these pages are so wildly divergent that as stereotypes they almost cancel each other out. Remember Rod Stewart's "Maggie," who keeps him out of school with her insatiable libido? She'll rock your world, but she'll devour you whole. Then again, as any long-married man will tell you, she's lost interest in sex altogether. On the other hand, she wants it so bad she's grateful to get it—according to numerous young repairmen.

As in every area of female sexuality, the truth is hidden beneath so many layers of social conditioning and media imagery that it's difficult to discern myth from reality. We haven't been seriously exploring women's sexuality from our own viewpoint long enough to know the truth, and I suspect that fifty years from now stories about older women's sexuality will be a lot different than the ones in this collection, simply because we will have evolved further.

In putting together this anthology, the most important thing to me was that the stories be honest, to show how we ourselves see and experience sex in the late twentieth and early twenty-first centuries. I'm sick to death of baby boomers claiming that we're so different from our ancestors as to comprise an entirely new species—one that won't age, gracefully or otherwise. You know what I'm talking about: all those books that tell us we're still smart, sexy, strong, and gorgeous; that if we eat right, exercise, and do our kegels we'll still be jogging and fucking beyond a hundred; that we need never show (much less feel, God forbid) the ravages of time. While it's true that advances in medicine, technology, and the care and feeding of the human body have made it possible to stay healthier longer, we are still made of flesh and sinew, blood and bone: A body is still a body—and a kiss is still a kiss.

Some of the stories in *Ripe Fruit* express loss, sorrow, or even, as in "This Pussy Retired," complete secession from the sexual arena. This is intentional: I did not want this anthology to be an exercise in cheerleading, vapid celebration, or politically correct "empowerment." Women, young and old, deserve to know the whole truth—and the truth is a lot more complex than facile celebrations would reveal. Yet, even with a scrupulous editor purposely seeking out the more realistic and perhaps less thrilling aspects of the aging process, the overall tone of this collection still ended up being more celebratory than not: Older women *do* love and enjoy sex, sometimes more than they did in their youth.

One of the reasons for this is that we're no longer shy about telling our partners what we like in bed. The women in "Trooper" and "Lady Luck" have no trouble showing and telling their partners—who are much younger than they, and pick-ups to boot—exactly how to give them satisfaction. In "Looking Is Listening...and Shaving," the narrator confesses her fetish to a lover, on their very first night together. Yes, she's a little bit embarrassed, but she doesn't give the embarrassment much attention or power. The audacious Madelon of "Exorbitant Pleasures" feels no compunctions about creating intrigue to spice up her sex life. In "Riding the Face Train," an old broad not only sits on a younger woman's face at a sex party, but brazenly returns for seconds. No apologies for her, no coy hints or awkward giggles. By the time she's put in five decades, the lady not only knows what turns her on but feels entitled to get it.

Another thing about us crones: We're not so hung up on "sexual identity." I remember the youthful confusion and obsession with labels: lesbian, heterosexual, or, scariest of all, bisexual. Well, if this book is any indication, by the time we turn fifty we've gotten past this red herring and see it for what it is—just another barrier to pleasure. "A Wardrobe of Souls" examines this issue head on. The women in "Wild Roses" and "Buzzed" put it aside altogether to fuck whomever they damn well please. Again, no apologies. Short shrift is made of the partner's gender, or any political ramifications of the shape of their genitals.

Not so, alas, with body image, which continues to plague us. If we had problems liking our bodies when they were young and firm, what are we to do about sagging breasts, stretch marks, unwanted hair, and moles? The aging process is so cruel: Just when we're beginning to learn self-acceptance, our bodies challenge us to extend the concept beyond what's reasonable. Still, we don't let these feelings interfere with our pleasure. One woman hung up about her aging body discovers "The Truth" by jumping past her fears with two men who find her luscious, droopy tits and all.

Another painful aspect of the aging process: We realize that we took our youth for granted. ("Youth is wasted on the young.") The narrator in "Addressing the Intern Situation" puts it most elegantly: "Every time I flipped my braids over my shoulders, every time a drop of sweat came off me, men wanted to flock to drink it up. I had no idea. I thought I was just given this power and that it would last forever."

All the so-called wisdom we acquire from living past fifty inevitably causes some regrets. In "Send in the Clowns" one woman faces a lifetime of mistaken choices. In "The Art of Losing," another mourns the losses of time. And many stories, far too many to publish, deal with the ultimate loss: death. Only a couple of the stories in this collection—"Play mysty for Me" and "Wild Roses"—deal directly with death; but I received ten times that many starring the Grim Reaper. When pages wet with tears began arriving, I, who'd worried about being superficial, was rudely thrust into a morass of grief. But of course, I suddenly realized—what did I expect to find in this territory? As a character in the movie *Funny Girl* says, "That's life for you—someone's always dying."

The greatest bonus that emerged from this theme, and the biggest surprise, was the depth of the characters who inhabit the stories. In all the erotic anthologies that I've edited, never have I come across such a vividly drawn group of fascinating and memorable women. When called on to develop older female characters, writers created intensely interesting people. Because they live their lives and take their pleasure without apology or compromise, these women are characters with a capital C.

There's Nola, the cowgirl in "Every Baby Finds Her Legs," who turns down champagne for beer and travels in a male world with graceful self-possession. There's Ordella in "Cotton Gloves," a proper grandmother by day, a red-hot momma by night. There's the "fecund" Annie of "Daffodils," the take-charge big sister in "A Dowager's Hump," the friends-till-death-do-us-part of "Tell Me Everything." I've lived with these characters for months now, and I'm not likely to forget them anytime soon, if ever.

So allow me to introduce you to a group of extremely juicy women. May they give readers, young and old alike, hope for a fecund and self-possessed sex life well into a ripe old age.

Marcy Sheiner
Emeryville. California
February 2002

JANE UNDERWOOD

Tell Me Everything

"So what else is new?" Lena asks.

I switch the telephone receiver to my left ear, because after an hour my right ear is starting to hurt. Then I tell Lena about the job I applied for selling diet cookies.

"I know it's an oxymoron," I say, "but the woman swears the cookies are delicious and that she lost seven pounds and made three thousand dollars in three weeks."

"I could eat ten cookies right now while I'm sitting here talking to you," Lena replies in her I'm-getting-too-fat tone of voice. "But I can't sell. *You* can sell. Who would buy diet cookies from someone with these hips? I've gained ten pounds in the last ten days. You, of course, are thin as a stick. So what else? Tell me something juicy. Tell me something new."

Lena and I have known each other for twenty years, and this is our zillionth phone conversation. We first met while standing at a deli counter in San Francisco. I ordered a bear claw, she ordered a bagel with lox and cream cheese.

"What's lox?" I asked, turning toward the New Yawk accent.

"Lox," said Lena, looking intently into my green goy eyes. "You know, *lox*."

I didn't know.

We started to chat. Lena, like me, had just moved to San Francisco. She was from Queens. I was from Kansas. We were both in our mid-twenties, both lived in the funky Mission district.

We walked out of the deli together. When we got to the corner of 18th and Castro, I stopped at the curb because the light was red. There were no cars in sight, but I was a girl who had been taught to wait until the red lights turned green. Lena, on the other hand, had never waited for a light in her life, if she could possibly avoid it.

Lena is still faster than I am at crossing streets, but I am faster than she is at a few other things.

I know what Lena wants me to tell her now. She wants me to tell her whether I've had sex recently. That's one of the areas in which I tend to be faster than Lena—sometimes, anyway. Like when I'm on a roll between extended bouts of celibacy.

"There's nothing to tell," I say. "Yesterday I sprinkled all my carpets with nontoxic flea powder. It took me two hours down on my hands and knees."

"I'm impressed."

"Oh yeah, and I slept with Joe."

"You what?"

"I slept with Joe, but it was no big deal really. It was more of an aberration. You know, a one-time occurrence."

Joe is my ex. Our relationship is definitely over. It was over a long time ago. It cannot be resurrected, resuscitated, or reinstituted. But passion dies hard, celibacy can suck, and sometimes we all do desperate, stupid things. Lena already knows my history with Joe, of course, because she has been privy to every detail of my life since the moment we realized we'd be friends until death do us part.

Most men don't share such things with each other the way women do, and I don't get it. How can they go through life this way? Who do they talk with, other than their wives or girlfriends, about the daily stuff of life?

"How did it happen?" Lena asks. Her voice holds no hint of judgment.

I begin my tale. "Well," I say, "he showed up at Jackie's birthday bash. Can you believe that? He doesn't even know Jackie, but he knew a friend of a friend of a friend. Anyway, I drank a little too much champagne—OK, a lot too much—and we ended up back at his place slow-dancing by candlelight to a bunch of old Inkspots records. Joe has preserved his entire record collection, in mint condition. I mean, we were dancing to the original 45s."

"Does Joe even own a CD player?"

"He owns a tape player but not a CD player."

"What a Neanderthal. OK, so then what?"

"So I happened to be wearing my skimpiest summer dress, spaghetti straps, no bra, and as we're dancing, he slips the straps down off my shoulders, and I say to him, in a dumb giggly way because we also smoked some pot, 'Joe! What are you doing?' And he pulls the top half of my dress down to my waist, reaches up, cups my bare breasts in his hands, and says to me, 'I'm doing exactly what I want to be doing.' As soon as he says that, I become completely, one hundred percent gushing wet. I'm talking sopping, all the way down my thighs. At that point I just lost the will to protest. So we kept on dancing, only now Joe's hands were squeezing my breasts instead of my waist."

"My God," Lena whispers loudly, "I'm creaming in my jeans."

"And *then,*" I say, "about half an hour later, we stopped dancing, and he told me to go stand in the middle of the room. And I started to shiver because...."

Here I pause for effect. Do men ever pause for effect? Perhaps. Male standup comics do it. Politicians who are giving speeches do it. But do men pause for effect when chatting one-on-one with their best friends? Do men really even *have* best friends?

"Because?" Lena prods. The static in the wires crackles and sparkles between us.

"Because...by that time all I was wearing were my new high heels."

"Get out of here!" Lena half hisses, half yells. "You mean the black ones with ankle straps that you got at the flea market last month for two dollars? Oh, my God, I love those shoes. Go on."

Do men talk to each other about their shoes? No. And yet shoes clearly are important, and they are not the same as sports. Shoes go on and off our feet every day. We don't just wear them to work. We wear them to and from sex, love, and all the rest of life. How can you not have anyone to talk with about your shoes?

"OK. So then he put on that same album. The cut where the woman sings the song without any words, the song that goes on and on and on. You know the one I mean, right?"

Lena moans a low, feral moan. "Yeah, I know the one. So then what happened?"

"I'm a rat, that's what. Joe dropped the pellet, I dashed through the maze."

"I want to go through the maze with you," Lena says. "Go back and start over from the very beginning."

I'm happy to oblige her. I don't mind going back through the maze. I love mazes. Most women do. Do men love mazes? I think not. I think that most men prefer to turn back as soon as they realize they have entered a maze—that, or karate chop their way through it. Unless it has something to do with baseball. But that can't be right, can it? Can that be right?

"I can't believe this!" Lena declares when I'm done telling her my Joe story. "But what do I know? I'm telling you, I want to tape this story so I can play it back to Marvin. Just say it over again and let me record it. I'm not kidding! I'm serious!"

Marvin, Lena's boyfriend, is dependable and true, which is more than I could ever say for Joe. But Lena rates her sex life with Marvin, on a scale of one to ten, as a two. On their first date, Marvin wore furry, pointy-toed leopard shoes, plus twenty-five airplane-wing pins on his cardigan sweater. Lena has never totally forgiven him for this.

Joe, I have to say, was a nine. With the addition of true love he would've been a ten. I decided to hold out for a ten, and I've been on hold ever since. These days, I'm just trying to keep from drowning in the waters of pregeriatric dating, as in: Sagging Siren Meets Potbellied Ladies' Man. Occasionally, though, one of these guys does manage to charm the pants off me. When that happens, a special part of my brain leaps to the thought, *Wait until Lena hears about this!*

Here's the thing: Much of the time, describing sex to Lena is better than actually having it. This is because Lena, like myself, is capable of picking up in her imagination where reality leaves off. She understands how important it is to see the full range of possibilities in every situation, even if those possibilities never come to fruition. Women like to look underneath things. We like to pick them up, turn them around in the light, approach them from all angles.

When Lena wants to hear a hot, voluptuous story, and I haven't got one to tell, I do my best to squeeze every last nuance out of an accidental touch at the grocery store, or a passing glance from the UPS man that could conceivably have been construed as seductive. Then I take these crumbs and arrange them on a platter for Lena to behold. Invariably, she exclaims at how delicious my meals—my sexual banquet—must have been. Lena knows how to be envious in a way that makes me feel good, not bad. Sometimes she even exaggerates her envy for the sake of making me feel better about one or more of my lacks. She exclaims over my supposedly enviable sex life because she knows that I am envious, conversely, of the fact that she lives with a man, even though he is Marvin.

The truth, and Lena already knows this too, is that although I'm glad I haven't settled for a Marvin, the tradeoff is that I often go through long periods of surviving on nothing but the aforementioned crumbs. Lena perceives these crumbs as meals because I dress them up for her with plenty of spices, sauces, and sprigs of parsley. I do my best to keep our conversations interesting.

Sometimes I have to remind Lena, at the same time that I'm reminding myself, that when sexually frustrated, one can channel the vast imbroglio of pent-up erotic energy into other worthwhile pursuits.

For example, I just got through telling Lena about how, not all that long ago, I bought the *Reader's Digest Household Hints & Handy Tips* for $12.95, in order to enter the *Reader's Digest* sweepstakes. The official contest rules said you didn't have to buy the book to enter, but does anyone really believe that?

"I've begun to master the fine art of stain removal and other acts of domestic repair," I said. "And did you know you can highlight your hair with coffee and fight ants with rosemary?"

"Yeah? Fascinating."

"I'm also making pomander balls."

"What are pomander balls?"

"Pomander balls. You know, *pomander* balls. For your closets. You stick cloves into oranges."

"Uh-huh. That's it?" I imagined Lena stirring her Earl Grey tea, gazing out her kitchen window toward her beloved garden, her mind drifting toward the weeds clustered around the jasmine, weeds that had suddenly become more interesting than what I was saying.

"Yeah, that's it. I mean no, wait. I almost forgot! Remember Tom? Tom the shy mechanic?"

"Of course I remember Tom. Tom, your old 'shy' boyfriend who never seemed all that shy to me. Tom who hung a seashell from your nipple back in 1977."

"Right. That Tom."

"He was slim but muscular, with great chiseled hands, and he had long brown hair that he tied back into a ponytail. He took you on a motorcycle ride out into the country on your first date, back when you didn't have to wear helmets, and when you got home and were sitting on the couch talking, he interrupted you mid-sentence to announce that he couldn't stop thinking about licking your clit. Later you went skinny-dipping at Lake Berryessa, and that's when he hung the seashell from your nipple. How am I doing so far?"

"Jesus, I can't believe you remember all that! Well anyway, I bumped into him last week when I took my car in for a smog check."

"You're kidding! Why didn't you tell me?"

"I *am* telling you. Now."

"Yeah, how many days later? But never mind that. So what happened?"

"I invited him over."

"And?"

"And we were having a nice conversation, and then his hand brushed my thigh, and then it brushed even more than my thigh."

"You're kidding. After all this time? It's been years!"

"Uh-huh."

"So?"

"So I saw him again the day before yesterday, and you'll never guess what he pulled out of his pocket."

Here I pause for effect.

"You're right," says Lena, "I'll never guess. So tell me. What did he pull out of his pocket?"

"A collar."

"Get out of here!" Lena says. "Oh, my God, go on."

"He made it especially for me. Nobody's ever made me a collar before, Lena. It was so sweet, I was touched."

"Get out of here!" Lena screams. "I can't believe I'm hearing this. Since when are you into wearing collars?"

"I'm not. I mean, not regularly," I say. "I don't think Tom would've even made it for me, if I hadn't told him about the time Jim took me as a slave on a leash to a Halloween party. Remember that party? I'm sure I told you about it. You know, that time when Melanie wouldn't go with Jim because she said she needed to lose ten pounds before she could feel comfortable parading around half-naked at a party, even though Jim kept telling her that she looked perfectly gorgeous just the way she was?"

"Vaguely. I remember it vaguely, though I still find it hard to believe that Melanie wasn't jealous of you."

"She wasn't. Not at all. They've got the parameters of their relationship all worked out. He's totally devoted to her, and she knows it. I was just doing him a favor, because he needed somebody to be at the end of his leash."

"Whatever. Oh wait, now it's coming back to me. Was that the time when you wore the slinky see-through dress and the feathery Mardi Gras mask made out of leather?"

"Yep. In fact, I never would've agreed to go without the mask. I would've felt way too exposed and embarrassed and a little silly wearing a collar and a leash. But with the mask on, it was OK. I could watch all the men looking at me, and I could boldly look back at them but still be hidden."

"So you think that the Halloween story was what inspired Tom to make you the collar?"

"That had to be it. Plus he likes to make things with his hands. I mean, he's an artist at heart, not a mechanic."

"That's very nice. So then what happened?"

"OK, so…oh, I forgot to mention one thing. Before he came over, he called me up and said, 'Put on a short black skirt with no panties on underneath.' Then, after he got here, and we were lying on the bed still dressed and talking, he leaned closer, ran his finger along my thigh, and whispered into my ear, 'I made something for you.' I asked him what it was, and he said, 'A collar. I think it's going to look very pretty on you.'"

"He really said that? Those exact words?"

"Verbatim. I swear it. Then he reached into his pocket—his pocket!—and pulled out a really soft black rope with a small loop at one end and a knot at the other. He wrapped it twice around my neck, then slipped the knot through the loop and said, 'My Boy Scout training came in handy for this project.'"

"His Boy Scout training?" Lena squeals.

"Uh-huh. Then he slips a finger under the collar and pulls me up onto my knees, very gently, and then, still holding the collar, he…."

"Wait!" Lena shouts. "I'm getting wet again. I need to get my tape recorder. I want to play this back to Marvin. I want him to hear every word of it. He has absolutely no idea that sex can be like this. I'm telling you, he's a great guy and I love him, but he hasn't got a clue."

A few seconds later I hear a click and a whir.

"All right," says Lena. "Go ahead." The tone of her voice is richly textured with her knowledge of my past and her interest in my future—her fascination with it, her commitment to it. This interest is a caress that coaxes, that urges, that offers me the ultimate gift: the gift I have always yearned for but never totally gotten from any man.

"Tell me," says Lena with an intensity and a focus that reaches down into the very depths of my soul, "everything."

EMMA KAUFMANN

Rome

She is waiting at a table in the hotel bar, all chrome and mirrors, staring blankly ahead of her.

Why on earth had she let herself be talked into coming here? Oh, please, Mummy, Saskia had pleaded, it'll be so much fun. We never spend any time together. It'll give us a chance to get reacquainted. And so, reluctantly, she had let herself be persuaded. Then, on their very first night here, Saskia had gone to the hotel disco, had met someone called Anthony, and had hardly been seen since.

A man comes into focus, sitting at another table, looking back at her. He's about her age, well-dressed, strands of gray running through his chestnut hair. Catherine lowers her eyes, unwilling to make contact. Not that she hasn't enjoyed the attention from the Italian men while she's been here—she has: the low whistling in the street, shoulders nudging against her, their hot breath on her face as they lean in, whispering, *Bella! Bellissima!*

It had been exhilarating to feel their dark eyes peering out at her from the shaded shop fronts as she walked through the narrow streets, the sun beating down on her. Only yesterday, she had gotten completely lost, and a handsome, wiry man, deeply tanned, had stepped out of one of the doorways, frightening her a little, and asked, "You are lost?" and she, flustered, had replied, "No, I'm all right, thank you," before hurrying on, her heart pounding.

But that was outdoors. She had savored the unthreatening contact with the local men, who could be shooed away with a wave of her hand. This was what she hated—men who, like her, had time on their hands. Men in between business meetings, who sensed a kindred spirit in her, someone with whom they could while away a few hours before their plane took off, carrying them back to their wives and kids.

He has walked over and is standing next to her table.

"Hello," he says pleasantly. She glances at her watch. 1:20. Where on earth is Saskia? She had said that she would bring Anthony along and they would all have lunch together.

"Can I buy you a drink?" His accent is foreign, but she can't place it.

She shakes her head. She doesn't want to offend him. She supposes that if she were looking for a little fling, then he would be quite a suitable specimen.

"Thanks, but I'm waiting for someone," she says hastily, thinking that the excuse sounds hollow. She can hear Saskia's voice in her ear—Saskia was always trying to set her up, ever since she'd divorced her husband when Saskia was eight. *Don't be so picky. Why don't you give the guy a break?*

"Are you sure?" says the man, raising an eyebrow quizzically. She nods.

So, she's choosy, what of it? Since her last relationship ended a year ago she has tremendously enjoyed being single, she is perfectly content with her life. Now that Saskia is away at university, it is pretty much perfect. Or so she tells herself. She twists the stem of the empty wineglass in front of her and stares at it. When she looks up, the man has disappeared.

"I'm sorry we're late." She smells a waft of perfume as Saskia bends down to kiss her. "Anthony was nice enough to take me to Prada," she says breathlessly, straightening up and shoving her Jackie O sunglasses back over her long blonde hair. Looking at Saskia's peachy skin, her toned body wrapped in a tiny slip of a dress, Catherine once again feels old, dried up, ancient.

"Your daughter certainly knows how to shop, Mrs. Fielding. My feet are killing me."

She stands up to shake hands with this man, this boyfriend of her daughter's, and when they make contact her stomach lurches. It's a strange moment, because he's still talking and she's not taking in a word. Everything passes in slow motion. She watches as Saskia laughs at something he is saying, while all the time she is drawn to him, helplessly, like metal filings toward a magnet.

"Oh, please call me Catherine," she says. The disconcerting thing is that he's returning her gaze. He too has had a reaction. His hazel eyes widen, his brow furrows, he grips her hand more firmly, and his mouth—the shape somehow so utterly familiar to her—opens and closes as if he is about to say something more.

Dimly, she notices that Saskia is looking at her oddly. "I'm starving," Saskia says. "I can't be bothered going out again. Shall we just eat at the hotel?"

"Yes. Yes, of course," Catherine says, finally pulling her hand away and picking up her handbag, sneaking a glance at Anthony. Why does she feel as if she has seen him somewhere before? Saskia has told her that he's twenty-six, has lived in Rome for a year now—yet she is sure she hasn't seen him while she's been here.

As they walk into the restaurant and take their places at the table she has the oddest sensation, as if she can't breathe. It's so humiliating to feel like this, her whole body opening up to him, like a flower unfurling under the sun. It's not that he's particularly good looking, but when he smiles her pulse quickens; when he runs his hand through his cropped, sandy hair she knots her fingers together under the tablecloth, feeling an unbearable friction all over her skin.

She talks about the museums and art galleries she has visited during the long afternoons when Saskia was out with him and he listens, mesmerized. It's as if he is no longer aware of Saskia's presence.

"It's such a shame," says Saskia, breaking up some ciabatta with her perfectly manicured fingers, "that we have to go back tomorrow."

"I don't know about that. I've had just about enough of the Italian climate. I think I'll be glad to get back to Berkshire, to the miserable English summer they've been having back home."

As Anthony picks up the bottle of red wine, Catherine looks at his long fingers, the back of his hand matted with honey-colored hair. She can almost feel them, slipping into her pussy, first one, then another, making her tingle. She sips her wine. It tastes of metal, of nothing. Her tastebuds have withered. All she is aware of is the blood pounding in her brain, and a need, a desperate need, to go to her room, to lie down.

"Order the *linguine con cozze* for me, will you," Saskia tells Anthony. "I really need to pee."

Catherine feels a sense of desperation, and is about to follow Saskia to the toilet to avoid being alone with Anthony. She half rises, puts down her napkin, sees Saskia winding her way through the tables, when his hand closes over hers.

"You seem awfully nervous," he says, turning her hand over and letting the tips of his fingers rest in the center of her palm. She pulls her hand free.

"I don't feel too well. It's the heat."

He laughs. "You don't recognize me, do you?"

The waiter is approaching now and asks her what she will have. She picks something at random. He looks at her with a puzzled expression as she tries to formulate the words, *raviolacci alle erbe,* but they stick in her throat. Anthony gives her order in perfect Italian, and the waiter nods in comprehension. She is grateful to him for helping her out but is also acutely aware that he must find her unsophisticated compared to her daughter.

"Have we met somewhere before?" she asks, as soon as the waiter has turned away.

"You've no idea what a crush I used to have on you," he says.

What on earth is he talking about? She picks up her fork and rolls it between her thumb and forefinger before placing it back on the white linen tablecloth. Saskia will be back any minute, she thinks, lifting up the fork again and stabbing it into the tablecloth.

Anthony moves his chair closer.

"I don't..." she says, stumbling over the words, "have a clue what you mean."

"You used to date my dad, Craig Peterson." His leg brushes hers and the fork clatters to the floor.

"Oh?"

Yes, of course, she thinks, relieved. That was why he had seemed so familiar. This strange sensation, that she has been struggling to explain ever since she met him—surely now it can be explained away? She barely remembers meeting him, as a sixteen-year-old boy, but now that she looks more closely she realizes that he is a sexier, younger version of his father. That was why he stared when they first met, simply because he recognized her, and for some reason had not wanted to mention it in front of Saskia. What a stupid old fool she was for thinking that he was attracted to her.

"Yes, I think I do remember you," she says. His hand grips her thigh and she laughs nervously.

"You look even better now." She looks into his eyes and knows now that he is serious. She is not altogether sure that she wants to be wanted.

He pulls out a card and scribbles on it. She sees Saskia returning, waiting impatiently, fiddling with her hair, for a dessert trolley to be pushed past her.

"How about catching up on old times? Will you meet me later?"

"Don't be ridiculous," she says, plucking the card out of his hand and trying to push it under her side plate, but missing and watching it fall to the floor. His knee presses against the silky length of her inner thigh; he pushes her skirt up with his hand, insistent.

"About four?"

"It's impossible," she whispers, moments before Saskia slides into the chair on the other side of him. The warm pressure of his leg retreats.

"I see you two have been getting acquainted. I hope you're not telling him all about my bad habits?"

"No, of course not, darling," Catherine says, bending down to the floor to retrieve Anthony's card and place it in her handbag. She looks at his trousers, charcoal gray, eyeing his crotch, gulping down air. When she finally straightens up, he is leaning toward Saskia. She feels an unexpected stab of jealousy.

She has no idea how she manages to get through the meal, but if she acts strangely, Saskia does not comment on it. At last it is over and he has left. She tells Saskia that she is going to lie down, but Saskia, a little drunk from the wine, insists on dawdling in her room to talk about Anthony.

"What do you think of him?"

Catherine sits down on the bed and kicks off her shoes. "I don't know. He seems very nice. Is it serious?"

"God, no. Just a bit of fun. He's so adorable." Adorable is not a word that Catherine would have used to describe him. "Plenty of cash too, of course."

Catherine stretches out on the bed. "Well, I'm pleased for you. Now, let me get some rest." She just needs to go to sleep and by the time she wakes up her head will be clear and the surreal events of the past hour will have passed.

Waking at half past three, she gets up and knocks on Saskia's door. No reply. She takes the elevator to the ground floor and exits the hotel.

She hails a taxi and in broken Italian tries to read the address from the card. She is furious to find that sleep has not dampened her curiosity or her ardor. The taxi driver looks at her blankly, so she hands him the card. Finally he drives to Anthony's address.

And now here she is, standing nervously outside a door heavily decorated with iron swirls, on the third floor of an ancient apartment block. Not a sound is heard. She rings the doorbell and he lets her in. She blurts out, "Saskia. She's not likely to come here?"

He pulls her into the hall and closes the door. "No. She doesn't know about this apartment."

"I don't know why I'm here," she says, taking a few steps and peering through the open door into his bedroom, at the enormous bed, the gray and purple striped sheets half pulled off.

"Let's not talk. We don't have much time. I said I'd meet Saskia at eight."

As Anthony unbuttons her blouse her vision blurs. "I want to, but what about Saskia?"

He kisses her and she trembles, all thoughts vanishing. Once they are naked on the bed and he begins to touch her she becomes totally relaxed, limp as a rag doll. He covers her breasts and back with kisses, then strokes her thighs, rests his mouth in the hollows at the back of her knees. She closes her eyes and descends into blackness, the pleasure almost unbearable.

His lips are resting on her eyelid.

"I had a real thing about you," he whispers, "and what made it worse was that you never seemed to notice I was alive." His hand moves over her breast, his fingers circling the nipple, increasing the friction, bit by bit. She sighs. *Don't stop.*

"All these years you've been in my head. All this time I've been looking for a woman like you. Then by chance, you turn up. I could hardly believe it when I saw you today."

She smiles. "It's certainly some coincidence." But she is in no mood to let him wander down memory lane. Her body is aching for him. They only have a few hours and she needs to make the most of it, to indulge herself, to wring every ounce of pleasure from the experience.

Greedily she drags her tongue down his body, along the thick chest hair. Naked, he is nothing like his father, or at least she can't remember what it felt like having sex with Craig. Their union had lasted less than a year and had not been particularly memorable.

She feels like a starving person as she lowers her head to his crotch, almost devouring him. The smell of his cock, that heady scent of musk, instills in her a state of total wantonness. Taking him into her mouth she drags her wetness over his stubbly chin, shudders as she feels his mouth find her pussy, open her up, and slide his tongue inside. After a while it feels as if she is being turned inside out.

After the first time she comes, she slithers off the bed and he falls on top of her. He ploughs her from behind, his skillful fingers all over her, caressing her breasts as she struggles up on all fours. She moans, coming a second time. After that she loses track of what they are doing, only that she is dissolving, breaking apart, every particle of her body swollen with desire. She is satiated, then the next moment her pussy goes rigid and the urgent craving begins again.

She doesn't feel self-conscious at all. She is only aware of the hairiness of his chest, his balls, his legs. The soft hairs caress her whole body, the sensation enveloping. Decadently, she plays with herself while he looks on, intently. She feels like a queen.

Now she lies against him, spent, her fingers sunk into his chest hair, looking up at his head, flopped back on the pillow.

"You were incredible," Anthony tells her. "The way you move...."

"Let's not spoil things by analyzing them." She gets up and looks at him. "Besides, don't you have to meet Saskia soon?"

He sits up, rubs his hair so that it stands up like a cockscomb. "I could cancel. We could spend the night together."

She pulls on her underwear.

"No. She'd wonder where I'd gotten to. And besides—"

"What?"

"Nothing." Even after what she has done, the stark fact remains that Saskia is more important to her than Anthony. It would become too tricky if she came clean to her daughter. She finishes dressing, then walks to the mirror set in the wardrobe door. She picks up his hairbrush from beside the bed and brushes her shoulder-length hair until it glistens like burnished pewter. His words float into her mind...*crush...on you.*

She stares back into her hooded eyes that someone—Craig?—had once compared to a bloodhound's. Anthony is reflected in the mirror, his head propped up on one arm. She still wants him, but knows that she will never see him again.

"Saskia needn't find out," he says. She walks over and places a finger on his lips.

"Shh. Don't say any more." Then she leaves.

• • •

The next morning she sits next to Saskia on their flight to Heathrow.

"Did you have a nice time with Anthony last night?" she asks, carefully opening a tiny carton of cream and pouring it into her coffee.

Saskia looks down at the glossy magazine in front of her. "It was OK. He seemed a little distracted," she says petulantly, turning to look at Catherine. "He's the strangest guy, I can't work him out at all. All that money he spent on me, you would have thought he'd have wanted something in return. I would have been happy to...." She blushes.

"Give him a little something in return for the Prada handbag?" Catherine sips her coffee.

"I just don't understand why he didn't try. All he seemed to want was a girl who could make small talk with his clients."

"I didn't hear you complaining at the time."

"Don't get me wrong, we had a wonderful time. That's the thing. I can't find any real fault with him."

"The perfect gentleman?"

"Yes, exactly. If he weren't so sexually unresponsive I'd consider him pretty much perfect husband material."

"Mmm, he certainly sounds like it," Catherine says, holding the coffee cup in front of her mouth and biting her lip in an effort to suppress her laughter. But Saskia has seen her.

"Mummy! What are you laughing about? What's so funny?"

"Nothing, darling," she says, remembering the ragged cry he had made when he came. "Nothing at all."

SALLY BELLEROSE

Daffodils

I am vainly, passionately in love with my garden. I consider each crocus bud to be swelling by the grace of the sweat that dripped off my neck while I planted last fall. The curve of the tulip's leaves are the curve of my back, straining with the pitchfork over the compost heap.

I have an ex-lover, Annie. My old girlfriend appreciates my vanities. She's a fecund woman of fifty-five. *Fecundity*. God, I love that word. A word that celebrates the muck and mire we all spring from, the richness of life. A word you can use without feeling corny about the filling, swelling, bursting going on inside and outside of you. A lusty word for lusty women. Like everything else in nature that's alive and kicking, my ex-girlfriend and I know a sexy season when we feel it. Spring is fucking time. Since we broke up, there have been some years when I don't see Annie all winter long. But you can bet your last tube of vagilube she's going to show up at my front door some time before and as sure as taxes are due, smiling as if she never ever did one wrong thing. She's the first sign of spring—soft, moist, and furrowed.

This year Annie came on April first, All Fools Day. I know because my present, love-her-madly-till-death-do-we-part-girlfriend left for a conference in Erie, Pennsylvania, that same morning. My girlfriend's tracks were still fresh on the driveway when, knock, knock, knock, Annie's at my door.

We sit quietly in the living room. I pour coffee. Her body, full on my couch, extravagant, is what my grandmother would have called pleasingly plump. In fact, Annie looks a lot like my grandmother, except her hair is not gray. Annie dyes her hair red—not auburn, red. It's one of those days when the light is so bright and the air so clean that everything seems possible. I look out the window. I see my neighbor's rusty trash cans lying on their sides near the border of my garden. The damned kids have thrown them over the fence again. When I smile at the sun bouncing off the dirty metal barrels, I know that Annie and I are going to end up naked.

It's always the same. We start out polite, acting like we aren't affected by the bulge in the daffodils anymore, pretending we don't have some unspoken pact to celebrate the rituals of spring together, year after year. We're dying to find out what changes and what remains the same, but we start out slow, just in case one of us has decided that we should quit while we're ahead.

Annie and I were born the same year, in the month of April. We met in the spring, twenty-two years after our separate births. We were young together. We were young together until we reached forty-six. Then we weren't together and we weren't young. Middle-age: I've never been able to wrap my mind around that season of life. It's not what I expected. I thought middle-life would take over and make me respectable, settled, comfortably bored. Now Annie and I are both fifty-five, on the cusp of old age, approaching old-ladyhood as unsettled and wanton as we were thirty-three years ago. Annie says you're only as old as you feel. Well, I feel fifty-five springs horny.

I look at Annie, wrinkles deepening around her eyes as she smiles at me. I see old familiar lust forming in the lines at the corners of her mouth. She brings her coffee to her lips. There's a fold inside her elbow that I don't remember from last year. Annie, we're turning into old women with desire tucked into the bends and kinks of our skin.

Old women. I like the sound of that. I touch my neck, my skin warm and loose. Old women, sitting on the couch unfolding. I like the feel of it. Especially in spring. Spring has a way of honoring the layers of life that came before. The thicker the blanket of dead leaves, kitchen scraps, manure, and snow, the more succulent the hyacinth's new shoots. I like having all those winters, all those springs backing me up. It's good that I'm still alive. I'm just starting to get the hang of life. It's mostly the dying at the end part that I'm having a hard time adjusting to.

I lean back on the couch and close my eyes. Annie sits quietly beside me. She touches my hand. Softly her fingertips turn over my memory. I think of Annie's hot breath on the back of my neck, her fingers reaching around my waist to unzip my jeans from behind. I don't think of us as any age. I remember how the sweat forms in the small of her back as she moves on top of me and calls my name. I try to remember where we found the guts to take these liberties so long ago. Even youth doesn't give two women license to do these things together. Maybe age stops asking for permission.

I open my eyes and smile at Annie. The older I get the better my long-term memory gets, and I can't remember Annie ever asking for permission to do anything. Maybe she was old before her time. She never asked me if she could sleep with other women when we were together. We had a deal. We were doing the don't-ask-don't-tell thing long before the military got the idea.

Sleeping with other women wasn't why we broke up. Our deal worked out fine, for the most part. It was good we broke up. It was getting so we weren't being nice to each other on a day-to-day, everyday schedule. It was time to go our separate ways. So we did.

"Let's see the garden," Annie says.

We walk out to the yard. We gossip among the crocuses. They're in bloom, tiny things, only six inches from the ground, but they're full of themselves, screaming yellow and purple. The first to flower, brave little darlings. There's a chill in the morning air. Still, you can feel it's going to be a warm day. The ground is damp. It feels nice to sink into each step just a little as we walk. Annie compliments me on my tulips, marvels at how many there are, more than last year, more than the year before. They're all up, awake, out of the ground, seven or eight inches high. The leaves are striated green and rusty red, profuse and pushing. They're not ready to bloom. They have maybe a foot more to grow and gallons of sun to drink before they're good to go.

It's the daffodils that grab us, stop us in our tracks. We stare for a full minute before we walk toward them, our mugs of coffee steaming in our hands. The daffodils are swollen, not one bloom actually open among one hundred. They're straining. They want to get on with it, bad. They're tired of waiting. You can feel their impatience: just a little more time, just a little more light, a little more sun. Something inside them is pushing. Open. This is the time. Open. This is the place. No shame. They stand in clumps, leaves turning toward the sun. If it was rain, they'd be just as ready. They know who they are, what they want.

Annie and I stare at each other and sip. Annie presses the warm mug to her cheek. The coffee steam rises. I brush my cheek against my cup and stare at Annie. It's the morning sun, it's the season, it's me, that makes Annie's face glow—but it's something else, too. Annie's happy. She's happier then I've seen her in a long time. She's in love, not with me. She has a new lover. I'm not guessing. I've met the woman. Nice woman. She makes Annie happy. I wonder what kind of deal Annie has with her new lover. I don't ask. Annie doesn't tell.

I push Annie's new lover out of my mind. I push my own lover as far out of my mind as she will go, Erie, Pennsylvania. The light is at that certain slant that Emily Dickinson doesn't describe. It's the *fuck it, this is the only moment that ever was or ever will be* slant. It hits Annie full in the face. She really is illuminated. She doesn't blink. She looks me straight in the eye.

"I want you bad," she says.

We walk back to the house. We sit on the couch. It's still warm where our bodies had been a few minutes earlier.

This time there's no space between us. Annie pulls my face to hers. She kisses me, full on the lips. I snuggle my face between her breasts. I love her skin, especially the *V* between her breasts. The skin there is more furrowed and wrinkled then the rest of her. Beyond the *V* are the places where the sun doesn't shine, pale, tender. I like those places, too.

I trace my finger down the leathery skin of one breast and up the leathery skin of the other. I like the feel of her skin on my fingers. I can see through her blouse, the dark mound of her nipple is swelling up, a hard little seed that I want to swallow. Her bra pushes her breasts together. I put my hand between them. Warm. Soft.

"Ah," Annie says and kisses the back of my neck. She slides her hands down my back into my jeans and kneads the muscle of my ass. She always does this. I always want her to do this.

Annie gets on top of me. I feel her full weight. Mouth to mouth, breast to breast, belly to belly. Her hips plant me further into the couch. My hips reach up to her. She slides both hands under my ass, takes a firm hold of each cheek, and pulls me even closer as she pushes down. We get a rhythm going, a dance. We move, her belly, my belly, her thighs, my thighs. I can feel the soft fleshy mound between her thighs and the hard bone beneath pushing into me, my own flesh and bone pushing back. We're touching everywhere, pressing every place we're able to press. The pressure and the movement get more intense. Our tongues are in and out of each other's mouths. Our hands are grabbing, pressing, kneading any piece of flesh we can work except the one spot that wants pressing most. Our pants are down around our knees. I have one leg completely free. My legs are slightly parted beneath her. She could lift up and slide her hand between my legs. I could reach up and find her hot and wet, too.

She's working me. Everything in its time. I'm so wet. I'm so ready to get wetter. *For God's sake, girl, hit the spot. It's time. Come on, honey*. I want it both ways, to be full, completely filled up, and at the same time completely empty, all the way open so that it all spills out. *Touch me, girl*. I want to explode. I'm squirming under her.

The phone rings. Ignore it. *Keep moving, keep moaning, keep your flesh heaving against mine, Annie*. The phone rings again, unnatural intrusion, blasphemy of the rites of spring. Annie's mouth is on my breast now. She's biting my nipple. *A little harder, baby*. Oh, Annie. That's exactly right.

The answering machine clicks on. My voice, "Sorry we can't come to the phone right now. Please leave a message at the sound of the beep." The machine is on the end table, six inches from our heads. It's turned up full volume because my hearing's not what it used to be. I try to reach and shut it off, but it falls to the floor. My girlfriend's voice comes blaring over the damned thing. "Hey, baby. You out in the garden? Plane's delayed. What a gorgeous day to be stuck in the airport. Hope you're enjoying it. Love you. Call you when I get to Pennsylvania." Click.

Annie makes a valiant effort to ignore the disturbing sound of the busy signal coming from the receiver that's fallen from its cradle. She keeps right on playing with my breast. But for me, there's a line where pleasurable erotic pressure becomes "stop right now" pain. It's the point where you hear your girlfriend's voice, talking sweet on the answering machine, while your ex-girlfriend has her teeth sunk into your right nipple.

I feel a stabbing ache from my nipple to my crotch. My body stiffens up like frozen road kill. Annie tries to soothe me. She tongues my nipple softly, strokes the side of my face. I try to melt back into her, but I'm chilled to the bone. A shiver runs up my spine.

Annie sits up. She doesn't try to hide her annoyance. "Sandy sounds well," she says.

"Jesus," I say. "Jesus Christ Almighty."

"What's *he* got to do with it?"

"Sweet Mary."

"Well, that's a little better."

I sit up next to Annie. "Sorry," I say weakly.

"I thought you and Sandy had an arrangement," Annie says in exasperation, rearranging her magnificent breasts in her bra. She glares at the answering machine. "Progress," she says. She picks her blouse off the floor. I watch as her fleshy breasts slowly disappear under checked cotton, button by button. I stand on one leg, trying to pull the other leg of my jeans and my panties up at the same time. I fall back onto the couch.

Annie stares at me, "Look at you. You're shaking. Poor baby." She puts her arm around me. She's more concerned than annoyed now. I put my head on her shoulder.

"Sandy hates the arrangement," I whine.

"Wasn't it Sandy who used to carry on about compulsory monogamy?"

"That was five years ago when she had the hots for her sister's neighbor. She's decided that open relationships work better in theory than in practice."

"All theory. No action." Annie sighs. "Never mind. I still love you, you sexy thing." Annie knows me well enough to know it's going to take me quite a bit of time to unthaw again.

I say, "Shit."

Annie stands up, pulls on her pants, tucks in her blouse. "I'm going home," she says, "to finish this business we started together all by myself."

She holds my face between her hands and gives me a suction cup kiss on the forehead. That's what I like about Annie, she takes life as it comes. She's not angry, still a tad irritated, but what the hell, she's got the right.

"Thanks, Annie," I say. "I love you too."

She moves toward the door. I'm a lump of deflated libido, limp on the couch. I watch her through the window as she walks toward the daffodils. I watch her bend at the knees and lean forward. Her sturdy thighs support her. Her butt sticks out. This posture suits her. Her curves perfectly complement the landscape of the garden. Does she know that I'm watching her?

She sure does. Beautiful, mellow old girl. She's trying to direct my attention to the flowers, but I'm looking at her. Her smile is upside down. The garden is only a backdrop; Annie's the focal point. My spirit rises with her as she stands, waves at me, and points to the flower in her hand. Her grin gets closer and closer as she walks back toward the house. I turn the knob. It's warmer outside than it is inside. The warm air spills through my door. Annie offers me a daffodil, fully bloomed, from my own garden.

DOROTHY B. TYLER

The Truth

In retrospect, I'm not sure which response I wanted to hear. The thought of baring my frumpy, fiftyish body before someone who knew me when was almost as unsettling as the thought of climbing into a hot tub still dressed. OK, so neither of the guys was quite as svelte as he might once have been either, but it was different for me. Because it was me. I had spent the entire first half of my life using my body as my calling card. I was all too aware that it wouldn't open many doors for me anymore.

It was equally weird that neither my husband nor I had even thought about it in time to suit up. When Evan had told us that he planned on a soak in his hot tub for muscles sore from partying too hard, we had both jumped at the opportunity to join in. It was only as we were leaving Evan's spare room that I asked Dale if we needed to return for bathing suits. Dale gave me a look as blank as mine, and we decided to wear our towels and see what Evan said. The fact that he was obviously naked when we got there was the best clue as to what his answer would be, but we asked anyway.

"Suit? Suit yourself."

Evan kept right on reading his book.

So, dropping my towel, and stepping into the hot water, I felt some relief, and the anxiety wasn't nearly so bad once I realized that he was so engrossed in his book that it probably wouldn't have mattered if I had walked into the room stark naked, rather than wrapped in a towel. Of course, once the anxiety went away, the depression settled in. I was well aware that there had once been a time when Evan would have done his damnedest to see what I had—but that was back when I had something to see.

"Stop it, Ange." Dale knew me too well. He had given up trying to convince me that stretch marks, sagging boobs, and a droopy ass didn't bother him—that he still found me sexually attractive in spite of a belly that pouched out like a beach ball instead of sinking in like a washboard. But he could see that I was thinking about it again, and it must have bothered him. It usually did.

I stuck my tongue out at him and picked up the book I had brought. Holding it up high, I could almost convince myself that, if I couldn't see them, they couldn't see me. Which was a pity, really—because I wanted to see them. Well, maybe not Dale; I was pretty familiar with how he looked. But Evan was a curiosity. I had known him for quite a few years and had seen him in good times and bad, thick and thin, as it were. He had entered his midlife as comfortably as I had, but he still sported a cock—and I had a never-ending need to know how every man was equipped.

I had sneaked plenty of looks through the years—enough to know that the outline was impressive enough. But there's nothing like the real thing, and outlines don't tell the whole story. There's no way to be sure about the details like circumcision, ball hang, relative shape and size. And anyway, I just liked to look.

For a while it was quiet, with no sounds but that of turning pages. Evan hadn't turned on the jets, and it made reading easier not to have to deal with the splashing of bubble makers. But those jets were the soothing lotion we needed for our out-of-shape aches and pains, so it wasn't long before Evan announced that he was going to turn them on.

There went my cover.

Carefully not looking at either guy, I put my book down behind me and leaned my head back, closing my eyes. That was a big mistake. To get my head to rest on the rim of the tub, I had to scoot my butt further along the bench and drop down deeper into the water. Two things happened simultaneously: The buoyancy factor of big tits kicked in to pop my butt up off the seat, and my feet, slipping out from under me, managed to ram directly into a crotch. It was Evan's. And he wasn't little. And he was interested in something.

I would have had a smart comeback ready, but I was too busy drowning. Going under water with your foot on a friend's semi-erect penis tends to cause one to gulp something other than air. I got a mouthful of chlorinated water and sank, afraid to splash and flounder my way to even more embarrassing contacts. Not to worry, though. Dale was always the cool one, and so was Evan—maybe that's why they got along so well. Nothing much ruffled their feathers; they always seemed to know what to do. I had no more than taken that mouthful and begun to sink when I had four arms around me, hauling me up to the surface.

Four arms. A fantasy come true. And I was coughing my lungs out.

Both guys kept their hold on me and pulled me out of the water, laying me down on the cold tile.

"Turn her over, Evan." Dale's voice was so matter-of-fact, you'd think they were inspecting a used car. I felt hands on my ass, turning me over onto my belly. Since Dale was up near my head, I assumed that was Evan on my ass. Christ. This was not going the way my fantasies did, that was for sure. All I needed to make this a perfect fiasco now was to fart.

Well, at least I didn't do that.

Dale held me down by the shoulders until he was sure I was breathing well on my own—which took some serious concentration on my part, because Evan hadn't let go when he turned me over, but kept his hands on my ass. He had big hands. Of course, I have a big ass.

"Feel OK?"

"Yeah," I managed. "Sorry 'bout that."

"Dale." Evan still had his hands on me. "I don't think I've ever seen a butt blush before. Have you?"

"That's my Ange. She never does anything halfway."

I felt like a prize cow at a 4-H fair.

"Can we get back into the water now?" Even the translucent nature of water seemed better than the stark reality of my bare butt hanging out. Is there any less secure feeling than lying naked, face down and red, while two seemingly nonchalant men discuss the color of your ass?

We all climbed back in and I sank slowly this time, to make sure I knew my buoyancy limit. I also kept a firm grip on Dale's thigh, just in case. Again, going on the theory that if I can't see it, it isn't there, I closed my eyes and tried to relax.

"I'm disappointed in you, Dale." That was Evan.

"Oh? Why?"

"You lied to me."

Considering Dale's well-earned nickname of "Mr. Straight Arrow," this was quite an accusation. It warranted opening my eyes and sitting a little taller.

"Lied?"

"Yes." Evan was leaning back against his side of the hot tub, looking at Dale. "You told me she had a great ass."

Dale carefully removed my hand from his thigh and reached up to close my open mouth. "Excuse me, darlin', but I've got to go defend your honor. The heat must have gotten to his brain."

"No," Evan continued. "I would never call *that* a great ass. I'd call it—magnificent. Glorious. Superlative. Outstanding. Marvelous. Grand. Matchless. Incomparable. But never just 'great.'"

Dale sat back down. "I bow to your expertise. I must plead negligence. Being as enamored as I am with her breasts, I failed to give her ass the respect it is due."

I wish I could record my own snappy comebacks to all this, but I was struck dumb—not a state with which I was familiar. But they were talking about *my body!*

"Really?" Evan looked at Dale in surprise. "Now, I had you figured for a pussy-man myself. Didn't know you were so focused on the milk glands."

"Ah, yes. Pussy. Well, Bud, while her ass may be marvelous and her breasts to die for, it's what's between her thighs that makes her the angel of every man's dreams."

"I find that hard to believe. Great ass, boobs, *and* twat, all bundled into one slice of woman? Nope. I can't buy it."

Dale turned to me with innocence in his eyes. "Sorry, Sweetmeat, but your honor is at stake here." He got out of the tub, reached two hands under my armpits, and hauled me up to the rim. Sitting behind me, straddling my thighs with his, he reached around, put a hand on each of my upper legs, and pushed. What the hell was I supposed to do? They were taking this so matter-of-factly that it would have felt like raining on their parade to protest. And, anyway, I couldn't come up with any words. Had they planned this, or what?

So there I sat, Dale behind me, holding my legs wide open, Evan in front of me. Looking. Dale kept his big hands on top of the meat of my thighs, thumbs toward the good parts, and Evan slowly came closer. My juices started to flow.

"Well, I've got to hand it to you, Dale. Unbelievable. Ass, tits, and twat. Almost perfect."

"Almost!?" For a first-time stab at entering the conversation, that was the best I could do. And my voice came out as a high-pitched squeal.

Evan looked up at me, deadpan serious. "Just because it looks good doesn't mean it tastes good. You'd be surprised."

"Oh." It was a good thing Dale was behind me then, or I would have melted back into the hot tub.

"Nectar. The sweetest nectar. There is no finer anywhere. You can trust me." Dale pushed himself firmly up against me, and I could feel his reaction to the conversation poking my backside. He brought his thumbs together to touch the hood of my clit and ran them lightly over the length of my cleft. I about came right then and there.

"Well, normally, dear friend, I wouldn't think of doing anything but trusting you. But then again, you did call it wrong already with her ass, and that puts your say-so in jeopardy. I'm afraid I just can't take your word for it. There's only one way to be sure."

Evan moved in. Dale didn't help much—well, actually, he helped a lot. Evan. Not me. Dale pulled me back to lean against him, spreading my thighs as wide as they could go, using his thumbs to open a pathway for Evan's tongue.

And what a tongue it was. He kept it long and flat and pressed hard against my cleft, licking upward with a slow, steady pressure. Pushing aside the folds of skin, he reached my clit after about a year and a half and flicked it softly.

That was the first time I came.

Fast, even for me. The shudders would have doubled me over if Dale hadn't had such a firm grip on me, but he was ready. As Evan traveled my valley, Dale steadily pulled me back against himself, raising my thighs even higher, enough so that he managed to lift my butt entirely off the rim of the hot tub.

"Can you hold her there, Buddy? I do love a pretty ass." Evan helped Dale out by cupping my ass himself, and lowered his head again. This time he started his licking lower down and lapped gently at the rim of my ass. I did my damnedest to climb backward over Dale's shoulders, to give Evan as much access as I could. Funny, how you can be as close to someone as I was to Dale and still be afraid to ask—but he had never shown much interest in my ass, and I always thought I might like it.

I was right.

"I think you may have hit the mother lode there, Evan. Think you can get her set up for me?" Dale was as hard as he had ever been and was rubbing his cock against my entire body. Just the thought that he might be interested in trying out a new entry point put me over the top again.

That was the second time I came.

"The way she's flowing now, she's getting herself ready without much help from me." Evan ran a thick thumb from the mouth of my cunt to the rim of my ass, taking about a pint of girl juice with him. He used it to massage me open and dip a finger inside.

With a finger in back and his thumb buried in front, Evan managed to hold me like a bowling ball, first rocking his finger in, while his thumb slid out, and then reversing the moves. Dale kept lifting my ass higher and higher, pulling me back to lie over him until his cock sprang free beneath me. That must have been some kind of signal, because the instant Dale sprang free, Evan lifted me up and balanced me over Dale's rigid member. That's when I lost track of who was doing what where. All I knew for sure was that there was a slow, steady pressure as a warm, hard cock slid into a well-lubricated ass. *My* well-lubricated ass. And I discovered that I was right—I liked it. I really liked it. I mean I *really* liked it.

That was the third time I came.

By then, I was pretty much out of it as an active participant. I was fairly sure it was all going according to some kind of plan—Dale's efforts to inflate my ego, maybe. I could give a flying fuck. As long as it never ended, they could do whatever they wanted.

Apparently, whatever they wanted involved more than just Dale's getting off, because, while I was in the throes of ecstasy, riding Dale's cock as Evan tongued me with an expertise he could have marketed, the boys managed to maneuver me back onto the tile surrounding the hot tub. Evan removed his tongue and Dale his cock as they rapidly did some flipping and rearranging. Trust me, I was shocked at the loss, but, considering the fingers that remained active on all the good spots, I didn't have a whole lot to complain about. Almost before I could draw breath, I found myself lying over Evan, whose very nicely proportioned member (I *still* hadn't had a good look at it, dammit!) was poised at my pussy, and I could feel Dale ready to slip back into my rear door.

The realization of what was about to happen shocked the shit (figuratively speaking only, thankfully)—and the breath—out of me. Which was probably a good thing, as both boys began to enter me at the same time, and with the same slow pace. I started sucking air in time with them, and, if my lungs hadn't been emptied first, I would have broken something. I managed to reach my lung capacity about the same time they each reached penile capacity. That's when I started to yowl.

You know, every cock novel I've read describes double entry as a seesaw thing—one guy pushes in while the other guy pulls out. Not these two. They hit the perfect "in/in" rhythm from the get-go. Both in all the way together, both withdrawing almost out together. The drag on my clit was maximized and unbelievable.

That's when I stopped counting orgasms.

Talk about your out-of-body experience: I was on such a sexual high that I wasn't really sure what was happening. Dale and I had been together for nearly twenty years before I'd ever felt the almost telepathic connection that taught me what he was experiencing while we fucked. But that night, I became as close to Evan as I ever had with Dale, and, for a brief moment, I found myself inside each of their heads. One minute I was lying between two energetically pumping men—the next I was on top, pushing into the tightest hole my dick had ever entered. Then I found myself underneath the weight of two hefty friends, barely able to breathe as my cock got buried in the sweet darkness of a well-lubed pussy, pressing my more sensitive side against the pounding penetration of my best friend.

Dale's gut-wrenching cry brought me back as I felt him explode up my ass. He finally broke the rhythm, pushing impossibly deep inside me, holding himself there as he pumped load after load after diminishing load, hands tightly gripping my ass, body arched away.

Evan never stopped. As Dale slowly pulled out of me, Evan flipped me onto my back and raised my legs over his shoulders. "My turn," he whispered, picking up his pace. I closed my eyes to imagine better the clenching of his ass as he rammed his cock in deeper. Deeper. Impossibly deep. Just as I began to realize I couldn't take much more, Evan growled, "Oh, Christ! Oh, sweet, fucking Christ," and pulled me up tightly as he stopped all motion, face contorted with the pain of ecstasy. What a beautiful face.

Spent, the three of us lay side by side on the tiles. Soon enough the change in our friendship would hit home. But, for the moment at least, I knew what Dale meant about my sexy body. If I could bring two men to this—if they could bring *me* to this—then there was truth in Dale's lies about me. Sweet, sweet truth.

RACHEL HEATH

Looking Is Listening and...Shaving

I met Felicia at the last Deaf Social. She was at the other end of the room with a bunch of young folks. It was a big room—more than sixty people were there—but I noticed her. My type. Long black hair flowing down her shoulders—and I could tell by the way she flung her hair and moved her hips that she was a sexy one.

Her group was listening to Rita Morales tell about the Balkans. Then Kevin Morales talked about their daughter's graduation.

I'm an old lady, I reminded myself. Plus I'm probably not even her gender. A teen-aged boy called her Mom but that doesn't mean anything—so many queers have kids.

I was talking to Gladys and Chuck; Gladys gave the run-down on AIDS and Magic Johnson, Chuck about Donald Trump's new girlfriend and Ivana's book. Harvey talked about the Operation Rescue fanatics. Harvey talks slowly, but everyone makes an extra effort to encourage him; he was raised oralist so he has trouble Signing.

I'd already said my hello, how-are-you's to Trudy, my ex-"roommate," and Carmen, her girlfriend. We don't have to actually go up to each other like Hearings do since we can talk from a distance, but we can't avoid each other either since we all attend the same Socials.

I've gotten used to seeing the two of them. Trudy left me over a year ago. Carmen is a nice lady; I don't hate her. I'm really quite sorry when she says she injured her foot last week and that's why it's in a splint.

Trudy's gone back to work part-time. She's also put on weight, which doesn't look good on her, since she's only five feet tall. Really, she's getting *fat*. But she's still dramatically good-looking, her plentiful snow-white hair swept to one side and up. Like her hair all over, I can't help but think.

I was talking about the Pentagon trying to resist budget cuts when I saw Felicia telling a joke about Star Wars and asteroids. Since we were talking about the same thing, I saw my chance and invited her over.

As she and her son made their way through the knots of people between us, I got a better look at them: poor guy, he had a terrible case of acne. He was dressed in a kind of preppy uniform, a white shirt and tie, jeans, his dull brown hair cut '50s-style short.

Felicia was a different story. Her coloring was perfect, from my point of view: fair skin, black eyebrows, and a detectable mustache (always a good omen). Her coal-black hair had some white streaks but she was young; she couldn't be over forty. A nice body, just a bit plump. Her powder-blue jeans were ripped up and down, reminding me of a picture of Cher—now *there's* a lady I could really do something with.

After mutual introductions I asked Felicia and Gary why they'd come to this Social. I knew it was their first in this area because I've been to every Deaf Social since I retired. Now that Trudy's split, I don't know what I'd do without them; it's all Hearing where I live.

"I just moved. For a new job," Felicia replied. "I'm an accountant."

"How about you, Gary?" I asked, thinking, Felicia's probably straight. And I'm too old for her.

"I'm going to a junior college right now," he said. "I'm a Hearie so I might work as a translator."

"You'd be a good one," I complimented him, quite sincerely. "I'd never have guessed you weren't Deaf. But kids who are raised by Signers...was your father Deaf too?"

Felicia answered for him. "His Dad was Deaf but we broke up when he was little. My daughter, Gail, was exposed to as much Sign as he was, but she's very poor at it, since she doesn't use it often. She was embarrassed about having Deaf parents when she was growing up."

"I'm sorry."

"Gail's doing fine, though. She's an X-ray technician. I'm proud of her even if she used to be embarrassed by me."

"She's not embarrassed by you anymore, Mom," Gary added.

"Do you work, Sue?" Felicia asked. She wore two little rings and a bracelet—with a woman symbol. She also had a tiny woman-symbol for one earring.

"I'm retired but I used to be a Deaf counselor for high school kids," I said.

"Are you married?" Felicia asked.

"Never have been," I tell them, feeling a twinge: I think of myself as divorced—abandoned. But I'm not out to the people at the Socials. In some of the bigger cities Gay Deaf have their own Socials, but not here.

"I know a lot of people like that," she said, and paused before adding, "especially women."

It's a hit. Gary laughed knowingly. Not much to look at, but he's smart.

As Felicia and I exchanged TTY phone numbers, I suddenly wondered: but what if it's *already* shaved?

Felicia is bisexual. A weird thing—we Deafies don't even have a word for it yet; we're still finger-spelling it. She divorced her husband because he drank. Also, she was starting to realize how she felt about women.

She was married gay-style but her girlfriend was a flirt and also very jealous (this is according to Felicia). Another time she lived with a Hearing—it was a guy—but then he lost interest in learning Sign, and that had been his reason for being with her.

"My son knows," she said, "because I came out to him when he asked me if I was a lesbian. He suspected because I was so close my girlfriend. Also, because we fought so bitterly. I haven't come out to Gail yet. Like I said, we haven't been that close. During her teen-aged years she rebelled by joining one of those religious fanatic churches. Anti-feminist, homophobic—when she had the TV on PTL or the 700 Club, I used to be glad I was Deaf since I didn't have to listen to those idiots."

"Is she still that way?" I asked.

"Oh, no. She came to her senses. Gail belongs to a pro-choice group that gets women past the Operation Rescue protesters. I should come out to her, I probably will soon."

When I confessed my fetish to Felicia, she blushed and started laughing. She reassured me that she wasn't offended, it was just that she never expected to attract anyone by having so much body hair. "I've always been self-conscious about it. I used to torture myself with wax."

I waited hopefully.

"I'm glad it's not the hair on my head, Sue," she continued. "I couldn't let you have that."

I was wearing stockings and garters and a lacy white teddy—that's what she liked—and I got the stuff together while she undressed: clippers, shaving cream and razor, pan of water, washcloths. I put a fat blue pillow in the middle of the bed and a beach towel across that.

Naked, Felicia lay on her tummy across the big pillow so that her bottom stuck up nicely. She held her head against another pillow.

There it was: a jungle of thick black hair down the crack of her ass.

I went to work with the clippers first. When she wriggled, I leaned over and warned her, "Stop, you're going to make me cut you."

She turned to say, "OK" and her elbow hit the pan, but luckily she didn't knock it over, just swished the water around.

I started shaving, very carefully, aware of my pussy juice warming. With each stroke, I rinsed the razor off, then shaved the next segment. Oh, I thought excitedly, she's got so much hair! I had one cheek shaved, washed, dried; I examined it to make sure—no stray hairs.

Pausing, I savored the sight of the one cheek so nakedly white against the primitive black brush of the other.

Then I shaved, washed, shaved, until both buns were hairless. My nipples tingled. I kissed her bottom; the skin shivered under my lips. She started playing with herself. Her hips moved from side to side as she masturbated.

I lay on her back, my chin on her shoulders and my pubis moving against her clean bald butt. Felicia's chest vibrated—giggling. I moved my legs further apart, trying to catch all the ass I could.

Sniffing the musky oil of her perspiration, I kissed and sucked on her shoulder. We rocked and shimmied, and I slid my hands underneath to play with her breasts. The hard tiny bumps of her nipples reminded me of raspberries.

I pushed and bounced against her ass in excitement. Our legs rubbed together, bearing down and flailing, and tears started hotly in my eyes. Her breath sped up. Her bottom swayed slowly and sensuously. My short fingernails dug into her skin as I bounced harder and faster, faster, slowing down, then speeding up, faster and faster until I came against Felicia's beautiful naked ass.

I kissed the nape of her neck gratefully. There was a pronounced red mark on her shoulder—I'd given her a hickey. Trying to catch my breath, wiping the perspiration off my forehead, I rolled off her and she turned onto her back.

"Now, it's my turn," Felicia said. She drew her knees up and opened her legs.

"Didn't you already come?" I asked.

"Yes, I did, but it was a small orgasm and I want a big one this time," she said, her hands trembling a little as she talked. "Seconds are usually best for me and I want as good an orgasm as *you* had, pervert."

I put my face on her very warm pussy. The clear fluid ran thickly along her lips and gave off a rich, spicy odor.

Her hands caressed her bush as I gently sucked her clit, then pushed my tongue into her vagina and around her wet lips, slowly and for a long time, the way she told me she liked it.

"Kiss my thighs," she said, "the inner thighs."

I moved my mouth down, kissing the inside of her still-furry thighs. Tufts of curly hair waved under my tongue like tall grasses in a breeze.

Felicia got my attention with a tap of her foot. "Now, eat me, Sue." I returned to her hot, open sex. My face was on her pussy licking around—not on—her hard little button, when her hips started grinding again, faster but with long pauses.

Her hand nudged the top of my head, so I licked inside her cunt. She put her fingers around her clit and she came, a slow, wonderful take-your-time shudder/freeze/shudder/wild twist with her cunt throbbing around my tongue.

Afterward, clinging and slippery, my face still bathed with her love juice, I asked, "Did you come good enough this time?"

"I think I was loud enough to make both of us Hear," she replied. Then we rested together in silence, our hands too tired to talk anymore.

PAIGE MATTHEWS

This Pussy Retired

Scenario One

I'm in bed with Dirk, a man of thirty-four—young enough to be my son, who is in fact thirty-six. Where we met and how we got here doesn't matter.

Dirk has long, flowing hair parted in the middle, and a brown beard to match, giving him a look reminiscent of paintings of Jesus Christ, a look that was popular among men during the sixties. His forehead is smooth, his alert blue eyes radiate honesty. I run my hands over his strong biceps, his muscled thighs, my hands thirstily drinking in health and youth. Even his breath emits a scent of innocence. I feel as if I've entered a time warp: This is what my lovers used to feel like, this is what *I* used to feel like. Strong, young, and healthy—whether fucking or making love, it was with joyful vigor. Not that we ever noticed—we mistook our youth for the natural order of things, as if it would always be this way. As if we were immortal.

With Dirk I feel intensely nostalgic—for all the young men I've ever slept with, as well as for the girl I used to be—and I begin to cry. Although I am responding primarily to Dirk's physicality, it is not for youthful bodies alone that I weep; it's also for my more innocent self. Soon I'm recalling all the lost and dead lovers, feeling acutely all the years gone by, and keenly aware of how very little time lies ahead.

Dirk is kind, patient with my tears. He's enjoying being "appreciated," as he puts it; he and his same-age lovers take youth for granted, so he doesn't experience himself as particularly youthful. How could he? None of us ever do: Not having experienced the aging process, we have nothing with which to compare ourselves in our youth.

I cannot stop crying, can't focus on the fun of sex; I'm too caught up in feelings of loss. What began as an adventurous roll in the hay has turned into an exhausting and painful experience. I resolve never again to rob the cradle.

Scenario Two

A friend sets me up on a blind date with a slightly older man, sixty-two. During dinner I assess his bedroom potential (not everything about me has changed with age!). Tan hairy arms, sexy blue eyes. But I can't stop staring at his quivering jowls, or the brown liver spots on his hands; I am almost repulsed. Inwardly I admonish myself: After all, he'll have to face my hideous varicose veins; his hands will brush against the little moles sprouting beneath my sagging breasts. I'm a victim, I tell myself, of our youth-obsessed culture—an intolerant, politically incorrect old lady. I resolve to overcome my ageism and, though I am not terribly attracted to Dave, I sleep with him just to prove that I can.

But Dave can only get it up for my mouth; every time he tries to fuck me, his cock deflates. We make jokes; we commiserate about age; at least we're comfortable talking about it. I end up sucking him off while pressing my clit against his shin, and we both have orgasms. Afterward I feel disgusted and empty. I resolve not to sleep with anyone unless I'm consumed with passion.

Scenario Three

Jerry comes around to see me; it's been several months, during which he's slept with dozens of women, none of whom is aware of the existence of the others. He's thoroughly exhausted from sneaking, lying, and juggling his life around.

Jerry is, like me, fifty-four, but he looks ten years younger. Tall and handsome in a classic American way, he is also intelligent, sensitive, and funny. Still, he's often confessed that he knows his abundance of women has more to do with sociological factors than him personally: Attractive, smart, single men are a dying breed—especially in our generation. "Let's be honest," he jokes with charming modesty. "I get points just because I can walk and chew gum at the same time."

We sleep together, and, as always, our sex is passionate, almost violently so. He's got a rough way of kissing that feels like murder; he pins my arms over my head, thrusts himself in and out, attacks my mouth in a frenzy of need. When he comes, he looks directly into my eyes, dissolving into a vulnerable little puppy who calls my name like an incantation. After a brief respite he fingers me until I come; he's learned the precise formula for getting me off, and later cracks jokes about knowing not to deviate in the least little word or movement from the routine.

We lie together companionably and talk for half an hour; then Jerry leaves, most likely to go service the next woman on his list. I squelch my desire for him to stay, knowing that if I pressure him he'll disappear for a while, if not for good. He's made it clear that if I fall in love with him, if I become just another female demanding time and attention, it's lights out, baby. I treasure our friendship. I love the way we make love. Still, this is, to say the least, not a terribly satisfying relationship. I resolve not to sleep with Jerry anymore.

Scenario Four

On my fifty-fifth birthday I decide that the thing to do is cross the gender line. It's been more than twenty years since my one passionate lesbian affair; since then there've been a few women here and there, but nothing to write home about. The truth is, I am, in this area as with aging, politically incorrect: The number of women to whom I've been attracted can be counted on the fingers of one inexperienced and very rusty hand.

I've been sharing coffee and lunches with Teresa, a fellow writer, on and off for a year now; she's in an open marriage with a man and considers herself bisexual. She is exactly my age, a gorgeous redhead, earthy and sexy. I drop a few hints, and within a few weeks we're in a hot tub pawing at one another. I find that it's like riding a bike, and delve into her pussy with unbridled enthusiasm. I make her come, she makes me come, we have a fine time.

But we never do it again. Her schedule is such that she's only free in the afternoons, which is when I write; I much prefer the lonely evenings for lovemaking, which is when she must tend to hubby. I suppose that I could give up a writing session; when I was younger, sex almost always took priority over work. But now I am unwilling to give up one single day of writing for the sake of physical pleasure.

I don't decide to "become celibate"—it just happens. Between antidepressants and menopause, my libido goes south. To my shock, this comes as a relief: I spent half my life following my pussy into compromised and even dangerous situations. I ended up in self-destructive relationships with inappropriate people for the sake of hot and steady sex. I am appalled to find that I'm now perfectly willing to give up sex—but there it is.

I continue to masturbate, a hasty affair with a vibrator, summoning up images of the arrogant and studly Jimmy Smits. I've discovered that celebrity fantasies, unlike those of former or potential lovers, help me come quickly and efficiently—and, most important, without emotion.

At least once a week I dream about ex-lovers. One night I get out of bed and make a list, beginning with my first, at sixteen. They total over seventy. I linger over each name, remembering. Some memories make me sad, others make me laugh, a few make me shake my head at my young impulsive self. I store the list in my computer so that when I'm seventy or eighty, should I live so long, I can refer to it. I frame photos of my top three lovers, one of whom is dead, and place them around my apartment. Slowly I face the truth of what has happened: Although I swore that I'd never become a sexless old lady, that is exactly what I have become.

Several years ago I read that Gloria Steinem was relieved to find her sex drive drastically reduced because it simplified her life; this appalled and frightened me at the time. Now I understand.

I understand other things as well—for instance, the lyrics, wistfully sung by Maurice Chevalier in *Gigi*, "I'm so glad that I'm not young anymore." I make an analogy to amusement park rides: I feel the same about sex as I do about a roller coaster full of thrilled, screaming teenagers; I too loved roller coasters once upon a time, but now they make me sick to my stomach.

I cultivate a new self-image: that of the bonsai tree, pared down to bare essentials, no flamboyant flowers or leaves waving in the wind to attract attention. No desperate luring of bees, pollen, sunlight, rain. Just here. Existing. Still. Peaceful. *Here.*

TERESA NOELLE ROBERTS

Trooper

Tracy pulled over before the trooper turned his siren on. No point in running away. She'd been nailed cleanly doing close to eighty in a fifty-five zone. Still, she couldn't wipe the smile off her face. The fast drive had cleared her head enough that she'd be able to send her book to New York in the morning. The advance would cover more small-town traffic tickets than even her reckless driving habits were likely to accrue. At fifty, Tracy O'Rourke wasn't a household name, but her alter ego, Anastasia Roman, was found on best-seller lists and bedside tables everywhere. *Publishers Weekly* called her the hot-sex queen of historical romance. Her great-aunt Agnes called her a disgrace to the family. She was proud of both.

The trooper adjusted his sunglasses and swaggered over to the car. Tracy sucked in her breath and belly, thrust her breasts forward unconsciously, then caught herself and stifled a nervous giggle.

She'd always been fascinated—no, make that aroused—

by the New York State troopers' uniforms. The high black boots; the snug-fitting, paramilitary olive shirt and trousers; the sunglasses that could conceal wolf eyes, vampire eyes—anything but human eyes—caught her in the groin. Always, though, in her run-ins with troopers, the uniform had been worn over something distinctly uninspiring.

This one couldn't have been more perfect if he'd been born out of her own word processor.

Tall, tanned to an almost Native American copper, dark brown hair that waved in defiance of the crew cut most troopers wore. Broad cheekbones, broad shoulders, narrow hips, and perfectly rounded ass. His uniform fit like spandex.

And, she saw as he approached the car, he was young. Hard to guess his age with those sunglasses on, but she'd say twenty-five, probably younger. He was trying to hold his mouth in a stern trooper's smirk, but it was still a boy's mouth, soft and vulnerable. She imagined it around her nipple.

Her nipples, which were already poking out of her shirt from the fast ride in the convertible, sprang to attention. She wished for a second that she'd worn a loose blouse instead of the tight-fitting tank top. As the trooper stared down at her through dark glasses, she changed her mind. His eyes were unreadable behind the glasses, but a flush was spreading over his cheekbones—embarrassment, arousal, or both? He had definitely noticed her. She wanted to pull him into the car and rip his clothes off, but decided it wouldn't be a wise idea.

"Do you know how fast you were going?"

"Oh, about seventy-eight." She handed him the

license, registration, and insurance that she had ready. She touched his hand a little longer than was really necessary and stared, half-smiling, into his hidden eyes.

"That's awfully fast for a road like this one, Ms...." he glanced down at the license, "Ms. O'Rourke."

"I'm a fast woman." *Oh God, what a cliché!* "Don't mind me, I'm a little nervous. I know I was speeding, but I have this awful habit of going out for a drive when I'm trying to think through something, and I just get out of control."

The trooper shook his head. "It sure is an awful habit. I'm going to have to give you a ticket, and from the look of your conviction stub, your insurance company is going to be a little bit upset with you."

"I must subconsciously enjoy dealing with men in uniform." She tried to catch the words, but her hormones seemed to be moving faster than her brain.

"You're from Philadelphia?" She nodded. "Just passing through?"

"I'm staying in the area for a few days."

"Visiting friends?"

"No. I'm staying out at Johnson's Cabins, down by the creek; I was on my way back there now. Why?"

The trooper grinned. "I know it's none of my business, but why in the world would anyone want to hang out here?" He gestured to the farm land around him. "There's nothing to do, and if you want peace and quiet, there are lots of prettier places to go."

"That's why I'm here." She turned toward him, leaning forward so that her breasts were practically, but not quite, brushing his hands. Her nipples strained to close the gap. He shifted—not away from her.

"I'm a writer. There are too many distractions in the city, so when I have a project to finish, I find some small town famous for absolutely nothing and hole up in a motel for a while." She leaned a little closer, thinking, *I can't believe I'm doing this,* thinking, *but my heroines do it all the time and their lives are much more exciting than mine.* "In fact, I'm almost done with a book. If you finish giving me my ticket and let me go soon, I should get it done by dinnertime."

He took off his sunglasses. His eyes were light blue, startling in the deeply tanned face. Wolf eyes, husky eyes, eyes that were obviously boring through her clothes. "It must take a long time to write a book. I bet you want to celebrate when you finish."

"You're right." *Oh, why can't I just take this man now?* "I don't suppose there's anywhere around here to party?"

"Nowhere decent closer than Oneonta, and that's thirty miles away. And the way you drive sober, I don't want to even think about you DWI."

"That's why I got a bottle of champagne while I was out." She pointed to the bag on the seat beside her.

"Champagne's better with someone to share it. And it's not good to drink alone."

"How do you know I don't have someone with me?"

He leaned down as if to kiss her, but stopped inches from her face. "Because you came up here to be alone. And because you've gone from alone to lonely by now or you wouldn't be so friendly to me when I'm about to give you a ticket. You're not even trying to talk me out of the ticket, you're just talking." He pulled back, trying, she thought, to pretend he hadn't been flirting.

She took a deep breath. What the hell, he's probably married, he's more than twenty years younger than I am, and he'll probably laugh, but I'm never going to be in this town again and I haven't been this turned on by an actual man, as opposed to one of my own fictional creations, for ages. "You're right. I am lonely, and champagne is much more fun with a friend. What time do you get off duty?"

"Seven." He flushed up to his pale eyes, but Tracy saw from the way he half-turned from her that he was trying to hide a raging erection. Or maybe trying to flaunt it: She never would have noticed if he hadn't moved.

"That's too early. I won't be done by then. Come by around, oh, nine-thirty or ten. I'm in cabin twelve at Johnson's. And wear your uniform, if you don't mind. It's very becoming."

He stammered, "Yes," and headed back to his car.

"Don't forget to give me the ticket," she called after him.

He turned, smiling a dazzlingly white smile. "Oh, I wouldn't forget your ticket, Tracy. I love fast women, but not when they're driving. Someone has to keep you under control." He jingled his handcuffs, laughing.

Tracy pressed her legs together, tightened her pussy, and gripped the steering wheel with white knuckles as a near-orgasm quaked her body. When he came back to hand her the ticket, she was under control again, but she saw in his eyes that he'd noticed the tell-tale flush revealed by her low-cut shirt.

The laptop all but smoked as she typed the last incendiary scenes of her latest book: The encounter with the cop had stimulated more than her body. When she read back over the words, the last clench as Justin and Moira declared their undying passion and true love, there wasn't a thing she wanted to change.

The knock at the door came at 9:30 precisely.

She set the manuscript pages down on the desk. She hadn't really expected him to show up, but she was ready.

Her trooper was in full uniform, as she'd instructed, and carrying two more bottles of champagne. "Too much of a good thing is better," he said, "as long as no one's driving."

"It sounds as if you're planning to stay." She took his hand and felt the shock of something not quite the texture of human skin, something less personal and in its own way more erotic. He was wearing black leather gloves.

"I thought you would like these."

"I do."

"Once in a while I have good instincts." He tossed the champagne onto the bed—the cabin was small enough that he could do that easily—and took her face between his leather-gloved hands. Big hands, hands that covered most of her face, hands that could snap bones if he wanted them to, but were touching her as delicately as another woman might. Leather feathers stroked her face, her throat, her collarbone.

Tracy's bones were melting. She wanted to scream for him to hurry, to touch her breasts, to peel off the jeans that were becoming increasingly confining, or to just stroke her right through them, leather and denim transforming the touch of skin on skin. But she didn't want him to stop what he was doing. He was shy and kinky at the same time; boyish romance and black leather. She'd never known her cheekbones were so sensitive.

Knees rubbery, she reached out, clutched at his hips, pulling him closer, but not close enough to feel his erection. She wanted to feel that and more, but not yet, and she was afraid that if she gave him a signal to move faster, he might move too fast, end this beautiful torment. He was so young he'd probably recover quickly—but she wanted to make this last.

The pants were some kind of unappealing polyester, nubby to the touch, but snug enough that she could tell he wasn't wearing anything underneath. She explored the tight muscles of his hips and buttocks, brushed something cool, metallic. The handcuffs. Her gut twisted, raising her to a new pitch of excitement.

He made a scarcely human noise. One hand slipped to her breast, brushing it. The other twisted into her hair, with a roughness searing and startling after his gentleness, and forced her head back. The kiss burst on her like something out of one of her own novels. Kisses had always been pleasant, fun, a nice prelude—but nothing like this.

How had she missed out on kisses like this?

They were grinding together. Joined at the lips, they tried frantically to connect the rest of their bodies right through their clothing. His tongue was doing such interesting things to the roof of her mouth that Tracy hardly noticed her blouse being unbuttoned and pushed aside.

He pinched one nipple between his leather-covered thumb and forefinger. Had she been less aroused, it would have hurt. As it was, the sensation walked the knife-edge between pleasure and pain, desire and fear—it made her writhe and rub her crotch against his hip. All her nerves seemed to be in her breasts. His thumbs circled her nipples, first gently, then hard enough to bruise.

Then he chuckled. At first, he laughed right into her mouth, then broke away from the kiss and went on laughing, though his hands kept doing a distracted version of their magic on her breasts.

"What's the joke?"

"I just realized I was about ravish you, if you didn't do it to me first, and I never even told you my name."

"Don't." She put her hand to his lips. He licked it. "Maybe later, but not now. Oh, my. I'd forgotten my fingers were so sensitive."

"I think," he said between nibbles, "that all of you is sensitive."

"I need a drink."

"Nervous?"

"Just thirsty. Besides, we have all this champagne."

And I have to breathe. She ran around looking for glasses.

He set down his champagne long enough to remove her blouse, then picked up the glass and splashed some on her breasts. "Oops. Better clean this up." He swirled his tongue around her nipple, then took another swig of champagne.

"Take your clothes off," she breathed.

He looked startled.

"A request, not an order—unless you'd rather have an order. I'd like to see you naked." She traced the outline of his erection with one champagne-dampened finger. "But leave your gloves on."

"Only if you leave your boots on." He stroked her thigh-high boots approvingly.

She laughed. "Let me run into the bathroom. I'll be out in a second."

Seconds later she was posing in the doorway, wearing the boots and a black silk G-string.

"Stay right there," he said. "You might need something to hang onto."

He knelt before her and caressed the boots, molding them to her legs. He kissed, nibbled, stroked her thighs until she wanted to push his face into her and tell him to get on with it. But she didn't. She gripped the doorway and moaned and swayed against him. Finally, he put his mouth where she needed him. The silk still lay between them, a moist, breathing barrier; the tantalizing work of his tongue wasn't quite enough to drive her to the edge. She hung on to the pulsing, crazy sweetness as long as she could stand it, then started to pull the G-string off.

He snapped the fragile silk with one tug.

"Let me sit down," she begged.

"Too much for you?" He followed her to the bed, nipping at her ankles playfully.

"No." She grabbed his hair and pulled him up to eye level. "I want you to fill me up with your fingers while you're eating me, and I want to see you going into me, with the gloves."

He glanced at his hands dubiously. "I don't want to hurt you."

"I'll let you know if it hurts," she said huskily, and kissed him. "But I don't think it will."

Almost too gently, he circled her clit with his finger. It throbbed and tickled. "Now," she choked out. "Put them in me. Two or three." As he slipped the first finger in—so cool and rough, little seams of the gloves tickling in odd places—she panted, "All at once, hard!"

She was so wet that three of his big fingers slipped in easily; she moaned and ground her hips against them. He worked them in and out, grinding her slowly, leisurely, almost as if he didn't notice her moaning and begging for mercy. Her moisture glistened on the black leather. It didn't feel that different from bare fingers, but the sight of leather made all the difference. She was twitching all over with little orgasms—not the big, obliterating kind, but the kind that were just enough to make her beg incoherently for more.

"More?" One finger of his other hand, ungloved, eased into her ass. Then he started licking.

She fell back. The first orgasm pulled a scream out of her that startled her lover for a second—fortunately, not long enough to lose his rhythm. The second—or was it a continuation of the first?—got her bucking, rubbing herself shamelessly against his face and hands, hungry for more. After the third, she lost count, and some time after that, she lost consciousness, for all practical purposes. She was a giant clitoris and pussy and asshole, being pleasured, twisting and wrenching in sweet agony, spilling sweet and salt all over her trooper. Finally, she lay still, half-conscious, panting, drenched in sweat.

When she had enough strength to sit up, he was lying back on the bed, hands behind his head, grinning like a very happy fool. His penis was erect, very thick with a jaunty tilt to it. She wanted desperately to put her lips around his cock.

She did.

He groaned and tangled his fingers in her hair. He was slick under her lips, and she tasted the first hints of semen almost immediately. She was so sated that she sped up; she didn't think she was ready to take him inside so soon after all those orgasms.

"No," he said. "I want to be inside you. You felt so good to my fingers and tongue, so tight and hot." The blood pounded in her ears so that she hardly heard the last words, but she let him roll her over.

He slipped into her; she surrounded him. For a few seconds, they lay still, enjoying the way they fit together. Her muscles tightened around him, and she began to move.

Her body was outside her conscious control, riding a wave of red and purple. He relaxed at first, letting her do the work; her striving against him raised her excitement level. Then he began slamming into her, hard, making the ridiculous, wonderful noises that men make.

She didn't think she'd be able to come again.

She was wrong.

He stayed half-hard inside her even after he collapsed on top of her, worn out. When they rolled apart and she licked away their combined juices, his cock jumped valiantly—but she didn't have the energy to do anything more than admire it. They finished the champagne, drinking straight from the bottle, and collapsed between the damp sheets to sleep.

Tracy woke up with a start. The digital clock blazed 12:46 A.M. What had happened? The trooper slept on his back, one arm over his eyes, the other flung across her. She slipped out and sat up to look at him.

He was spare and hard like a jungle cat, not a trace of fat under the smooth young skin. His cock was at half-mast. He would need only a little encouragement—but she wanted it different this time. She wanted to do him, to wallow in his beauty. She'd be happy to just admire him for a while. It would be nice, though, if he weren't quite so relaxed, if his muscles were tense and his cock bulging. But if he woke up, it would be hard to convince him to lie back and let her do the work.

She remembered the handcuffs. He'd probably wake up, but it was worth a try.

As quietly as she could, she slipped off the bed and found the handcuffs and key. She picked up both their belts to secure his legs to the bed frame.

She expected him to wake at the touch of cool metal, but he was sleeping the sleep of the young and well-fucked, and barely twitched. She sat back and surveyed her work. Heat, a crazy kind of bubbly, exhilarated champagne heat, zinged in her veins.

When she tried to spread his legs, he woke up in a panic. She narrowly avoided being kicked in the face before he realized what she was doing. Then he smiled in a nervous way and nodded, giving his assent. He kept up a token struggle, just enough so that she felt a kind of victory when his legs were spread and tied to the bed with belts.

Tracy stood, put her hands on her hips, and looked at him. His muscles were tense now with anticipation and stood out, even more defined than before. Too bad there wasn't some way to secure him standing on tiptoes with his hands cuffed and stretched overhead, putting maximum tension on all of him—but this was good enough.

"Nice," she breathed.

His cock quivered. He licked his lips. "What are you going to do with me?" he asked. She wasn't sure if his nervousness was play or for real. She hoped it was partly for real.

"Anything I want to." She ran her nails lightly up the inside of his thighs. "Is that understood?"

"Yes, ma'am." He looked away. His erection was fading.

The nervousness was real, then. Disarmed, naked, bound, in a room with a woman he barely knew, the trooper was a scared young man. She wanted power from this encounter—power, yes—but not the power of fear.

"I won't hurt you," she promised, "except I may nibble a little too hard." She bent down and nibbled a delicious ear, then spoke into it. "I'll lighten up if you yell. I just want to play." Her hands roamed as she spoke, and she felt some of his resistance fade. "If anything I do turns you off, say *red*."

"Safeword," he murmured. She raised her eyebrows and he added, "Hey, I may be young, but I read a lot."

"Good," she said. "Have fun." She ran two fingers across her labia, then put them to his lips. He sucked eagerly, and her whole body throbbed. She could have started riding him then and there, but she held back.

She wanted to kiss, stroke, and otherwise enflame every possible inch of his skin, until his whole body was as sensitized as his penis. But there was no way she would have the patience, not in the state she was in just from seeing him helpless before her. She straddled his face, just out of his reach. She opened her pussy lips, ensuring that he would have a good, tantalizing view. Two fingers of her other hand circled her clit. She could bring herself off in about thirty seconds, but she took her time, enjoying her rising arousal, the frustration on his face, the way he strained against his bonds to reach her.

"Let me," he begged.

She shook her head. "Not this time. Just enjoy watching." She ran her slick fingers over his lips and he sucked them.

"I do enjoy it," he said. "Do you like being watched?"

It was becoming difficult to talk. "Not...always. It just seemed right tonight.... Ohh!" She threw her head back and convulsed as an orgasm took her over.

She kissed him deeply on the lips. Their tongues engaged, and again she wondered where she'd been all her life not to know that kissing could feel this great. She worked her way down to his chin and around his face—up to the eyes, the cheekbones, the forehead—then back to his lips. She traced his jawbone with her lips, then his right ear, where she settled in to see if, as she'd read somewhere long ago, you really could make someone come with prolonged earlobe stimulation. Her hands stroked the insides of his arms and played in the fur of his armpits.

Either he couldn't come from earlobe play or she wasn't quite patient enough, but they had fun trying. She nibbled her way down his neck toward his lightly haired chest, and detoured at the armpit. No deodorant, just healthy young man smell—clean a few hours before and now nicely rutty. She licked the salt sweat and he squirmed.

"No one's ever done that to me before," he said. "Then again, no one's ever done a lot of the things you do." She kissed his mouth again, then clamped her lip over one flat little nipple.

She rolled it between her lips and flicked it with rapid hummingbird movements of her tongue, while she teased the other with her fingers. Men didn't, in her experience, usually relate to their nipples very well—they just didn't know how much fun they could be. Ten minutes later, judging by the state of his erection, his flushed, sweaty condition, and the way he was begging for mercy, her trooper knew.

She licked down to his navel, then worked her way up again, kissing every inch of his ridged belly. "You're going the wrong way," he moaned, trying to move her head down by writhing. It didn't work. She intended to enjoy every inch of his magnificently muscled belly first.

She did, then blew a raspberry in his belly button and kissed her way down. When her lips brushed his pubic hair, she raised her head a little and blew warm breath on his cock and balls before sinking her teeth into his hip bone.

His hip and buttock muscles were well-defined, even to her tongue.

He was frantic now, arching against his bonds, begging. Still, she was resolute, exploring his thighs with hands and tongue, biting the backs of his knees, stroking his hairy calves, nibbling his Achilles tendons. One by one, she sucked his toes, each one for two minutes by the digital clock. She was yearning to be filled, yearning for him to touch her again—but she was also determined to keep this up as long as she could. She worked her way deliberately up the other leg.

She parted his buttocks with her hands, squeezing the muscles, digging in her nails.

Finally, she took him into her mouth, where his cock seemed to leap and grow. He was trembling and moaning inarticulately. She played him as long as she could. "Please," he begged her, "please, please...."

"Please what?" She raised her head just long enough to say the words.

"Please...."

"Please what?" She licked him like an ice-cream cone. "What do you want?"

"Please...let me come."

"In my mouth or my pussy?"

He didn't answer, at least not very articulately, so the decision was hers. Giving the head of the penis one last playful kiss, she mounted him and started to ride.

He felt huge inside her, and he wasn't even trying to move, just letting her do what she wished. Part of her wanted to drag it on, but the feel of him, the sight of his face contorted with an agonized desire, and the rut smell filling the room, made that impossible. She saw an explosion behind her eyes and moved wildly to catch up with it, grinding herself against him. When the orgasm overtook her, it was long and hot and almost painful, the kind that left her sprawled limp and drained on his chest. She nearly didn't hear his harsh cry through her own screams.

Just before she dozed off, Tracy mustered the strength to unlock and untie the trooper. Almost unconscious himself, he threw an arm around her. "What's your name?" she asked drowsily.

"Dan. Dan Brady."

"Nice. Irish," she muttered, and fell asleep.

JOLI AGNEW

Cotton Gloves

Myrlee heard the car tires crunching the gravel driveway. A surge of relief flooded her veins. *Ordella's home.*

Glancing at the bedside clock, Myrlee noted the time. *Almost midnight. How long does a Mother's Day dinner last?*

Knowing Ordella's children, they probably tried to keep their mother overnight. The kids hated their mother's relationship with Myrlee. Hated Myrlee. They never brought the subject out in the open. It was not something they wanted to discuss. To know. Just the idea of their mother having a sex life upset them.

The scratching of a key in the lock alerted Myrlee. She stayed in the bedroom; she didn't want Ordella to know she'd waited up for her, that she'd worried all day.

Ordella entered the silent house. Myrlee was comforted by the sound of her partner's clicking heels. Comforted—yet her heart pumped with anticipation when Ordella entered the bedroom.

Myrlee faked sleep, watching Ordella through half-open eyes. She needed this moment to see what kind of mood Ordella was in. She was hoping horny, but Myrlee seriously doubted it. Her lover was probably exhausted.

The hall light streamed into the bedroom, casting a soft glow on Ordella. She looked beautiful in her hat and dress. Elegant and refined, aloof and regal, like an African goddess. This wasn't the woman Myrlee knew intimately. She couldn't wait for Ordella to strip off the clothes and expose the earthy, sensual woman underneath.

Ordella reached up to pull the long pin out of her white wide-brimmed hat. She took off the hat and ran her gloved hand through the tight, graying curls.

She tugged the fingers of her startling white gloves, short pulls starting from the little finger to the thumb. Myrlee felt each tug deep in her tummy. She watched, mesmerized, as Ordella peeled the elbow-length glove off her brown hand and started on the other one. Myrlee didn't think she could handle the innocent undressing.

"Ordella?" Myrlee murmured.

Ordella's head turned sharply. "Did I wake you up?" she whispered, tugging the glove off and tossing it onto the floor. "I'm sorry."

"No, no. I'm glad to see you. I've missed you." Myrlee winced at her own words. She hadn't wanted to reveal that. She made a show of looking at the clock. "It's midnight. I guess you had a good time."

"It was good to see all my kids and grandbabies." Ordella kicked off her leather shoes while unbuttoning her yellow silk dress.

"What did you do?"

"What we do every year." The silk slid down her curves and pooled onto the floor. "It's a tradition."

Myrlee tuned out Ordella's description of the Mother's Day breakfast, the church ceremony, and the outing at the National Zoo, allowing the melodic flow of her voice to coast over her tightening muscles.

"Those grandbabies of mine wore me out." She unsnapped her creamy white bra. Her full breasts burst out into freedom.

Myrlee stared at the amazing sight. Desire blazed through her chest. She never got tired of seeing her lover's naked breasts. "And how were the kids?" She didn't really want to know, but she felt Ordella would like to talk about her two children.

Ordella rolled her eyes as she shucked off her panties. Myrlee bit her lip to prevent herself from purring. "Monique wants me to baby-sit a couple of times this week."

Myrlee swallowed a sigh. Knowing Ordella, she'd agreed, whether or not she had the time. "And DeShaun?"

Ordella sighed. "He asked me for a 'loan' again."

Myrlee's full lips twisted in anger. What was wrong with Ordella's children? The day was supposed to honor their mother, and all they did was try to get something out of her. It was just like any other day.

"What did they give you?" Myrlee asked, recognizing the huskiness in her voice.

"My grandkids gave me some artwork that I promised I would display prominently on my refrigerator." Ordella's white teeth flashed in the darkness as she smiled, sending a curious warmth through Myrlee's heart. "Monique gave me a necklace and DeShaun got me flowers. Oh, and they all gave me a corsage."

Myrlee's mouth slackened as she watched Ordella walk to the dresser and remove a nightgown from the drawer, an old present from one of her kids. A granny's nightgown.

Hmm…seems Ordella is still in grandmother mode.

"Don't bother putting that on." Myrlee's voice came out as a seductive growl.

"Huh?" Ordella stopped and looked over her shoulder. "What?"

"That nightgown will be off of you in a matter of seconds," Myrlee promised.

Ordella turned around and placed her hands on her ample hips. "Is that right?" she teased.

Myrlee flipped a corner of the blanket. "Come here so I can give you your Mother's Day present."

"What are you talking about?" Ordella sauntered toward the bed.

"OK, so only children and fathers give the presents. But I think it's time to start a new tradition."

"I like the sound of that." Ordella crawled into bed. She opened her arms and cradled Myrlee close. Their lips met. Ordella placed soft, sweet kisses on the edge of Myrlee's mouth. Myrlee nibbled Ordella's pouty lips. She slicked her tongue along the crease of Ordella's mouth. Ordella surprised her by brushing her lips across her cheek and forehead.

What is going on? Where is the wildness? What happened to the down-and-dirty, raunchy Ordella?

Ordella splayed her hand on Myrlee's throat. She trailed her fingers down to Myrlee's small breast, cupping it gently before stroking along the slope, then brushed her thumb against Myrlee's hardening nipple.

Myrlee gave up kissing her lover in hopes of transforming her back into a wanton woman. *Damn, her kids did a number on her today. Ordella sees herself only as a mother and grandmother. She's forgetting about being a woman. A purely feminine woman.*

"Suck me," Ordella muttered hoarsely, pushing her breast into Myrlee's face.

Myrlee greedily latched onto Ordella's nipple, drawing deeply on the hard brown nub. She frowned as Ordella stroked her hair.

This gentleness has got to stop. Myrlee began to suck and chew Ordella's breasts. Her hands trailed Ordella's rounded bottom. She grabbed and squeezed, desperately wanting to provoke a response.

"Yes, baby. Yeah, just like that," Ordella crooned.

Baby! Uh-uh. Nope. This is not going to work. Myrlee pulled away from Ordella's breast and slicked wet kisses on her stomach, her mind whirling in confusion.

Nothing is working. I want to tear away this nurturing and save the sensuous woman suffocating inside.

An idea trickled into her mind. She paused, inhaling the cinnamon scent of her lover. There was something that Myrlee had wanted to try. Wanted, but had been too scared to carry it out, too embarrassed to demand.

Was this the right time for it? If Ordella wasn't ready, would this caregiver personality stay intact? Would it freak her out?

But if Ordella was ready for it, ripe for it, then the woman she knew and loved would no longer be trapped.

The nurturing, motherly image would melt away.

Myrlee didn't want to ignore the mother aspect of Ordella—it was a part of her, part of how she viewed and lived her life. How could she honor that aspect of Ordella and at the same time make her forget it for a moment?

It was risky. Very risky. Maybe she should wait until tomorrow.

No. She was going to do it now. Remind Ordella that she was more than a caregiver. More than a mother and grandmother. She was Ordella—a strong, sensual, feminine woman.

"Lie on your back," Myrlee said.

Ordella looked at her quizzically, but quietly obeyed.

"Wait right here," Myrlee softly commanded. She slid off the bed and searched the floor. The pure white gloves shone in the darkness. Myrlee scooped them up and returned to the bed.

She straddled Ordella's waist, grinding her pelvis provocatively into her soft stomach. Myrlee wrapped her fingers around Ordella's wrists and stretched her arm above the headboard.

"We're going to try something different tonight," Myrlee announced.

"Like what?"

"Hold still while I tie you to the bed."

Ordella's eyes widened. "Uh...I'm not sure about this."

"You've been curious," Myrlee cautiously reminded her. *Please don't say no.*

"Yeah, but...." Her voice trailed off with indecision.

"Hush. If you can't take it, just say the word 'flower.'"

Ordella hesitated. "OK."

Myrlee tied her hands to the spindle headboard with the gloves. She did her best not to make them tight; that might make Ordella panic.

"Are you comfortable?" Myrlee asked.

"I think so." She pulled against the gloves. Her fingers flexed and bunched.

With a feathery touch, Myrlee trailed one hand down Ordella's arms. Ordella twisted violently.

"Stop that! It tickles."

"Sorry." Myrlee smiled wickedly. "I won't be gentle anymore."

"Good," Ordella said with a challenging smile.

Myrlee descended on her like a starving woman, wiping away Ordella's superior smile. Her hands roamed Ordella's voluptuous curves while her tongue plundered inside her mouth.

That luscious mouth. As a mother she'd kissed away the hurts and sung her babies to sleep. Now Ordella's mouth did nasty things. Her tongue could bring Myrlee to the edge of heaven and back.

Myrlee slid down to Ordella's throat, sucking and biting, placing love bites on the elegant brown skin. Ordella's guttural groans sparked a wet excitement inside Myrlee.

She moved to Ordella's breasts. They were large and full, slightly sagging with age and years of breastfeeding. Myrlee preferred them to younger, perkier breasts: They were more beautiful and intriguing. She rolled one nipple with her tongue and the other with frantic fingers. She pinched the nipple and listened to Ordella groan with savage pleasure. Myrlee ran the sharp edge of her teeth against the sensitive nipple. Ordella arched her spine, pulling herself upward, but the ties held her fast to the bed.

Myrlee continued nipping and tweaking Ordella's nipples at a fast and furious pace. She watched with fascination as Ordella tossed her head from side to side.

"Damn, Myrlee. Oh...damn."

She licked and slicked her tongue down Ordella's stomach. Behind the dark brown flesh lay the womb where she'd carried her children. Now her womb twitched and vibrated with lust.

Myrlee poked her tongue into her navel and Ordella screeched with surprise. Myrlee didn't linger, intent on exploring what hid beneath the wiry thatch of gray curls. Inhaling Ordella's female scent, Myrlee dove her questing fingers into her wetness. Ordella bucked at the invasion, her womanly thighs quivering with need.

"Please...please."

Myrlee tormented her with her fingers. Ordella in ecstasy was a breathtaking sight. "You're quite a woman."

"Now, Myrlee! Now!"

Myrlee attacked Ordella's womanhood with gusto, munching and slurping, pressing her face deep between her spread legs. Ordella hooked her trembling knees over Myrlee's bare shoulders and bore down on her mouth. Myrlee wildly claimed Ordella, who twisted and yanked at the bindings, desperate to take control, yet finding her position intensely arousing.

Ordella soon became wild. She bucked and thrashed, moaned and begged. She swore with astonishing vulgarity as her body gave in to exquisite submission, and she came violently, screams of release erupting from her straining throat. The aftershocks of Ordella's orgasm were just as powerful. Gulping for air, she closed her eyes and succumbed to the tremors of her exhausted muscles.

Myrlee climbed over Ordella and pulled the gloves free. She inspected Ordella's wrists. They felt tender but the ties hadn't cut into the skin.

Myrlee stretched out on her side of the bed and gathered Ordella close.

"Just give me a minute," Ordella murmured.

"Ssh. Later. Go to sleep."

"Didn't you like—?"

"I loved it. I loved giving you your Mother's Day present."

"What? I have to wait another year for that?" Ordella teased.

"We'll see," Myrlee responded lightly, already planning when she could tie Ordella up again. Try something different, like in the living room...or the bathroom. Myrlee gritted her teeth, throbbing with lust. "We'll see."

JOANNE MILLER

The Clockmaker

Some years ago, when I lived in the city, a lover had given me the gift of an antique silver wristwatch. I hadn't thought about it, or him, for some time. But lately, I've been thinking a lot about the choices I didn't make.

Not that he would have been a good match for me. He was new to America, recently emigrated from Italy, and he was much more daring and open, much more fearless than I. And I suspected that his affection for me was based more on permanent citizenship than true love. But how can one be sure, really? A few months after saying good-bye to the silver watch man, I met and married my husband.

Although it's hard to believe now, my courting-husband-to-be couldn't keep his hands off me, always telling me how beautiful I was, giving me his full attention and concern. It was wonderful.

He and I are little more than roommates these days—polite, friendly, and living in our own separate worlds. I suppose I should accept passion as a thing of youth—the years have worn down my physical beauty, it's true, but I have other equally attractive traits that he never seems to notice. I feel invisible, which conjures up what-might-have-been.

I hadn't seen the silver watch for many years, but while looking through an old storage case, I came across it. Since my daughter was about to turn twenty-five and had been hinting for a new watch, I considered fixing the one I held in my hand. If reparable, it would be perfect—she appreciated antiques, especially art deco. Like me, she valued the craftsmanship that was a part of so many artifacts of that era.

I set about finding a repairman in the usual way, with a telephone book and a prepared battery of questions. One fellow I called, who listed himself as a specialist in antique clock restoration and rebuilding, answered my questions in a heavy German accent. I pictured him, snowy-headed and gnome-like, hunched over his worktable, a Disney version of the Old European Craftsman—Geppetto with cuckoos. He worked out of his apartment in the next town and specialized in timepieces of this type. Since his prices were neither more nor less than anyone else's, I decided to give him a try.

His apartment was in an undistinguished older two-story building in a quiet suburban neighborhood. The maples lining the street were already beginning to show early fall color.

When he opened the door, I was astonished to find that he was probably less than thirty years of age. Barefoot, wearing baggy shorts and a T-shirt, he was roughly as tall as I, but with disproportionately large hands, feet, and head. He was obviously very shy, looking into my face infrequently as we talked. His English, though heavily accented, was excellent, and very precise. Something about his eyes engaged my attention right away, and during his hurried glances, I could see that the iris in his left eye was divided into two colors—hazel-brown, and blue. His eyes were large, and he had a sensuous, well-formed mouth. I stared at it a little too much when he spoke. Because he was so casually dressed, I felt odd, as though I were intruding at an intimate moment, though that was not really the case. The apartment itself was very small, with the bedroom serving as a workroom, a galley-type kitchen, and a narrow single bed in the living room, neatly made up. No television.

He took the watch into the bedroom and beckoned me to follow; the room was painted a bright white to reflect the light, and was as spotless as a laboratory. Neat rows of small plastic boxes containing cog-like wheels, numbered faces, crystals of various sizes, and tiny bronze instruments were aligned on either side of a large lamp with a magnifying glass attached. As he examined the watch under the light, his eyes would swing to my feet, my hips—never my face. These stolen looks excited me. That odd chemistry—nature's drug that makes the brain servant to desire—was spreading like a fine vapor in that tiny room, inhaled with every breath of our polite interactions. I couldn't believe this was happening.

"I'm concerned about the cost," I said, though I really wasn't. I wanted to retain some control. My heart was racing. This was ridiculous.

"I assure you that it would not be more than you wish to spend," he said formally.

I left the watch with him, planning to return in a few days, and I hurried out of the apartment.

He popped up in my thoughts throughout the next week—the way his muscles bulged beneath the baggy clothes, his mesmerizing eyes. I wondered what his skin smelled like. Ridiculous thoughts and peculiar longings sneaked into my day-to-day routine. Feelings I barely remembered. My husband's well-ordered life, up at six, home at seven, failed to diminish my peculiar new mental toy. I concluded that I was bored, and must find some new outlet. Knitting, perhaps—until I could content myself with grandchildren.

When I returned to pick up the timepiece, the clockmaker answered the door in dishevelment again, and looked at me indirectly. The watch was ready.

I followed him into the small room and he sat on the stool, holding the watch in his open hands like an offering. He told me the repair price; it was nearly double what I had expected to pay. "That's far more than you told me it would cost," I said.

"It was necessary to put a great deal of time into the work, more than I expected. It needed considerably more attention, being unused for many years." He went on to explain what he had done, the extra work that was necessary, and so forth. "I would not do less than the best work for you," he said.

"Money is a problem for me." I don't know why I told him that. What was I trying to prove? "I don't think I brought enough." I nervously fiddled with my bag, fumbling with the clasp. He put out his hand and closed it over the top of my purse. This time he looked at me steadily and directly.

I had my back to the wall near the door, and he was seated two feet away in front of his worktable. His look shot through me as if he had hit me in the solar plexus and knocked the wind out. He lowered the purse to the floor, pushing it aside with his foot. There was now nothing between us. I felt completely naked.

I raised my arm and hand across my breasts protectively. I could see the pulsing bulge growing in the front of his pants as his eyes followed my hand. I looked at the floor, my breath coming in short pants. He didn't say anything, but looked at my arm and nodded. I remembered another room and another seated man—the young Italian, so many years ago.

My hand went to the top button on my blouse. I felt numb—yet at the same time more excited than I had ever been. I unbuttoned it, and went to the next until I reached my waist, then dropped my hands to my sides.

"Don't stop," he said.

I pulled my blouse apart, exposing the front of my bra, and undid the remaining buttons. I pulled my bra up, dragging up then pushing down on my small breasts. His hard look made my nipples stiffen and my breath quicken even more. His hand moved to the front of his shorts. Gently he stroked his erect penis, wrapping his palm around it. He unsnapped his shorts, and delicately pinched the zipper between his fingers, pulling it down and spreading it apart to expose his white underwear. The tip of his deep red penis protruded from the top. He gestured to me.

I moved toward him, my hands by my sides, my breasts jutting out under the elastic of my bra. He reached up under my skirt and tugged at my pantyhose. I rolled the hose down to my thighs. He put his hand flat across my pubic hair, and I pressed into it. I moaned. I never took my eyes from his. He forced my damp pantyhose down to my knees. I took off one shoe and one side of the panty hose.

All this time, he had not moved from the stool. He pulled his shorts and underwear down to his knees, and sat down again, his stiff, throbbing penis bobbing with each movement. It was big, like his hands and head, as big as my forearm.

He wrapped his fingers gently around my hands and pulled me toward him; I opened my legs and squatted down over him, guiding his hard penis into my creamy opening. The tip rubbed against my clit and slid into the greedy mouth of my cunt.

I had gotten looser over the years, but with him, it didn't matter: I had to push to take him in. Every millimeter sent an electric pulse of pleasure up our bodies. I was afraid I couldn't take it all. Once, I pulled up, suddenly conscious of what I was doing and where I was. He quickly placed his hands on my hips and guided me slowly, further down his pole, until I rested above his shiny pubic hair. God, I felt so filled up! He kept his eyes on my breasts, but his hands went around to pull my butt in closer and impale me further on his stiff cock.

Then he began to move, pushing himself into me, groaning softly with each wavelike thrust. I opened my legs further and ground my clit into his abdomen, wrapping my arms around his shoulders and pressing my tits into his face. He grabbed a breast, then pinched the nipple hard as he continued to rhythmically pulse his hips back and forth.

"Wait a moment," he said, "just a moment."

"No, no," I moaned—my orgasm was coming on like a herd of mustangs. "Don't stop, oh please."

"Oh," he said, "yes!" as if surprised. He held my hips slightly away from his and thrust more quickly. I spread my legs to the maximum, accepting and meeting every thrust. He pushed himself into me with a grunt, and his big cock jerked with each spurt. I closed around him, thrusting myself into him a final time, and came and came and came.

We sat there a few more moments before disengaging. He looked at me with gentle tenderness, and touched my arm as I rearranged my clothing. "You owe me nothing," he said.

"I owe you everything."

I left the payment on his kitchen counter on my way out, watch in hand. In the car on the way home, I could smell delicious sex, and feel the wetness on my thighs. I would have expected to feel guilty, but I didn't. I felt full of life. I felt defiant. Passion wasn't only for the young—and however I could get it, starting with trying to light a fire under that old-fart husband of mine, I wanted to try.

I knew that there was no future for the beautiful clockmaker and me, but I'll tell anyone who asks about his magical ability to bring new life to antiques.

MARCY SHEINER

Send in the Clowns

My panties are soaking wet. I've been walking around the mall for the past two hours, shopping on automatic pilot, remembering last night's lovemaking with my husband.

My name is Margie Cassena. Mrs. Frank Cassena. I'm fifty-seven years old and have been married to Paul for thirty-five years. We raised four children—three girls and a boy—and have two granddaughters. By the time they're all done I expect we'll have something like fifteen or twenty grandchildren, and to that I say, the sooner the better.

Most of these years our marriage has been what you'd call happy. We've had our share of tragedies, the worst being losing our second baby to crib death. And there were some rough years when we almost didn't make it. During the '70s we smoked a lot of pot, popped a lot of pills, and went to "house key" parties where the husbands threw their keys into a bowl and the wives fished them out, each woman going home with the owner of whichever key they got. Two years into this insane trip, Paul and I separated—but within six months we reunited, stopped all the nonsense, and had our fourth child.

Paul's retired now. I never had to work—had my hands full with four kids anyway—but I did manage to do a bit of writing, and even got a few poems published in literary journals, which made Paul even prouder than it made me. We're not rich, but compared to the majority of the world's population we certainly do live well. Paul built our house when he first got into construction, and over the years he added on to it. We own a few rental properties. When I left for the mall today he smacked my ass playfully and said, "Don't spend all my money," and I laughed, knowing that he loves it when I spend "his" money.

Of course we fight; what couple doesn't? We fight as passionately as we make love, sometimes both at the same time. Yesterday was a whopper. The subjects of our fights change, but they usually follow a predictable pattern—Paul does something stupid, I curse and scream at him, he curses right back, I walk away crying, and a few hours later he apologizes. Last night when he came to me full of remorse, with flowers no less, he promised he'd make it up to me. I know what that means. It means I get to be a pillow queen, to just lie back and take it; that the sex is all for me.

He led me to bed, wouldn't even let me take a shower though I was grubby from working in the garden. He undressed me, fastened my wrists and ankles to the bedposts with his own ties, wrapped another one around my eyes, and washed my pussy with a warm soapy cloth. I begged him to take the blindfold off, because watching him during sex is one of the biggest turn-ons for me, but he said it was staying on till after he had a chance to eat me. Then he spread my legs wide and cleaved my pussy with his tongue, knowing exactly how hard or soft or fast or slow to go, following the cues of my moans and wiggles almost instinctively. After so many years, our sex is like a long, familiar conversation, with little surprises thrown in now and then to keep things interesting.

He buried his mouth in my cunt and drank my juices—and let me tell you, I was flowing like a river. He ate me for a good half-hour, until I was dying to come—and we both know I hardly ever come from being eaten. Paul long ago gave up trying—thank God. When we were first married he used to dive in like a maniac, insisting that I at least try to come that way—but he's finally learned that I'll come my own way in my own sweet time, and lets me be.

Finally he loosened one of the ankle ties and one of my wrists so that I could climb on top of him. I sat down on his throbbing dick, and pulled off the blindfold. I love to sit on his cock and look down at his face; I can see the teenage boy I fell in love with beneath the middle-aged face, the hard, rippling muscles under the recent layers of fat. I confess that I love just as much to watch my own silhouette on the wall—with my long hair flowing and my back arching, when all you can see is a dark shadow without wrinkles. Hell, I look almost like a teenager again myself.

I leaned forward so that my tits were hanging in his face. He took one in each hand and growled, "Mine. I own them."

"Yes. Yours. All yours." Ferociously I ground my cunt against him. My jaw slackened and my eyes lost focus, and that familiar orgasmic feeling moved through my cunt; slowly my insides undulated, radiating waves of pleasure up and down my arms, my legs, my toes, my fingers. Paul rolled me over then and thrust furiously, harder and faster, with my cunt contracting around his cock. I watched his face scrunch up with that exquisite feeling. "I'm coming, babe," he said. His cock stiffened, and then bathed my cervix in hot semen.

He curled himself around me, one hand on my breast. "Do you know how lucky we are?" he murmured into my ear.

"I know how lucky *I* am."

"*We're* lucky, babe, *we* are. Because we still love each other."

I took his hand from my breast and kissed each of his fingers, then drifted into a blissful sleep.

If this sounds too good to be true, that's because it is. The real story is, I am a fifty-seven-year-old woman living alone five hundred miles away from my only child—a daughter—and my two grandsons, whom I constantly and achingly miss—so much, in fact, that I'm thinking of moving to be closer to them. It will be perhaps the thirtieth move of my life, each one aimed at improving my circumstances in some way—which it will. But as I know all too well from experience, the improvements will be temporary, until new problems surface to replace those that the move has resolved. I support myself as a writer, thus am perpetually broke. (I would say I am poor, even, but that would be an insult to people who live in real poverty.) I am terribly lonely. Oh, I have friends, a few so beloved I would die for them. I get laid maybe five times a year, by ex-lovers or "fuck buddies" or newly met men who come and go with the breeze.

Paul Cassena is real, all right—but he's some other woman's husband. He's *The Boy I Left Behind*, who turned out to be *The Man Who Got Away*.

Paul pursued me relentlessly throughout our high school years and beyond—and just as relentlessly I ran away. To an insecure teenage girl, he seemed overbearing: everywhere I went, everywhere I looked, there was Paul Cassena, staring at me with pathetic, bovine eyes, telling me he loved me, pleading for a date, a kiss, eventually marriage. A few times I burst into frustrated tears, begging him to leave me alone: Today what he did would probably be called *stalking*.

But Paul was a lively, funny, sweet boy; the real problem was that I didn't think enough of myself back then to value anyone who would love me, and so I didn't trust that he really did. Instead of giving Paul a chance, I fell in love with sadists, or with handsome boys devoid of personality, none of whom returned my affections. At nineteen I broke Paul's heart finally and ultimately by marrying one of the sadists. The marriage lasted six years.

I could paint my life in happier terms. It has certainly been interesting. I've been in the thick of the big issues of my times, and have been intimately involved in some significant social changes. I've met some of the most intriguing people of my generation. I've loved people on all points of the gender continuum, some ferociously, some now dead, some of whom I still love. I've had mind-blowing, life-altering sex; my only regrets in that department are the times I said no.

But two weeks ago, modern technology brought Paul Cassena's words into my e-mail in-box, into my heart and my brain and my cunt. In just two short weeks we've rehashed the past, speculated on what might have been, and confessed intimate thoughts and feelings.

Paul's been married to his second wife for over twenty years; they have three kids and a passel of grandchildren who live nearby. He lives three thousand miles away from me, enmeshed in family, business, and friends. It is eminently clear that this relationship can go nowhere—unless, perhaps, the real Mrs. Cassena were to die. But I refuse to hope for a future, even in fantasy, based on another woman's death.

Yes, I have just returned from the mall, my panties wet from the fantasy of fucking Paul in our marital bed. But believe me, my cunt is not the only part of me that's wet.

BERTICE BERRY

The Erotic Adventures of Jim and Louella Parsons

It all started when Jim couldn't get it up. I guess I should find another way to say it, but we just country folks. That's how we put it. That was two months ago, and he been 'fraid to try ever since. Anyway, we been married for twenty-six years and have had more than our share in the love department. We youngish still; both in our fifties, and we got a lot of love left. I told Jim just that, but it didn't help none. In all our years of marriage ahead and three before, I have never seen him so upset. Jim has a lot of pride. He don't like the idea of not being able to do his business. I stopped trying to talk sense into him and did the next best thing.

Now, I had learned years before not to take stock in none of those women's magazines. Their sex tips usually included some food or saran wrap. Jim didn't like nothing too messy. He said the only thing he wants wet is me. Anyway, whenever things were tough with me and Jim, I pray that God will give me strength, make me humble and show me where I'm wrong. Then I talk to the ancestors. I talk to them like they still alive, too. I just do it in my sleep. They always know the answers. This time I call on the women: my mama, Aunt T, and Grandma Sadie. They a hoot.

Mama say, "Hey, girl. Don't say a word. We know just why we here."

"Uh huh," Aunt T say. "Jim can't do the do."

Grandma Sadie tell them to hush. She say, "*They* men weren't too good *no* time." She say it's better to have a man who have it but lose it all the way once, than one who never lose it but only halfway does it the rest of the time.

Now I laugh. Grandma Sadie tell me that our problem is that we done got way too comfortable with each other. She say we hit it every Wednesday and sometimes on Sunday (depending on how good my fried chicken is). Until then, I didn't know about that connection, but I vow to take more time with Sunday dinner from that point on.

Mama say, "Girl, you need to spice things up a bit, fix your hair and put on a little makeup."

Mama know that I ain't into nothing too fancy, but I remind her anyway. Aunt Sadie say I need to learn some other positions. She say I got the wife and the mother part down pat, but I need to be a bit more whorish in the bedroom.

Grandma Sadie say, "Hush. Good loving ain't in no makeup, and it certainly ain't in no slutty ways. If the man want a whore, he pay one."

Grandma Sadie say the loving in the bedroom is in all the things you do before you get there. She also say me and Jim are real good to each other, better than most, but we need to find each another all over again.

I ask her what she mean, and she say, "Girl, when the last time you rubbed that man's behind?" Before I can act shocked or tell her "never," she say, "Uh huh, that's what I'm talking about. Jim knows what he got, and he thinks he knows how he likes it. What makes a man hot is making his woman hot. He thinks he knows just what to touch and how to touch it. In all the years you've been married and all the time you were sneaking before, Jim ain't had to figure out too much. He made you happy in bed because he made you happy in life. But girl, there's a lot more you should be doing."

At that point, I want to ask what, but I hear Jim getting up so I do too. I roll over and see Jim lying on his stomach. I can tell that he's feeling badly because it's Wednesday, and in the morning he's usually feeling like he want it. Most times, but not always, he gets it too. Usually, I wait for him to come to me, but this time I go to him. I rubbed Jim's behind slow and soft at first. I hear him moaning real low.

"Mmm, baby, that feels good," he say.

I rub it some more and he turn over. And I see what I haven't seen in a long time. Mr. Jim, that's what I call him, is standing at full attention. Jim so excited he can't wait to say hello to Miss Lou. That's what he call me down there, on account of my name is Louella. Jim open my legs quicker than he usually do. He ain't wait to see if I'm ready, but I don't care, seeing his joy make me too happy to say anything. As soon as Jim try to get in Miss Lou, he loses himself.

"Dammit, God dammit," he say.

"Take your time, baby," I tell him.

I start rubbing his behind some more, but Jim too shamed to try again. He mumble "sorry" and get dressed and go on to the job he has had for as long as we been married. I pray that he don't lose that too.

After he leave, I go back to sleep so I can ask Grandma Sadie what I need to do. As soon as I get there, they're waiting.

"Girl, I told you. You need to be more seductive," Aunt T was saying.

"Hush up, girl," my mama told her. "Can't you see she feels badly enough?"

"Look like to me she ain't feeling nothing at all," Aunt T said, laughing.

"Be quiet, y'all," Grandma Sadie told them. "Baby, listen and listen good. I'm gonna give you the magic you need, but you got to add the spice to it. Like I said before, you've been doing the same thing the same way for years. You need to get to know every inch of that man's body and what really makes him feel good."

I tell her I thought I did. She say Jim and me don't know what we like 'cause we ain't had it. I don't say nothing 'cause I figure she on the other side. She got to know more than I do.

She say, "Baby, what I'm gonna tell you take patience and your 'bility to follow through. You got to do just what I tell you. How you do it is up to you, though.

"Tonight," she say, looking me right in the eyes, "you and Jim sit on this bed and talk about everything you think you want to do or have done to you. It's gonna be hard, but all you can do is talk. Don't touch no matter how hard he get. Tomorrow night you can touch each other, but you can't touch it. Then, the next night you can touch it, but don't taste. Next night, taste but don't enter. Then, on the last night, get ready to go in."

That night, Jim came home tired as always. I cook him his Sunday chicken dinner, and it ain't even Sunday. Jim smile at me real sweet, but say, "Baby, I don't want to try...let's give it some time."

I tell him, "Fine. I don't want to, but I do want to talk."

I take Jim into the bedroom that I had cleaned real good. I had the bed linens changed and sprinkled my best perfume on them.

"Sit down, Jim," I say. "Now, Jim," I say, "for years we've been doing things the same, but we gonna try something new."

Jim start to tell me how tired he is, but I tell him to listen. He ain't really seen me like that, but I know he like it. I sit him on the bed and undress him real slow. I never did that before either. When I take off his pants, I let my fingers touch him real lightly, but I remember what my grandma say so I stop myself. Then I undress. Now you got to believe me when I say this. I don't think I've ever been naked in front of my man with the lights on, so all this is making him crazy. I'm not as fine as I used to be, but he didn't see with the lights on then so all he knows is now. I sit on the other side of the bed, and Jim thinks I'm asking for some.

I tell him, "Tonight, baby, we just gonna talk. Tell me what you like, and I'll tell you. Tomorrow you get to touch me, but you can't touch me now. Friday you can touch and Saturday you can touch it and taste it. Sunday, after church, if you still want to, I'll let you in."

With that, Mr. Jim came right to attention, and I was so wet I coulda slid right off my bed. Just that little bit of talk done got us hot and ready, but I know that I gotta do just what Grandma Sadie say. So I start.

"Jim," I tell him, "I love the way you moan. It's telling me that it's good. I love the way you pull my knees apart, but I wish you would stroke my thighs and play with my breasts more and my nipples. I know they ain't like they used to be, but I still got feelings. I love your kisses too, but I wish..."

This takes me a while to say, but Jim jump up and say, "What, baby? Just tell me."

Finally, I get to it. "I wish you would kiss Miss Lou. I want you to put those big lips of yours right down there. I want you to kiss it and put your tongue on it."

I was shamed to say all that, but Jim says, "Alright, baby." He was about to do it right then, but I tell him it gotta wait.

Then I say, "Jim, I need you to touch me more. I want you to put your hand on my head like you used to. And Jim, years ago you used to smack me on the behind a little. I won't mind if you do that too."

Jim sure enough was grinning. So was I. Talking about it made me want to climb on top of him and ride him to kingdom come.

"Jim," I say, "it's your turn."

Jim ain't say nothing, but I open my eyes to see his hand is holding Mr. Jim and giving himself some good love.

"Jim!" I say, "You gotta wait." I declare. I have to call him three times before he comes to.

"Oh, yeah. Okay. Sorry, babe. Seem like I kind of got lost."

"It's your turn," I say.

Jim say okay and tell me things that make me want to lose my mind. "Baby," he say in his deep voice, "I want you to act like you can't wait to get it."

"I can't," I almost yell.

"Well, sometimes it seem like you just doing your duty."

I don't say nothing 'cause I know I got something to learn. I want to talk back too.

"Tell me what you want. Say it right in my ear. I want you to tell me it's good, that it's always good. I want you to put your mouth all over me."

I'm blushing now, but I try not to show it.

"Everywhere. My chest. I got nipples too, and I want your mouth on them. Baby, I want you to put Mr. Jim in your mouth too. I want you to suck him and lick him good. I been scared to ask you for it, but we talking, ain't we?"

Jim stood up and started fondling himself again. "We gotta wait, baby?"

I say, "Yes."

"I know. I just want to show you how I want it. Is that okay?" Jim ask. He hold Mr. Jim up with one hand and start stroking slowly with the other. "Take your mouth up and down like this, baby," he say. "Start slow and then suck harder and faster. You can touch my balls, too."

That make me want to laugh, but something tell me not to. Jim tell me to suck it 'til he say he want to come. Then he want me to stand up and bend over. He say he loves taking me from behind, but he don't do it too often because it seem like I don't like it. Now I know my grandma was right because I only remember Jim doing it twice, and both times it was so good I commence to crying. Jim must've thought I was sad, and I was too old-fashioned to tell him otherwise. I'm thinking all of this and look over to find Jim done come all over himself.

"Jim, we s'posed to wait," I say. Jim kiss me like he ain't never kiss me before and goes to sleep right there in my arms.

The next day Jim wake up singing, and so do I. He calls me three times from work, something he used to do back when we just got married.

"Can't wait to touch you," he say.

"Me neither," I whisper.

That night, I undress Jim again, but this time I lay him on his stomach. I open up some baby oil I found in the back of my cupboard and pour it all over his back.

"Mmm, that's nice," he say.

I rub his shoulders and back and down to his waist. I knead his strong back like I'm making bread.

"Yes, woman," he says between strokes.

Then I pour baby oil on his behind and down between his legs. I rub his behind and slip my oily fingers between his cheeks. It must feel good because he snatches my hands and tries to take me right then.

"Not yet," I whisper in his ear.

"Oh, woman, you driving me crazy," he say.

"You don't know the half," I whisper back.

"Who are you and what have you done with my wife?" he say, laughing.

"Lay down, man, and let me finish my business."

I oil his legs and rub them hard, front and back. I touch everything but Mr. Jim. Jim trying to get me to, but he know we gotta wait.

"Alright, woman," he say, "your turn."

He lay me down and pour oil right in the crack of my behind. He rub my behind until I think I can see Jesus. I moan, and Jim moans with me. He rub everything but Miss Lou. I gotta tell the truth and shame the devil. Jim rub my feet so good I think I will die. I didn't know feet could get you so wet. He start at my feet and work his way back up. When he get to my breasts, he could have asked me to run down the street buck-naked, and I mighta done it! He rub my breasts in a way that lets me know he has done it before, but not with me. I forgive him right when the thought comes to me. I know that he wasn't getting this from me, and part of that is my fault. Besides, we been too far not to know how to forgive. Jim must've somehow felt my thoughts because he starts to cry. I tell him it's okay and hold him. We rock each other 'til we fall asleep, oily and wet.

The next day was my grocery shopping day. I got up and took a long, hot shower, fixed my hair, and put on a little makeup. Dora, who works down at the market, say, "Girl, you look like you been getting some on the side." I want to tell her to hush and that she needs salvation, but I just grin. I couldn't help it, but something about what she said makes me feel kinda proud. I push my pride back 'cause I wasn't looking to fall and say, "Thank you." That got folks whispering and I let them. We live in a small town. I know folks gonna think and say whatever they want anyway.

That night, Jim came in smiling, holding flowers, and it ain't even my birthday. This our night to touch Mr. Jim and Miss Lou, and neither one of us can wait. Now, I have always had my husband's dinner on the table for him when he gets home. With the exception of the birth of two of our five children, his meal has always been waiting. This time though, I meet him on the porch. I give him some cold, tart lemonade and kiss him right on the mouth. Miss Brown from across the street is looking, but I don't care and neither do Jim.

"We better go in," he say.

"Let her go in if she don't like what she see."

Miss Brown must've heard me 'cause she did go in, but I saw her curtain pull back and her eye peeping through. Jim sit next to me on the porch step.

"I get to touch it tonight, don't I?" he say right up next to my ear.

His hot, sticky breath on my neck make my nipples stand out at attention and my behind got real hot. Before I could answer, Jim shock me by slipping his hand up under my dress. Now it was already dark so I know Miss Brown couldn't see nothing, but all of this is new to me. I was sure surprised, but I had one for Mr. Jim too. He reach under my dress and find me naked as the day I was born. I didn't have on a stitch of underwear.

"Louella Givens," he say, calling me by my maiden name.

I grin, and Jim commence to laugh like I ain't heard in years. He pull me by the hand and take me in. We didn't make it to the bedroom though. Good thing the children are grown and moved out of town 'cause otherwise, they'd seen more than they ever wanted to know. Jim lay me down right on the living room carpet and pull my dress up over my head. He start to kiss my breasts, and I remind him that he couldn't use his mouth 'til the next day. He shook his head but said he wasn't going to argue. He grab my breast with one hand and start playing with my nipple with the other. It feel too good to be true. I didn't know my nipple had that much life left in it. Then I take one of his hands and put it down on Miss Lou.

"You full of all kinds of surprises, ain't you, woman?" Jim say.

He rub across my thighs real light for what seemed like hours. I want to scream, "Touch it, man!" but I learned the importance of patience. By the time Jim stroke the hairs on Miss Lou, how I want to skip over the next few days and get right to it. Jim stroked the inside and whispered in my ear, "I love this pussy. This is my pussy."

My husband had never talked like this to me before. Three days before I would have been shamed to hear this kind of talk coming from him, but that night I couldn't get enough. He stroked the inside of my kitty until it was hard as him. I was moaning and hollering like I was crazy. Then, when Jim stroked my spot, which by the way I wasn't aware of before then, I squirted all over the place like a man. I was shaking so hard, Jim came right through his pants.

"Woman," he said, "what have we been missing?"

I was panting hard and smiling like a madwoman. Jim carried me to bed. I felt too weak to touch anything he had, but it was okay. I slept until twelve midnight exactly and awoke to find Jim sleeping like a baby. I waited until one minute past and pulled Mr. Jim out of the slit of his PJs and commenced to sucking him the way Jim showed me. Jim must've done thought he was dreaming 'cause he was moaning something 'bout, "No, I'm married. Please don't."

He opened his eyes and saw my mouth on him. I was looking right in his eyes. His head rolled back and he let out a moan that probably made Miss Brown across the street come to attention.

"I'm coming, baby." When he said that, I climbed on top of him and rocked slowly, allowing him to come inside me. Jim arched his back and yelled, "Sweet Lord, thank you."

"Yes," I said, "I'm coming with you."

We must've both passed out 'cause when I came to, Jim was lying next to me, grinning in his sleep. He woke up and smiled and started kissing me all over. He kissed as high as possible, and as low as possible. I stood up and bent over, and we did what we both like. We made love all day long. I fell asleep in between lovemaking and I saw my ancestors.

"Girl, you was supposed to wait," Aunt T said. "You never did know how to wait."

My grandma smiled. "Girl, hush. Sometimes rules are made to be broken. Besides," she added, "y'all been waiting over twenty years to get it right."

"Thank you," I told them.

Jim must've thought I was talking to him 'cause I heard him say, "You wait—you ain't had nothin' to thank me for yet. Come here, woman. Let me taste you."

LAURA FEDERICO

Exorbitant Pleasures

She's come in before. She usually sits at one of the window tables and says nothing except to order tea. Just tea. She doesn't take off her coat, she pretends to read, and she leaves a ten-dollar tip. Every time.

"Wish she'd sit in my station for a change," I say to Roddy as she's leaving. Seems as if she hears that. At least, she turns around to look at me. She smiles.

"Uh-oh. I think you have an admirer," Roddy says in a stage whisper. That she definitely hears. The smile becomes broader—she almost laughs, pulling the door open and going out into the night.

"Thanks a lot, asshole." I punch him in the arm.

"You should've gotten her phone number," he says, shaking his head sorrowfully. "A girl's gotta get some every once in a while, eh? What're you saving it for—"

"—your wedding night?" I chorus with him, rolling my eyes. "Shut up, Roddy."

It's true I've been single going on...if you must know, almost two years now. But I'm pre-med at San Francisco State, and most of the time I just don't feel like taking my nose out of my books. I've explained this to him before—but Roddy, like most of the men who work here at The Attitude Café (all gay, obviously, with a name like that), never stops thinking about sex, and he can't see how anyone else could, either.

By the time I get off my shift at eleven, I've forgotten all about the Tea Lady, as we call her. So I just about jump out of my clothes when I see her outside, sitting in front of the café in a white Jaguar. She's wearing sunglasses, even though it's dark out—in fact, not just dark, but raining. She's drinking from a silver flask. Not just tea, I bet.

"Hello, Starr," she says.

I blink. "How do you know my name?"

"It's on your name tag."

I look down, but of course I'm not in uniform anymore.

"Oh," I say.

"Come for a ride with me."

I stare at her for a second, then look around. There's no one on the street at this hour, in the rain, on a Tuesday night, but us.

"A ride?" I echo blankly. I shift my backpack, squint in the rain.

"There's a place I know, not far from here. Very nice. You'll like it. What do you drink?"

Whatever's cheapest, I think, eyeing the flask. I look her over more carefully. She's in her early fifties, with soft ash-blonde hair that falls to her shoulders. She wears a shiny black raincoat, and an enormous diamond glitters on her finger. Married woman. Should've guessed.

"Thanks, anyhow. I better be going."

"No," she says, with surprising force. "No, I want you to come with me. You'll be interested in what I have to say. I promise."

"Yeah, well...." I look around for Roddy. Anyone. Damn, it is so hard to reject women.

"How much do you make waitressing here?" she asks, gesturing at the café. "Forty dollars a night? Sixty?"

"Uh." I clear my throat. Scowl at her. "Actually, that's none of your business." It's more like eighty to a hundred, minimum, and I resent her underestimating me. So now I really do take off, walking quickly down the dark shiny street, my head ducked against the rain. After a minute I hear the hiss of tires behind me. Shit.

"Starr, listen, this is not...."

"Leave me alone, OK?"

"This is not what you think."

I make a gesture over my shoulder: whatever. Two more blocks to the train station. Surely she won't drive alongside me the whole way.

"Will you come with me, hear what I have to say? I'll pay you."

Still walking, faster now, I look over my shoulder at her. "Jesus, lady!"

"I will pay you five hundred dollars if you'll have a conversation with me this evening, in a public place."

I stop. The car stops too. There is no traffic this direction, the streets wet and empty. What if this woman has a gun? What if she's just plain crazy? Would anyone hear me if I screamed?

She's staring at me across the interior of the car, the passenger window rolled down. The flask lies beside her on the seat.

"You're drunk."

"Drunk." She laughs. "No. Not drunk. Just desperate."

"No, thanks."

I start to back away and she says, very fast, "You could buy your way into medical school, if you just listen to what I have to say."

"How did you know—"

"Your boss told me."

"My *boss?*" This is getting creepier and creepier. "When the hell did you.... Who are you, anyway? What's going on here?"

"I've been wanting to meet you for a long time." I stand there, dripping wet, transfixed. "That's why I go into the café. One afternoon you weren't working, and your boss told me you're a student, pre-med, in class all day."

"And what the fuck business is that of yours? Listen, lady, I don't need this. I mean it. You need to go away now."

"Starr. This is legitimate. I am not trying to harass you. Please. I have something I want to tell you. I swear this is not a game, not what you think."

She swallows.

"Please," she says again.

"Then tell me now, fast. Tell me right here."

"This isn't how I wanted to."

"OK, forget it."

I turn away, head for the lights of the gas station

across the street. I'm pulling my cell phone out of my pocket as I walk.

"I want you to be...I want you to be my husband's mistress."

I stop.

"You want *what?*"

"I will pay you five thousand dollars a month. Tax-free. For as long as the arrangement suits you both."

This is not happening.

We stare at each other for several seconds. Then she says, "Get in the car where it's dry. I promise I won't hurt you." And again, "Please."

The interior of the salon is deeply plush in plum-colored velvet. Draperies, two love seats, fat ottomans with shirred skirts. Thick Oriental carpets underfoot, intricate mahogany wainscoting, antique maps framed in gold, and Tiffany lamps casting soft, magical light full of color. From here we can faintly hear the live piano downstairs.

We are on the second floor. The windows are heavily draped, muffling the sounds of the elegant restaurant below and, even more important, I suspect, blocking the view from the street. In the twelve years I have lived in San Francisco, I never knew this place—this *salon*—existed. Which of course is the whole point of it.

A woman had greeted us in the foyer. "Madelon. And a guest, how delightful." That was how I learned the Tea Lady's name. Our hostess was tall and severe looking, impeccably dressed, with ink-black hair pulled back from a chalk-white face, a gray chiffon scarf around her neck. We'd stepped inside, and I was immediately aware of my smell: wet wool, and hamburger grease from the café. I stood there with my schoolgirl backpack, soaked sneakers, hair plastered to my head. Lovely. Beside me, Madelon was tall—taller than I'd realized—and elegant in her shiny black coat.

"Starr Ayers, a new friend," she said to the hostess, who took our coats and ushered us inside. (And how did she know my *last* name?) Underneath her coat, Madelon was wearing a sleeveless, dark-blue crepe dress, a single strand of pearls.

She has obviously been here many times. The hostess, or whoever she is, knows what she drinks (Cosmopolitan straight up) and brings it on a silver tray before we're even seated. I order the same, trying to compose myself, wishing I could have gone home to shower and change before coming to a place like this.

But, whatever. I've decided that this is definitely an adventure. Wait till Roddy and the guys hear.

"I suppose we're doing this all backward." Madelon smiles at me, after my drink has arrived. "Of course, this is my first time...negotiating in this way. So you'll forgive me any awkwardness."

"Mmm," I say noncommittally. I sip my drink.

"Let me belatedly introduce myself. My name is Madelon Bernier. That is my maiden name. I've never changed it. My husband's name is Jefferson."

"And what's his first name? Do you have a picture, by any chance? I mean, if I'm going to be his mistress...." I look at her, deadpan. "Where is he tonight, by the way?"

She regards me for a minute. "He's out of town on business, actually."

"I see. And what kind of business is he in?"

"He owns his own company." She hesitates. "You understand that this is all to be extremely confidential, Starr? Whether we come to an agreement or not." She hesitates again. "You do understand that, I hope."

"Oh, sure."

Now she starts fiddling with the ring on her finger. Silence creeps between us. She gulps her drink.

She is a pretty woman, actually. She has a strong-boned face, clear skin, and widely spaced dark-blue eyes. Her mouth is full and soft. Her neck is long, the shoulders square, and her body is as slim as a twenty-year-old's. She looks like a woman who could have been—maybe was—a model when she was younger. But she would have been all hard edges then, sharp-faced, with the ambitious gleam in her eye endemic to beautiful young women.

But Madelon has softened, and there is a richness to her expression, a gentle wisdom, that only older women have. Something in her eyes makes me wonder what she's been through—how, for starters, she came to be driving a white Jaguar down a rainy street tonight, in pursuit of an off-duty waitress.

"Well, it's too bad Mr. Jefferson couldn't make this little meeting tonight, Madelon. I mean, what is the world coming to when a man has to send his wife out to do his pimping for him?"

She bursts into laughter.

"Starr," she says. "Starr, you are...I have to tell you, you are a rare one. I can't imagine how strange you must find all of this."

"No, you probably can't."

"I'm going to be honest with you...."

"Listen, Madelon," I say, leaning forward. "Do be honest, and I mean really honest. Because this whole thing has the feel of a drug deal to me, or white slavery or something, and I have to tell you I am a little bit creeped out here."

"It is an odd situation, to be sure," she says. Her tone is uncertain, and she twists the ring on her finger some more. "David and I have been married for twenty-one years. We have two sons. I say 'have,' but one of them died four years ago. Since then, things between us haven't been.... They've changed. It's difficult to explain. But perhaps," she says softly, "you're old enough to understand what I mean."

"Well, I hope so," I say, "if I'm old enough to be David's mistress."

She laughs again. Surprising me. "How old are you, if you don't mind my asking?"

"Twenty-nine."

"That's good. I thought you were younger."

"Yeah, it's my Audrey Hepburn gamine look." This time we both laugh.

Then she says seriously, "You're much prettier than Audrey Hepburn."

"Thanks. But there are lots of girls out there who are way prettier than me—and who, frankly, wouldn't have any trouble at all with this little exchange we're having. I mean, girls who do this kind of thing on their own. Like it's their chosen profession, if you catch my drift."

"But you're the one I want."

We stare at each other. "Why?" I finally ask.

"I like your look. I like how you conduct yourself—your style. I've watched you at work, at school."

"At *school?* You've seen me at school too?" I jerk in surprise and start to rise out of my chair. "What are you, some kind of stalker, for Chrissakes?"

"No, no, please," she says, placing a hand on my arm. "I was at the campus for a lecture once. That was when I saw you for the first time. I stared at you through the whole lecture. Something about you. Then I just happened to find you again, about three months later, at the café. I remembered you instantly."

"And you immediately thought, 'Now, she would make a lovely mistress for my David.'" I find myself sitting down again. Intrigued. Repelled. "So it's you that doesn't want to anymore, right? Not him?"

She swallows. "That's a long story."

"Well, I need to know. I mean, if I do this. If I *consider* doing this. Is he impotent? Is this, like, a problem between you two, or is it just one of you? You don't have to go into specifics, unless it's him. In that case, I would appreciate all the information you could give me."

"You are something else." She laughs, a little shakily. "Well, then—it's me. He's fine. He still wants to. He's not seeing anyone else—never has, actually, though I've suggested it." She coughs. "We've seen a counselor. She kept insisting that there was nothing to worry about, that couples often have sexual problems after an experience like we had—our son's death. But the truth is, I've never, um, I've never really wanted to. Not like some wives do. So. There it is." She looks me in the eye. "I've never told anyone that before."

"I'm flattered." I wince. This makes us both laugh again. I realize that I'm actually having quite a good time. Maybe Roddy's right—maybe I should get out more often.

"Well, as you can imagine, I've felt pretty badly about it, all these years," she says. "It's not that I don't love him. My God, I adore him—even now, after all we've been through, and all this time. I can't wait to see him at the end of the day. And he is a good lover, Starr: patient, warm, considerate. Oh, hell," she says, her eyes shining with tears. "Oh, it's been...it's been such a disappointment to us both."

"Yeah. I bet," I say gruffly. After a minute, without planning to, I reach over and put my hand on hers. Now what made me do that? It's the second time we've touched, and I am even more aware, this time, of how silky her skin feels, the richness of her perfume. I yank my hand back. "Sorry."

"No. No, it's OK." She closes her eyes briefly, touching them with her fingertips. Unobserved, I admire her hands—the French manicure, ooh la la.

Shit, I really have been single too long. I settle back into my chair, marveling at myself, at this whole scene. This will definitely merit a chapter in my memoirs.

At that moment, the hostess appears with more drinks. I notice my glass is empty. They make a damn good Cosmopolitan here, icy cold and tart. I reach for the second one eagerly, thinking, what the hell. You only live once.

"Cheers," she says, with her sweet, sad smile.

"Mud in your eye."

We toast. I gulp half of mine, then set the glass down.

"Listen, Madelon," I say, "I have to tell you something. Your David sounds like a sweetheart, and I am definitely of the school that believes everyone is entitled to a great sex life. I feel for him. And I feel for you too. But I'm not going to do this."

She sighs. Nods. "Yes. I didn't think you would, somehow."

"I'm sorry."

"No. Don't be. I asked you if you would come and discuss it, that's all. You've done that." She reaches for her purse.

"You don't have to pay me."

"Of course I do. I offered it. You would be silly not to accept."

I would be a fucking *moron* not to accept, I think. Five hundred dollars. That's a week's worth of shifts at the café. But I hear myself say, "No, really. I can't."

"Believe me. It was worth it." She finds the money, already folded into a neat wad, in her purse. "Please, Starr."

I wonder how many times tonight she's said, "Please, Starr." I am starting to like the sound of it.

"Tell me why it was worth it to you."

"Because." She's actually blushing. Holy shit, a fifty-year-old who still blushes! "Because of what I just told you."

"Which was what?"

"About the—about how I never liked...."

"Sex. How you never liked sex." She is holding out the money. I am ignoring it. "Well, Madelon, have you ever tried it with anyone but David?"

Her eyes widen. They really are the most beautiful shade of midnight blue. "No. I mean, not since I was married."

"What about before then?"

"Well...." Oh, good, she's blushing again. "Well, I mean in college...."

"In college what? Drink up," I say, nudging her glass closer. "The night's still young."

She laughs. A little hysterically, I think. Well, that's all right, too.

"In college I dated a few boys, of course. But we didn't really...you know."

"Go all the way? Please tell me you weren't about to say that."

"No, I mean—there was no relationship there. It wasn't like a meaningful...."

"Oh, give me a break! If you think you have to have a meaningful relationship with a person to have great sex, well...." I laugh. "I guess that explains a lot."

"Oh!" She's laughing too. "Starr, you're so...."

"Drink," I remind her.

She does. Her dark-blue eyes study me over the rim of the glass. When she puts it down she says, elaborately casual, "So I suppose *you* have sex just like—without a lot of preliminaries, much less a meaningful...the expectation of a meaningful...."

A grin spreads across my face. I put my hand on hers, run it up her arm. "Usually I like to wait till a woman comes to me, asking me to be her husband's mistress."

Our eyes lock.

"This was bullshit," I say softly. "This whole thing. You were cruising me for you, not him."

She goes perfectly still for a minute. Then she draws in her breath, slowly.

"How dare you."

"How fucking dare *you*. You follow me on the street, play all these coy games, offer me *money,* and give me this whole line about your poor beloved husband and his unmet sexual needs. What about *your* unmet needs, Madelon? Has he spent the past twenty-one years coaxing you to have extramarital affairs? Has he ever even asked you what turns you on?"

She stands up. "I don't have to listen to this."

"Kind of hits a nerve, doesn't it?" I stand up too. She's breathing so hard I can feel the warm air on my face. "How was it that of all the cafés in the city, you decided to hang out in mine? Not exactly in your neighborhood, is it? The place is Queer Central. The waiters give each other blowjobs in the bathroom, for Chrissakes. But you had no idea I was a dyke. Right?"

Our eye contact won't break. Then her eyes fill up with tears.

"Why are you doing this to me?"

I grab both of her wrists. "Why did you follow me?" I kiss her. Her mouth is soft and open. I pull back. "Well?"

She doesn't answer.

I kiss her again, slipping my tongue into her mouth. My hands move up her arms to her shoulders, her neck. I bury my fists in her hair. It feels like corn silk.

"Who has ever actually given a shit if you liked the sex you had with them?" I whisper. When I kiss her again, she cries into my mouth. I draw back. "How many years have you been faking it, exactly?"

I pull her down onto the sofa, kiss her until she stops crying. It has been so long for me, too, that I feel like I am drowning in her, in the taste of her mouth, in gratitude. She is pliant in my arms. I have no idea whether she's liking this or not. I know I am, though. When I finally draw back she looks at me with sparkling eyes.

Guess she liked it.

"What I mean to say, Madelon…." I bend over her, breathe into her mouth, lightly touch her lips with mine. My voice is very soft. "What I mean to say is, there are simpler ways to get laid."

I stand up.

Shocked, she remains still for a moment, pressed deep into the plush sofa, where I've pushed her. She struggles to sit up.

"I have to get home," I tell her. "If you ever want to find me, God knows, you know how to do it."

"Wait," she bursts out. "No. Starr."

"Do you want to come home with me?" I ask gently. "I'm not going to fuck you here, you know. It's kind of, um, like someone's living room." I glance around. We're alone. But this is, technically, a public place. "What'll it be, Madelon?"

"Wait. Wait here." Her voice is shaking. She slides past me, the crepe of her dress whispery, and goes to the door. She has a hell of a sexy walk.

The room is so quiet, with only the sound of the crackling fire and the muted music downstairs. I wonder where my coat is, if it's still raining outside. I wonder what she's up to.

She comes back in a minute, holding a little gold key.

"They have…rooms here," she says, blushing furiously. "Upstairs."

"There's *another* floor?"

There is indeed.

• • •

The room is all white—ivory, actually. The thick carpet, the layers of crisp sheets on the bed, the damask-striped wallpaper. Gold sconces, gold faucets in the bathroom. It's like something out of a movie set.

"Holy shit," I breathe, testing the mattress with my palm. How much does a room like this cost?

As if I'd spoken, she says behind me, "Don't worry. It's paid for."

"Oh, yeah?" I put my hands around her hips, pull her to me. "Is that included in the five hundred, or extra?"

With a little moan, she leans into me. Her mouth finds mine.

God, she's good. She's so, so good. Tastes good, feels good. My mind is spinning.

I find the zipper of her dress, pull it down. The silky skin of her back prickles. I run my hands over her, the delicate bones of her spine, her shoulder blades. Her skin warms, and after a minute she leans in closer. I can feel her give, feel her neck and back relax, her arms rising to hold me.

How have I lived without this for so long?

"Don't be scared," I whisper. I slide the dress down. It falls to the floor with that whispery sound, and she steps neatly out of it without letting me go. She's naked.

"God," I say involuntarily. I am so turned on my knees are shaking. I almost shove her to the bed. She falls backward with a little sound, like a squeak, and then laughs. Opens her arms. I fall into them.

I can't wait. I had planned (if you could call it planning) a slow seduction—her first time, after all—but fuck it, I can't wait, she's too good.

I shift onto my side and cradle the back of her head in one hand, and slide the other down the length of her, then up, back down again. I want to feel every inch of her. She's so smooth, smells so good; her heat seeps into me; I can feel it through my clothes. Her stomach muscles are quivering, her thighs too. My palm feels cool against her hot skin, passing over her in a fast tour—the warm hard place between her breasts, where I can feel her heart thudding, the curve of her waist flowing into the sharp rise of her hipbone. Her breasts, not large, not small, but just right, with their firm dark nipples: she shudders when I touch them, but I don't touch them for long. I am acquainting myself with her, but I know this territory. Her body is a remembered country, recalling all the others before her, all the ones I've loved (or at the very least loved to touch), going back to my first time, *my* first time. God, how I have missed this.

Madelon will love it, too. In fact, she already seems to. She's moaning now, lifting her hips. Her arms go tightly around my shoulders, her mouth lifted, open, urgent against mine. A part of me is surprised—am I really to believe that this is not just her first time with a woman, but her first pleasure in sex? I draw back, look at her for a minute.

"Please," she says softly.

Well, that's how all this started, isn't it—that word. I smile down at her. Gone, totally. Both of us. Her eyes are black with dilated pupils, her cheeks and lips flushed.

Strands of pale hair cling to her damp forehead. Yes, yes. Oh God, she is perfect. And real. This is really happening.

My fingers find the velvety moisture of her pussy and without thinking, unable to wait, I plunge two fingers in her, then three. My hand pounds in and out of her, and she takes it, drawing her knees back. My arm is titanic, invincible. I find the rhythm, find it and keep it. She's going to come fast. I slide a fourth finger into her and press the heel of my hand against her clit.

She screams softly.

We are both murmuring to each other—to the air, I think. To the sweet gods above, who allow this. Her whole pussy is swollen in my palm, dripping wet. Inside she clutches me, releases, clutches. Her muscles are so strong.

"I'm coming," she says. Her voice is muffled because her arms are crossed over her face, her breathing ragged behind them, little sobs breaking out of her. Juice gushes out of her, she grabs my fingers with her pussy so hard it feels as if they're going to break, and she almost leaps off the bed.

Yowza.

I keep fucking her until the spasms stop, and the inside of her pussy is soft and swollen. My arm is shaking with fatigue now—she came fast but I am out of practice—and my whole being is limp with gratitude. How could I have forgotten how much I love this?

There on the ivory bed, with a chandelier of cavorting cupids overhead, I make a solemn promise to myself: Starr Ayers, you will never go two years without sex again.

"Oh, my God," Madelon is murmuring.

I fall full-length on her, still clothed, beaming. Her eyes are closed and the lashes quiver. I kiss her.

"Not bad for your first time," I say. "Looks to me like you'll get the hang of it."

The dark-blue eyes open, just slits, and after a minute a slow smile spreads across her face.

"Is that a promise?"

It's a different voice—rougher, deeper. Not breathy, polite, high-class, as before. I register this without, you know, registering it.

"Yeah," I say. "To tell you the truth, it's hard to believe that that was really your first...."

I feel her stomach muscles rippling before I realize she's laughing.

"Oh, Starr," she says. She sits up, tossing me off her. "C'mon." She reaches for my belt buckle.

"No, that's OK. I don't like to, y'know, the first time with someone. But if you're up for another round—I mean, since you seem to be such a fast learner and all...."

She squints at me. "Funny. I wouldn't have taken you for a stone butch. For any kind of butch, actually."

"I'm not." Propped up on one elbow, I study her. "You're kind of up on the lingo, seems to me. For a straight woman." I add softly, "For a, you'll excuse the expression, frigid married straight woman."

She throws her head back and laughs.

I sit up. "You're a dyke. Jesus!"

She just laughs and laughs.

"I don't believe this," I exclaim. "How many times have you pulled that one, Madelon? Is that even your real name? How many women do you pick up and...."

"You're the first," she says, trying for a straight face. Then she cracks up again.

"This isn't funny."

I leap off the bed and stomp around, looking for my backpack and coat.

"Why isn't it?" She reclines languidly, watching me. Her long legs are stretched out in front of her, crossed at the ankle. Her blond hair spills onto her smooth shoulders. Naked as an angel. "I think it's hilarious. Do you realize what's happening here?"

I just glare at her. Jam my arms into the sleeves of my coat. Snatch up my backpack.

"You're pissed because you just went to bed with a lesbian."

"Yeah, but..." I grope. "Yeah, but you...."

Suddenly I start to laugh too.

Really, it's not funny.

Oh, but it *is*.

"I just wanted to make it interesting." She cocks her head. "Is that so awful?"

She gets up and comes to me. Kisses me deeply. I stop laughing.

"You have to admit," she whispers, "this was interesting. More interesting than anything you've done in awhile, I'm sure."

My legs are weak from kissing her, from the sex. I can still smell her on me.

"That's not saying a lot, Madelon."

"Most people's lives are boring. Yours, from what I can tell, is boring as hell."

"Hey, now," I say sharply. But after a second or

two the laughter bubbles up again. She's right. Oh God, is she right.

Her fingertips trace all the little bones in my spine, making me tingle. "You'll remember this for years. For the rest of your life, I bet."

"Yeah, but...mmm...." I bury my face in her hair. "But when you lie, it changes everything. The person can never trust that you...." My head is starting to spin again. I draw back from her. I shake my head a little, and my eyes clear.

She's laughing again. "So what?"

"So if you ever wanted to see one of your *tricks* again...."

"Tricks." She shrugs. "You just said it yourself."

And that, I understand, is my cue to leave.

At the door I turn and say slowly, "You had the room arranged. You had this all set up in advance. You know the proprietor. How often do you do this, Madelon? Just out of curiosity."

"As often as I want," she says, not flinching. "And it's never the same script twice."

"See you," I say softly.

I close the door behind me. The image of her, naked, golden-haired, a little smile on her lips, is one I'll keep, yes, for the rest of my life.

I step onto the elevator. As I'm borne swiftly downward, the sound of the piano music reaches me again, very faint.

Wait till Roddy hears about this.

• • •

It's not until later, after I've gotten into a cab (the white-faced proprietor, with no expression whatsoever, informed me one was already waiting for me in front) and have ridden all the way back to the Mission and to my life, to my dear little awful life, that I reach into my coat pocket for the first time, to pay the fare. My fingers fold around a wad of cash.

I don't have to count it. I know how much it is.

HELEN E. H. MADDEN

Lady Luck

The day I got divorced, I decided to celebrate by gambling.

My ratfink ex-husband had asked for a quick divorce in Vegas, and I had agreed. After everything else I'd been through, I didn't want to drag the matter out too long. It was to my advantage anyway—my ex was in such a hurry to run off with his new honey, he didn't seem to mind too much when I demanded the house, the car, and a hefty alimony payment. I cleaned him out pretty good, but I still felt cheated. Being on the receiving end of a divorce will make anybody feel like a loser, especially when your husband goes trotting off with a woman half your age.

I hate losing.

As soon as I signed the divorce papers I decided I needed to win something, anything. So I walked out of the lawyer's office with my first alimony check and headed straight for the nearest casino.

I spent the day wandering from one casino to the next, playing the slots, a few hands of blackjack, and occasionally shooting craps. I'd never gambled before, so I didn't really know what I was doing. I kept thinking I was bound to get lucky at some point.

Stupid me. I lost. By ten o'clock I was down to my last hundred dollars. I sighed and rolled my eyes, tucking the money safely away in my purse. Quitting now would be the smart thing to do, but I still had this hankering to win big. After all, I was recently divorced. Didn't I deserve to get lucky just once?

Just then I spotted the Lady Luck Casino, probably the only joint I hadn't been in that day. As I eyed the flickering neon sign above the door, I thought about my ex and how happy he was with his new girlfriend. I thought about the hundred dollars burning a hole in my purse. I thought about how badly I wanted to win. I shouldered my purse and walked resolutely into the Lady Luck Casino.

I had never been in a more depressing place in all my life. The lights in the main room were dim, which was probably good because the place might have looked even worse if I could have actually seen it. The air was thick with cigarette smoke, and slot machines lined the dark paneled walls as far as the eye could see. Only a few of them were in use—by some tired-looking women, who looked as if they were losing their will to live along with their money every time they pulled the handle. I shuddered when I realized how many of those women were my age.

The scene in the bar wasn't much better. A handful of old men sat around in battered red vinyl armchairs, nursing the poison of their choice as they watched various sporting events on the televisions lining the back wall.

Waitresses moved among the tables, collecting bets as well as tips. They were obviously the only people in the casino making any money.

The last thing I wanted to do on the day I got divorced was to spend it with professional losers who never strayed too far from their favorite one-armed bandit. I was about to turn around and leave when I noticed the roulette table.

Actually, it wasn't the roulette table I noticed so much as the guy running it. He was nice-looking, and young, maybe even younger than the little tramp my ex left me for. My heart jumped when he looked over at me and smiled. He patted one of the padded stools by the roulette table and motioned for me to come over.

"First time here?" he asked as I carefully perched on the stool.

"First time in Vegas, actually," I replied with a smile. Up close, this guy looked even better than I had first realized. He was tall and lean like a college boy, and he had thick, dark hair and big brown eyes. His uniform consisted of a crisp white shirt and a dark red vest that fit snugly over his chest, with a nametag that said "Tony" in neat gold letters. His black pants were practically molded around his long legs and a firm rear-end. I leaned forward a little and got a whiff of his spicy aftershave.

"Care to place a bet, ma'am?"

"Don't call me ma'am," I said. "It makes me feel old. Call me Amelia, OK?"

He smiled. "Amelia, then. Care to place a bet?"

"Maybe. I've never played this game before. How does it work?"

Tony pointed at the table. “You place your chips on any of these numbers. If you don’t want to bet on a specific number, you can bet even or odd, or you can bet by color. I spin the wheel, and we see if you win.”

“What’s the best way to win big?” I asked as I studied the table.

“Pick a specific number,” he said. “You’ll get more money back on that bet. Of course, it’s also the best way to lose.”

I winced. “Sounds risky. I don’t like losing.”

Tony shrugged. “This is Vegas. Around here, if you want to win big, you have to take some risks.”

I pulled twenty-five dollars out of my purse and tossed it on the table. “OK. Why don’t I start small first, and see how this game goes?”

Tony nodded and held up a handful of chips. “Sounds like a plan. What number would you like to try first?”

I laughed. “I have no idea! How do most people pick their numbers?”

“Well, usually they pick their favorite numbers, or they use their age, a birthday, their anniversary. Things like that.”

“OK. Let’s try twenty-seven then.”

Tony grinned and put the chips down on the table. “I knew it! Pretty women always start with their age.”

“My age? Oh no, dear! You don’t have a number on this table high enough for that!” I wasn’t joking. My fifty-second birthday was just around the corner.

“Are you serious? The highest number is thirty-six!” Tony stared at me, his mouth open. I thought he might be faking his surprise, but if he was, he was doing a good job of it. "I'm sorry. I, ah, I hope I didn't offend you."

I giggled and leaned forward on the table. "Trust me. Being told I look like I'm twenty-seven does *not* offend me."

Tony smiled again, then grabbed the roulette wheel and gave it a spin. I watched intently as the little silver ball rolled round and round until it came to a stop.

"Sixteen," Tony announced. "I guess twenty-seven wasn't your lucky number."

I sighed. "Well, that's no big surprise. Twenty-seven was the number of years I was married before I got divorced this morning."

Tony's eyebrows shot up. "You got divorced?"

"Yeah. My ex left me for a younger woman."

"You've got to be kidding. Why would any man leave a beautiful woman like you?"

I gave him a weary smile. "You're a nice guy, Tony."

On impulse, I leaned across the roulette table and kissed him. I meant for it to be quick, just a way to say thank you. Somehow, though, once my lips touched his, I just couldn't pull away. His mouth was so soft and gentle. When I finally realized what I was doing, I broke off suddenly, embarrassed beyond belief.

"I'm sorry. I shouldn't have done that."

"It's OK," Tony said. I was surprised to see he was actually grinning. "I like the way you kiss. We can do it again, if you like."

I shook my head. "Ah, no. I don't want to get you into trouble."

Tony gestured to the nearly empty casino. "Hey, it's not like anybody in here is going to pay attention to us."

I looked around. He was right. Everyone else was too busy losing their life savings to bother noticing one old woman molesting a handsome young dealer.

I slid off the stool. "I guess you're right. Still, I should probably go."

Tony grabbed my hand. "Not yet. Why don't you try again?"

"No, thanks. I've done enough losing for one day." I tried to pull my hand back, but Tony refused to let go.

"You picked one lousy number. Try again, but this time pick a good number, a number that makes you think of something you like. OK?"

I chewed my lower lip for a moment. "If I lose again, I get to go?"

"If you lose, you can leave. But you won't lose. Not if you pick the right number."

I settled back on the stool. "A happy number, huh? Let's see. What makes me happy?" I didn't have to look far for the answer. "How old are you, Tony?"

"Twenty-five."

"Put all of this on twenty-five," I said, pulling out another small wad of cash.

Tony took my money and put some chips on twenty-five. The wheel spun around again. This time, I only pretended to watch it: I was really staring at Tony. I let my eyes travel up and down his body, until they finally came to rest at his crotch. I'll admit, I wasn't very subtle, but hell, I'd already kissed him and managed to get away with it. His pelvis shifted forward a little and rubbed against the table railing. A sudden wave of heat shot through me. I imagined what it would be like to slip my hand between Tony's legs.

The wheel slowed to a stop. The little silver ball bounced a few more times before finally coming to rest.

"Twenty-five," Tony announced with a smile. He added an impressive number of chips to my little pile. "You win, Amelia."

I leaned forward, placing my elbows on the edge of the table. The neckline of my dress slipped a bit. I may not be as young as my ex's new girlfriend, but I still have firm breasts. Tony's eyes went straight to my cleavage as he handed me some of my chips.

"There's more here than I can hold in two hands," Tony said, adding hastily, "I meant the chips."

I leaned forward even further, this time undoing the top button on my dress. Tony licked his lips. I picked up one of the chips and started playing with it. "Want to help me pick another number, Tony?"

"Sure."

"What's your pants size?"

"Thirty-two waist, thirty-six length."

"You've got long legs, Tony. I like that. Place all those chips on thirty-six."

"You got it!"

The wheel spun again, and again I ignored it, continuing to watch Tony. He watched me watching him. My eyes came back to his crotch. It shifted forward and back again, rubbing harder against the table. A bulge appeared between his legs. It grew bigger.

The wheel slowed and stopped.

"Thirty-six! You win again." Tony added more chips to my growing pile. "You can cash out, or you can place another bet. What would you like to do?"

I hesitated a moment, then stole another look at Tony's rapidly growing hard-on. What the hell, I thought. I wanted to win big, and like Tony said, that meant taking a risk.

"Tell me something," I said as I popped open another button on my dress, Tony's eyes watching intently. "How long is your cock?"

"Uh...I'm not sure." Even in the dim light of the casino, I could see his face turn pink.

"You don't know?" I asked innocently.

Tony laughed a little. "I've never really measured it."

"Guess, then."

"Six inches?"

"That sounds like a good number to me," I said, stealing another glance at his crotch. I pulled out the last of my cash. "Place all those chips on number six, and add this as well."

Tony nodded and moved the chips. I handed him the cash this time instead of tossing it on the table, just so that I could touch his hand. I felt a little electric jolt as my fingers brushed his. From the look on his face, I guessed he felt it too.

The wheel spun. Neither of us bothered to watch it this time. I casually popped open another button and slipped a hand inside my dress. My fingers teased the nipple. It got hard fast, forming a little knot under the thin fabric. I was certain that Tony could see it. He didn't rub against the table this time. He used his hand instead, sliding it down to that sweet spot between his legs. My gamble was starting to pay off.

The wheel slowed and stopped. The ball came to rest.

"Six is the lucky number," Tony said, his voice a little rough. "You want to let it ride?"

"Not yet," I replied. "What time do you get off tonight?"

"Twelve o'clock." He began gathering up the rather large pile of chips I had won. "Is twelve your new lucky number?"

"No, it's yours." I leaned across the table and swept the chips toward me, giving Tony a clear view of what I had beneath my dress. "I'm cashing out and going back to my hotel room to change. I'll be back for you at twelve."

Tony just nodded. I took my chips up to the cashier. She looked a little startled at the open buttons on my dress, but she didn't say anything. She just counted up my winnings, and I walked out of the Lucky Lady with a lot more than I'd gone in with.

It took about fifteen minutes by taxi to get back to my hotel. As soon as I reached my room, I began stripping my clothes off. The dress I had been wearing all day was nice enough to get divorced in, but that was about it. I took a quick shower and then shimmied into the little black dress I had packed just in case I got lucky. I didn't bother with underwear. I stood in front of the mirror to see the results. The dress clung to my damp skin, showing off every voluptuous curve. Without a bra to hide them, my nipples stood out like two tiny gumdrops. I felt like a cat in heat. I hadn't been this aroused in years.

It was exactly midnight when I arrived back at the Lady Luck. Tony was waiting for me outside. As soon as I stepped out of my cab he strode over and took my hand.

"I just clocked out," he said. He slipped an arm around my waist and guided me back into the casino. "How about another game of roulette? I've got a special table set up in the back room."

I rubbed my hand across his chest. He had taken off the vest, and I could feel every muscle ripple beneath his shirt.

"Think I could win big?"

"Of course," he whispered. "You're a very lucky lady."

We walked to the back of the casino and headed through a door marked "Employees Only," down a narrow hallway, and into a dimly lit storage room. Tony pulled me inside and shut the door behind us, locking it.

"Nice place you got here," I murmured. The storage room was filled with old slot machines, blackjack tables, some barstools, and other odds and ends.

"This way," Tony said.

He carefully led me down an aisle past some abandoned Lucky Seven slots, kissing me along the way. We ended up at an old roulette table tucked away in the back corner. Tony pressed me against the table and rubbed his hard cock against my hip. A slow fire started in my groin and spread up through my belly until it reached my nipples.

"Take off your shirt," I ordered, already fumbling with the buttons. I couldn't wait to get him undressed.

Buttons flew off as Tony tore the shirt from his body. I was already working on his fly. I pushed his waistband over his hips, letting his pants fall to the floor with a soft thud. Then I ran my hands all over his body. I could feel his muscles rippling beneath his soft, smooth skin.

I buried my face in his neck and smelled the rich, warm scent of his skin. God, he was young and fresh!

While I explored Tony's body, he went to work on my dress. He slid the shoulder straps down and kissed my neck. Then he pulled the dress down to my waist, exposing my breasts to the cool air.

"I never had anyone tease me the way you did tonight," he whispered. "I thought I was going to come on the spot when you started playing with yourself out there!"

He brought a hand to my breast and played with the nipple. I moaned. Fire swept through me. "Oh God, Tony! I want more!"

Tony obliged by putting his mouth to the other nipple and sucking on it. But it still wasn't enough for me. I slid his boxers down over his hips, wrestling to get the elastic band over his erect cock. When I finally succeeded, his cock sprang free, bouncing up and down. I grabbed it and squeezed.

Tony moaned. He broke off playing with my breasts and grabbed me by the hips, lifting me up off the floor and onto the green felt surface of the roulette table. I leaned back and let him pull my dress the rest of the way off, then waited anxiously for him to join me on the table.

He kicked off his shoes and socks and climbed over the rail. "Care to place a bet?" he asked, leaning over to kiss me.

"I think I'd like to ride that number six now," I said, pushing him back onto the table. I rolled over on top of him and rubbed my clit against his hard cock.

We stayed like that for a good long while, grinding our hips together in unison. Tony continued playing with my breasts, alternately sucking and pinching my hard nipples. I squeezed his nipples too, and they grew hard and pink under my fingers. I couldn't get enough of that. My ex had never cared much for foreplay, and he hated being on the bottom during sex. This was a chance for me to finally indulge myself. I wanted it to last all night.

The fire inside me blazed hotter; I was going to come quickly if I didn't do something fast. So I shifted my weight and sat back on the table.

"You're stopping?" Tony asked.

"Just changing games." I straddled Tony's hips. "I want to play slot machine for a little while."

He laughed. "How do you play that?"

"I keep pulling on your handle until your eyes spin around and we hit the jackpot."

I grabbed his cock with one hand and stroked it. I slipped the other hand between his legs and massaged his balls. Tony arched his back and moaned as my hands went to work. I swear, his eyes really did spin. I stroked harder, waiting to see if they'd come up all cherries.

Tony was practically bucking underneath me now. I kept stroking and squeezing his cock until a tiny drop of semen welled out of the tip. He was going to come any second. Then, without warning, he reached up and grabbed me around the waist.

"We're going back to roulette now," he said, pulling me close. "You sit on my lap and I'll give you a spin."

He pulled my hips forward until they hovered just above his cock. I settled down on it slowly, shuddering with delight as he slipped inside. He was big, and the walls of my pussy hugged him tight as we rocked back and forth on the table.

We started out slowly, with me sliding up and down on Tony's hard cock, but soon I was moving faster and faster. I shifted my legs to wrap them around his waist, and my foot accidentally kicked the roulette wheel. It made a loud clacking noise as it lazily spun around a couple of times. Tony laughed.

"Round and round and round she goes," he sang. "Where she stops, nobody knows!"

He reached back with one hand and gave the wheel a furious push, sending it spinning.

"Your turn now." He grabbed me by the hips and brought me up high, then pulled me down hard and fast on his thick cock. I shuddered as he lifted me up and impaled me again.

The wheel kept spinning and I kept moving, up and down, around and around. I was out of control now, the fire raging inside me. I dug my fingers into Tony's back and fucked him as hard as I could.

"Come on, Lady Luck!" Tony whispered hoarsely. "Come to Tony!"

"I'm coming! I'm coming!"

He groaned and then pulled me down onto that hard dick of his one last time. I shuddered and exploded, taking Tony with me as we both hit the jackpot.

"Oh God, Amelia!" he moaned through clenched teeth.

The roulette wheel slowed and stopped.

Tony fell back on the table and I slumped forward against him, exhausted. We lay there for a while, panting. I listened to the beating of Tony's heart. I had finally won big.

"Want to play again?" Tony finally asked, brushing a strand of hair from my face.

I looked up at him and smiled. "You bet!"

ERIN CRESSIDA WILSON

Addressing the Intern Situation

We worked together. She was my husband's secretary. I knew it the first day she walked in. I saw the look on his face, as if the answer to midlife crisis had just walked through the door. She wasn't at all pretty, but she looked at me out of the corner of her eye as if to say, "Those ten extra pounds on you might as well be seventy, because baby, I'm twenty-three years old, without a half ounce of extra body fat on me, and I rule the fucking world." Check.

She was trouble. Throwing fits, taking sick leave, coming in late and hung over. Every time she'd come in tardy with a document, he'd scold her. The disciplining of this young secretary gave him new life. No, it wasn't Viagra, it wasn't a forklift for the flaccid flower; it was "Tricia," the secretary.

I had just turned forty, and you know the rest of the story. He was fifty.

When he "confessed," I couldn't bring myself to sleep with anybody else for a year and a half. When Tricia entered my life, the girl inside me stood up and left my dying ovaries, walked into Tricia's body, as my life expectancy dropped in the blink of an eye. I was suddenly old. With her entrance, I was officially no longer the cutest and youngest girl in the room.

(She's on the couch in his office, in the same position in which I first made love to him, straddling him, he has yanked her pink panties to the side and entered her, her stick legs are coming out of the dress, and this time it's her sloppy mouth and her childish arrogant way, going, "Yes, yes, yes," and she's wearing those braids, and they're slapping her face back and forth as she says, "Oh, God, oh, God, oh, God!" And he smacks his mouth and then slaps her ass, "Yes!" And when he paws her dress off and it rips, it's not my breasts that fall out and fill his hands, it's her tiny tits that can barely be cupped in a hand, and he pulls really hard on her nipples. She writhes every time he twists them. She's a good actress. And her faking it is what's even more of a turn-on.

Another time—in the bathroom stall of the men's room, the ugly beige walls, the smell of piss—she's fingering herself, kind of spastic 'cause she's gangly like a colt, pulling up her little slip dress, almost keeling over on her wobbly high-heeled shoes as he's standing there, squished into this stall, with his tool in his hands, just his zipper open, saying, "Yeah, baby," and with the other hand he's stroking his balls, trying not to lose his spunk too fast, as she says, "Oh, God! Oh, God, I'm coming!" Until her sloppy mouth opens up, and he beats off right into it.

You may think rape fantasies are disgusting, but nothing compares to a year and a half of fantasizing to the loss of my childhood. The disgusting sight of this old man screwing this birdlike girl who had not a brain in her head. Yes, indeed, that which I know, that which I now understand—in my body—is arousing. The degrading, humiliating screwing of a little girl like in porno books, yes, was my fodder. My breath would quicken, and my voice would break, echoing alone in my room. And I would lie in my bed, broken, empty. What before had been my beautiful body was replaced by what I had bought—the magazine image of the starved, twenty-three-year-old girl—the perfect woman of the twenty-first century. And she turned me on.

My finger still dipped inside me.

I remember being that girl, sleeping with married men. Yeah, I remember my flippant sideways stares, my disdain for feminism. Not understanding that I had the world by the balls because I was the fountain of youth. Every time I flipped my braids over my shoulders, every time a drop of sweat came off me, men wanted to flock to drink it up. I had no idea. I thought I was just given this power and that it would last forever. Rose petals and flowers flowing from my lips.

I gave her my dying breath; it's in her, he entered her. I still have some of it left over, curled up in a ball. Sometimes I open it up, sit under her like a tree. And I wait for just one petal to fall and anoint me. Because inside me, I still think I'm that girl.

LANA GAIL TAYLOR

Every Baby Finds Her Legs

Nola has two sons, Jack and Jared. Twin tall and twin lean. Same age as me. They bunk at the ranch house between rodeos. I think she's not going to tell them the truth. How I sleep in her bed. Nola shared that bed with their father for twenty-nine years. Nola does tell them, though, over steak and potatoes.

"Janie's bunking with me."

After a moment of the twins chewing in unison, Jack slams his hand on the table and I think, *Here we go,* and everyone gets quiet, and then Jack swallows hard.

"You mean you're a *lesbian?*" he asks. Jack can't look at his mom without getting red in the face. He doesn't look at me at all.

"Oh hell, who knows?" Nola retorts.

Jack isn't chewing his food now, just shoveling it in and swallowing. I fiddle with my fork under the table. Jared is gripping his beer glass. "Mom?" he asks. "Mom? What about Dad?"

I drop my fork and mutter "'Scuse me," then lean under the table. It's somewhere past my boots; I try roping it with my fingers.

"I loved your Dad," I hear, coming up.

"Why you going lesbian then?" Jack is frowning, not directly at me, not exactly, more like in general, but I fiddle with my fork some more.

Nola chuckles. "Where's Lesbian? North of Nebraska?"

I can't help but laugh. I think the twins laugh, too. A little.

At the breakfast table the next day, Jack decides that Nola is too old for me. Nola is in the other room on the phone with her brother, who lives in Missoula, Montana. I hear her shouting, "Damn straight!" and wonder if she's telling her brother too.

"When Mom was eighteen you weren't even a fetus," Jack says. "That's sick."

I look up from sketching, but don't say anything.

Jared starts in next. "When younger women date older men it's cuz they need a dad. You need a mom?"

They're both looking at me.

I keep sketching. The lines are light and not coming together. "Everybody needs something," I say.

"Maybe Mom's so freaked out about Dad dying she's gone nuts," Jack announces, staring off into space.

I want to kick him under the table.

Later I ask Nola if she's going nuts.

She busts out with a laugh. "We're all nuts."

The two of us are in the barn cleaning stalls, shoveling horseshit out, and then filling the animals' bins with fresh water, oats, and grain.

I ask Nola if I'm her midlife crisis.

Nola shakes her head, grinning. "Boys got a hold of you, huh? I don't believe in a midlife crisis. I believe in various twists in life."

I hesitate and then ask, "Do I need a mom?"

Nola stops shoveling and wipes her shining forehead with a glove. "Oh, hell, honey, Freud could be right or wrong. I know you lost your mom when you were small. I know I never had a daughter. Our age difference can mean anything to anyone, and so can our attraction to each other." Nola starts shoveling again. I smell hay and horse manure. Heavenly.

"I know you're here for a reason," she says. "And I know I love you all the same."

We bring the horses in from the pasture an hour later, including the mare and her foal. The baby shoves her nose under my arm, snorting and twitching her ears. I hug the foal's neck and tickle her cheek until she jerks away and trots back to the mare. Nola looks at me, throwing her gloves at the rack. I lean into her, watching the horses.

Cricket calls slip through the open bedroom windows and moonlight pushes in through the screens, illuminating two nude bodies with hips and breasts moving behind a gauzy mosquito net. My arms stretch across pillows and my middle lifts off the crocheted comforter to add to the friction of hair and skin and wetness. Nola is breathing against my neck. A heavy mane of hair falls into my face, neck, and shoulders. A breast slides across my lips and I latch on to the sugar-salt nipple—I don't want to let go.

Three months ago, I was at the track—quarter horse races. I was peddling sketches, set up just left of the north side bleachers, holding up a hand to shield my face from the sun while cowboys leaned in to peer at my drawings, or my cleavage.

"Will you take five dollars for that one?" A cowboy negotiates with my chest.

Five dollars? I try not to look as if he just said my horse is ugly. "I was thinking maybe twenty?"

The cowboy spit at the red dirt. "Are you famous, honey?"

Now it's as if he asked if my horse is lame. "No. I'm not famous."

The cowboy peers one more time at the sketch. "I'll give you five."

Put us out to pasture, why don't you? "All right." Five dollars is closer to rent than not.

About then I hear something above the rest of the track noise: a woman's voice hollering "Run, you big donkey, or I'll kick your ass!"

Up in the bleachers, row ten, the same woman shouting again: "*Ruuunnn,* jackass!"

I see a statuesque body dressed in boots, belted blue jeans, and a spaghetti-strapped shirt. The sun is behind her reddish-brown hair, lighting it up, obscuring her face. The woman's hands are punching the air. I grab a pencil and my sketchpad; the lines feel quick and light, scratching across the paper.

"I'll give you five bucks for this one," another cowboy offers.

Five again? I keep sketching. When the race ends, the woman notices my gawking. She watches me watching her and I see her face now: around fifty years old, beautiful. She stomps down the bleachers making more racket than a quarter horse getting into his hitch. She's at least five-foot-eleven. She comes to a halt beside me.

"Fucking hot out here today." The woman peers down at my sketch. "Where'd you see that babe?" She laughs heartily. "Hey, you're pretty good."

I smile, a little shy, a little embarrassed. "Thanks."

Another cowboy stops, scanning the drawings and then spewing at the ground. "This one's kinda nice. How much?"

I hesitate. "I guess...ten?"

The cowboy adjusts his belt buckle. "Ten dollars? Hell, that's a lot."

I squirm, ready to lower my price again, but the woman jumps in. "You get kicked in the head by your horse, cowboy? This gal is the next Tory Tolia."

The cowboy pauses. "How much is it worth, then?" He's looking at the woman.

"Hell, you got to pay at least twenty-five for an original piece like this." The woman never bats an eye. When the cowboy isn't looking, she winks at me. I'd never get that much for a sketch.

"All right," the cowboy agrees, and shoves twenty-five bucks in my hand. He leaves with his "original" and I'm staring at the money as if it isn't really there.

"Know what you need?" the woman asks me.

I shake my head.

"A little gumption."

I nod. "Yeah, maybe."

"Not maybe," she retorts. "Damned straight." Then she says, "Let's pack your stuff and grab a cold one." Damned straight. The woman tells me her name is Nola. I say I'm Janie and she says, "Yeah, that fits you, all right." Nola and the bartender go way back. He worked the rodeo circuit with Nola's husband from 1968 to 1977. They reminisce. I memorize the crinkles around Nola's blue eyes, the number of white strands lacing her auburn hair, the thin lips, her gnawed-down fingernails, the way she throws back a beer. I take out a pencil and start sketching her face on a napkin.

Nola looks at me. "How young are you, anyway?"

"Twenty-six. Is that young?"

Nola lifts her beer. "Hell, my boys are twenty-six."

"How old are you?"

"Fifty-one." She drains her beer.

"I like fifty-one."

Nola winks. "It ain't bad."

I lift my bare leg to her boot, bumping it. I feel the heat in my cheeks.

Nola eyeballs me. "What's this?"

I smile.

Nola grins. "Little Janie's hitting on me."

Nola mentioned in the bar that day that she needed help at the ranch when her boys weren't around. I told her, "I'll help," and for six months since, I've been shoveling stalls, loading hay, and exercising and grooming horses. Falling in love with Nola.

I'm there when Nola's best mare drops the foal.

The baby slips sticky wet red from beneath her mother's tail and then hits the straw, blinking her eyes, before immediately trying to get up. The foal finds her legs pretty fast. Nola's smile is glowing.

"She'll do fine," she says.

Most mornings, after our chores, Nola and I ride out through the meadow and into the mountains. Our horses stay surefooted on the rocky trail. In the evening, we drink beer and play cards on the porch and Nola is cheating. I slap the cards out of her hand and cuss her out.

Nola lets go with whoop. "Hell! That's gumption!"

I make my move before I go chicken shit—*gumption*—and I kiss Nola's mouth. We keep kissing, knocking into the card table, and then stopping, wiping our mouths, and Nola repeats, "OK, OK." She kisses me again for a long time without stopping.

Nola wakes up moaning into the down pillow that scrunches her face. She waits for me to bring coffee and then two cups later gets out of bed and lets out a belch. I grab my sketchpad. Nola's nude body stretches and ripples as my pencil mimics the curve of her swelling hips, the long legs on tiptoe, the blue veins visible under the skin of her brown calves, her soft belly pulling taut. I sketch her and I think she poses, but she won't say that, and the lines I draw come slow but sure, more defined than usual.

Nola takes a peek and tells me, "That's a keeper. I'll frame it. Hang it right there." She points at a spot above the bed and then winks, padding into the bathroom, turning on the shower.

I climb in after her. We soap each other down, wash one another's hair. I giggle and Nola giggles and then she presses me against the smooth porcelain wall while the water pelts our bodies and our mouths feel liquidy together. My hands cup her breasts with the round, ruddy nipples. I squeeze them; she squeezes my ass. Then Nola pulls away, tapping my freckles with a finger before using her tongue to trace the gold studs all the way around the cartilage of my ears. Nola likes the way I shudder when she does that, the way the nipples on my "horsefly-stung" tits pucker up. I like how my curves fit into hers, how she feels tall and warm and soft, and how her sleek, wet head leans back when I nurse on her nipples.

One of us shuts the water off and I leap from the shower, dripping wet and galloping into the bedroom, giggling, throwing myself on the bed and singing an old Cheap Trick song. *"If you want my love, you got it. If you need my love, you got it."* Nola follows me into the bedroom and I spread my legs for her, shivering. She leans over me, nuzzling my neck.

The next week, Nola's quarter horse, Sylvia, runs her first race. Nola's eyes are full of piss and vinegar and her hair looks wild and windblown as she stands on the bleachers, waving her fist, yelling, "Get in there, broad!"

I jump up and down and yell, too. "Don't let that pony beat you, baby!"

Sylvia wins the race. Nola glows in the winner's circle. She hugs Sylvia and kisses her nose. Then she kisses me.

Later, we hit a party. I'm wearing the dress I like—pink and clingy. Nola's wearing tailored slacks, a velvet jacket, and polished, knee-high boots. Her hair is pulled in a bun. Loose strands of dark auburn and soft white flank her face. The party guests sip champagne, except Nola, who demands beer right away. She introduces me around to her friends, most of them her age, some of them younger. Many exchange congratulations with her about Sylvia, and some eyeball us up and down. You *know* they're dying to figure us out, so Nola slaps my ass and says real loud, "What a goddamned babe!"

Nola tells everyone, "Janie's an artist. Let her sketch you sometime. You won't fucking believe how good she is."

Another lesbian couple shows up and Nola tells them, "I remember you wanted someone to sketch you two. Let Janie do it."

The women ask if I will sketch them making love.

I shrug and say, "Sure," and Nola drives us to the women's apartment. On the way, Nola has the radio on loud. She slams her hands in a rhythm on the steering wheel, bellowing, "Hey! You! Get off of my cloud!" I open my window so that a breeze blows over my face. In the street in front of the house, Nola kisses me pressed up against the car door. The metal behind me cools my feverish skin. Her mouth on mine is restless.

Inside, one of the women wears boxer shorts and a T-shirt. Her hair is short, her face tanned, her limbs slim and muscled. Her lover wears a silk robe, white socks. She has a round face and platinum blond hair. Her body is plump like a pony's. She prances around the room for her lover's benefit, and maybe ours, too. They're sipping Zinfandel wine, giving each other the eye and giggling. Nola asks for a beer. I think she is a little drunk.

I take my place cross-legged on the floor. The woman in the robe reclines across a futon, one breast falling through the loose neckline. She slips a hand between her bare thighs and watches her lover standing over her, toying with her nipples through the T-shirt before pulling the boxer shorts down, exposing a thick, black bush. The one in the robe fondles her lover's cunt, poking a finger through the slit and then pulling it out to nip at the juice.

Nola is slumped in a chair behind me. She has kicked off her boots and nudges her feet under my ass so that I'm sitting on her toes. She lights a cigar and puffs contentedly. I continue to sketch. The lovers are both on the couch now, making small noises, caressing, hugging. Soon they are humping feverishly, humming, then moaning. Nola plays with my hair. My pencil scratches fast, light and dark, sure, flowing.

Nola whispers, "Looks terrific, honey."

My favorite sketch shows the lovers afterward, limp and sated, one hand absently stroking a breast, another hand cupping a hip, and their limbs so intimately tangled I don't know whose is whose. The women nuzzle. I fall back into Nola.

I hold the last sketch up for the couple to view. They ask me how much. I look at Nola. She's blowing cigar smoke at the ceiling. Her eyes are closed. I think for a while, stalling, and then inhale and say, "Seventy-five." The women don't even flinch.

"We'll take it."

Outside I'm ecstatic. I'm kicking my feet, dancing. Nola grabs me when I fall against her and her hand twists inside my dress while she presses the small of my back. Our kiss is a combination of champagne and beer and cigar smoke, rough and impatient. Nola holds onto me, squeezing. I want to crawl up her body and ride her hips.

Nola releases me to open the car door. She directs me across the front seat and then mounts me, pushing up the hem of my dress. I open my legs, wrapping my naked calves around her boots, feeling the cool leather up and down on my skin. Nola reaches to turn the radio on. Roger Daltry sings, "You better, you better, you bet!" My lover takes hold of my hand, long fingers squeezing around mine until it hurts. She lowers her face. Breath rushes past the night air climbing my thighs. Her tongue wriggles against my underwear, licking at the silk, finding my erect clit and nipping it between her lips.

Her impatience is catching. I want the underwear out of the way. I start with them and Nola finishes, pulling them off. I'm open and warm-cool to the air, her lips, a tongue licking my clit. I sink somewhere salacious and urgent. When I come, the contractions are deep and slow, the spasms gripping then releasing my clit. My body shudders, stills, and then shudders again.

Nola is a tad more than drunk. I take the wheel. Wind blows in my hair. Nola says above the radio, "Every baby finds her legs."

I smile with both sides of my mouth. "I can't believe I told them seventy-five and they took it. Can you believe it?"

"'Course I can."

I grip the wheel, staring at the road ahead. "I love you," I gush.

"I know you do, baby." She yawns. "I love you an awful lot, too."

I continue blabbing, elated, unable to stop. "God, I can't believe seventy-five. Seventy-five! You know what I think? I think the twins are getting used to us. I think Sylvia is going to win all her races this year. I think I'm going to show. Maybe in a gallery downtown."

When I look over at Nola, she's asleep.

I wander out to the barn alone, inhaling the air tinged with earth, hay, and horses. I search the stalls for the mare and her foal. I remember when the foal never left the mare's side. Eventually, she began to walk short distances before trotting back, pushing her nose into her mother's side. Lately, the foal gallops to the end of the pasture, sticking her nose through the fence. She's getting taller, more surefooted all the time, and I wonder if Nola will sell her, or keep her around. I wonder how I will feel if the foal goes. I return to the house—the bedroom, the bed. The mosquito net flutters in a breeze. My skin feels hot. I can't lie still. I feel the weight of Nola on the bed, see her silhouette. I nudge across the crocheted comforter, into Nola's body, her lean, long body that is soft in many places. I nuzzle her in the gray light before dawn and then wake her, crawling between her legs. She holds my hair, stroking it, pulling me closer in. I feel as if I can fit through the curling pubes, the doughy lips, and the sticky, moist mouth. My face noses right up to her cunt, tongue curling inside the hole, and then my finger, more fingers. Nola's stomach rises and falls with the sound of her labored breathing and she grits her teeth, cunt pushing down on my fingers until her orgasm pops out, slick and warm on my skin.

Nola falls back to sleep, snoring. I lie next to her listening, holding onto her. After a while, my limbs stretch beneath the comforter and my body slips from under the liquid-silk sheets. My bare feet hit the floor square. I imagine Nola's smile. I imagine I'll do fine.

The twins are back from another rodeo. Jared says we're having a spitting contest and draws a target on the trunk of a tree outside. He explains, "If you hit the ground it don't count. Hit the tree and it's five points. If you hit the outside ring, that's ten points. Hit inside the ring and it's fifteen. Hit a bull's-eye and you get twenty." Jared looks at his brother and they both laugh.

Jared packs his cheek with chew and passes the pouch to Jack, who does the same. Jack grins as he passes the pouch to me. I dip a wad in my mouth and feel the burn behind my lip. My eyes water so that I see the twins through sun-spotted streaks. Jack asks, "Feel like a cowgirl yet?" and I ignore him. They're both laughing again. Jared fires and hits outside the third ring. Jack steps up next and hits between the outside and inside ring. He tries to convince us his wad is closer to the inner ring, but Jack shoves him and says, "Bullshit. That's ten."

I grab the porch rail, lean back, and then push my body forward, blowing through my lips and launching a brown string that splatters the tree square.

Jared's mouth falls open, eyes squinting as he looks at the wad stuck to the target.

Jack pushes his hat back, chew bulging in his cheek. "Hell, she got a bull's-eye first try."

Jared looks at me. "Mom teaching you to spit like that?"

"Mom ain't got that kinda firepower," Jack speaks up.

"I taught myself to spit," I answer. "Mesa County champion, 1993."

The twins look at each other and then at me. Jared whistles before Jack says, "Mom's got good taste in girls."

GILLIAN FITZGERALD

Play mysty for Me

When Karen turned fifty, her husband gave her a choker of Tahitian black pearls and earrings to match. She was a Halloween child, a true Scorpio, so they had dinner at a favorite restaurant, attended a costume party at Wicked Ways—an upscale, members-only fetish club—then made passionate love until three in the morning. The night glowed in her memory like one of the pearls on her necklace.

She had no memory of her fifty-first birthday.

Three months before, Matt was diagnosed with pancreatic cancer. By her birthday, he was bedridden and on morphine. She vaguely recalled spending the day in the downstairs den that had been turned into a sick room, with a hospital bed to make it easier for him and his caretakers—but exactly what she did there, other than love him and try to hide her grief, was a blank.

Two months later, Matt was dead, and she was a widow. They had no children, by choice, and Matt had planned his own funeral and handled the details that a death entailed while he was still alive. She threw herself into her law practice, concentrating on the problems of divorcing couples so that she wouldn't have to face the emptiness. After ten-hour days at the office, she headed for the gym for marathon workouts that she hoped would make her tired enough to sleep. She took on pro bono work for the local battered women's shelter. She cried herself to sleep more often than not. When the first urgent pain gave way to a dull ache, she felt guilty, as if she had betrayed Matt by not suffering more.

Sex wasn't even an issue. Her body was numb, as if she'd buried her libido with Matt. Whenever he'd gone away on business, she'd resorted to a vibrator. He had given her a Magic Wand with a card that read "How do you spell relief? H-I-T-A-C-H-I" Now there wasn't even an urge.

And she hadn't had many offers from appealing men. The old cliché that the good ones were all taken was a reality for women over fifty. The men who weren't in relationships of some sort either didn't want one or had so many problems that any sane woman would run as fast as she could—a brief series of bad dates set up by well-meaning friends and family members had convinced her of that.

On October 30th, she got a wake-up call: a package delivered by messenger, with no return address. The large box sat on her desk, a mystery demanding to be solved. When she slit it open, she was glad she was behind a closed door.

She lifted out a pair of custom-made red leather thigh-high boots with three-inch heels and a matching red leather corset and bikini wrapped in protective plastic. Intrigued, she looked into the box; the supple boot dropped out of her hand, thunking against the desk as she let out a stunned sob. An envelope lay at the bottom with "Karen" written on it in Matt's familiar scrawl. With trembling hands she withdrew the sheet of paper.

My darling mysty—

"mysty" was the name that Matt had called her in their most intimate moments. It was her name when she played bottom to his dominant. Karen Darcy, avenger of abused women, terror of deadbeat dads, was a bedroom submissive who loved to be spanked. She and Matt had had an equal partnership in every other area of their life together, but in the bedroom he was her master. She had reveled in his ownership—something that would have surprised her courtroom opponents, one of whom referred to her as a "femi-nazi."

By the time you read this, I'll have been gone for months. I wanted to give you one last birthday present, and one last order. In two days you'll go to Carte Blanche, where you'll have what you always call the works. I made the appointment. Then you will come home and put on the things in this box and go to the Halloween Ball at Wicked Ways. You will be my mysty one last time.

As my final act as your master, I order you to call Jamie Douglas, and tell him I am giving you to him for the night of Halloween. I am doing this because I love you, and because I don't want you stuck in the quicksand of grief. I know that, with your sense of profound loyalty, you are likely to regard sex with another man as some sort of adultery. The first time will be the hardest for you, but once you get past it, you'll be fine. You have a body made for sex and a soul made for love. You won't spend the rest of your life alone.

Call Jamie. Tell him you are my gift to him for All Hallows Eve.

Play mysty for him, and know that I still love you.

She sat at her desk and wept. The one thing they had agreed on when they'd embarked on their journey into D/S was that she would at least try to follow his orders. She would carry out his final command.

Jamie was the only man in their circle for whom she'd ever seriously lusted. He was eight years younger than she, six foot four, with dark hair touched with silver at the temples and a salt and pepper beard. He had green eyes and a sensual mouth, and the body of the stuntman he'd been before he'd gotten his Ph.D. and became a respectable professor of drama. She and Matt had played with him once, an elaborate scenario incorporating one of her Victorian fantasies. He was one of the few men she knew who could talk about his feelings without being awkward or sounding rehearsed. He'd been divorced for six years; his wife, who didn't enjoy the sexual games that Jamie did, had left him when she'd gotten a job in Seattle, and was happily remarried to a software maven.

I order you to call him.

When she got home she poured herself a double portion of Glenfiddich and downed it. Then she poured another. The worst he could do was say he wasn't interested. Matt couldn't blame her if he turned her down.

A half-hour and several drinks later, she called him, and got an answering machine.

"Jamie, this is Karen Darcy. Master Matthew's mysty. I'll be at the Halloween party at Wicked Ways tomorrow." She swallowed, hung up. And felt like an idiot.

By midnight, Jamie still hadn't called back. She crawled into the bed she had shared with Matt for almost twenty years and cried herself to sleep. She didn't know which scared her worse: Jamie taking her up on Matt's offer, or not showing up at all.

The next morning she took a shower, dragged on a blouse and jeans, and took a cab to Carte Blanche, stopping for a bagel at the deli around the block.

During the facial and hair treatment, she realized how much she'd let herself go. She should have colored her hair six weeks ago, but she'd been putting it in a French braid every day and hadn't really noticed. She'd stopped caring for her nails, and only kept up her skin regimen out of a lifelong habit.

Matt was right. She had given up on life. It was time to start living again.

She opted for a new long-layered haircut, releasing the curls in the thick, chestnut hair that fell below her shoulder blades. She liked the way it framed her face in a sexy tousle. She chose fiery red for her nails, and told the make-up artist to go all out.

She wore jeans and a sweater to Wicked Ways, and flashed her membership card at the door. They had a changing room, and several collared slaves to help those who preferred to dress at the club. Jane, aka gypsy, humbly begged Karen for the privilege of providing assistance. Karen slipped on lace-topped thigh-high fishnet hose, slid her legs into the boots that clung like the hand of a lover, and pulled on the leather panties, fastening the small gold buckles at the hip. Then it was time for the corset.

Jane closed the metal fasteners in front, then pulled the laces so tight that Karen couldn't draw a deep breath.

"This is gorgeous. A custom job?"

"A gift from my husband."

"OK, hon, you sit on the edge of the bed and get used to that while I make up my face. Then I'll tighten it up some more. So, do you mind me asking what brought this on?"

Karen swallowed. The corset wasn't tight enough to squash the butterflies in her stomach. "I—I can't talk about it, Jane. Let's just say, it's something Matthew wanted, and mysty is trying to obey."

Jane smiled at her in the mirror. "I'm glad. I've missed mysty."

The steel stays didn't allow her to bend at the waist, and Karen couldn't take a really deep breath—but each inhalation lifted her breasts enticingly, and the corset turned her opulent figure into a voluptuous hourglass. Kohl and gray shadow made her smoky eyes mysterious, and the red lipstick gave her wide mouth a full and pouty look. mysty looked out at her from the mirror.

For the first time she realized that she, too, had missed her alter ego.

The club was crowded when Karen emerged. She decided to see what was going on in the dungeons.

A leather-chapped blond man was using a bullwhip with precision on the back and thighs of a body-builder clad in a leather harness. In the cell next door, another couple was involved in an intense hot wax scene. The master turned his slave into a living canvas, creating fantastically intricate designs in myriad colors. Karen remembered the first moment when the wax was deliciously too hot, a rush of pain-pleasure that had sent her screaming into orgasm more than once. As she moved onward, she saw a tiny, delicate dominatrix using clothespins to turn her male submissive into a whimpering puddle of pleasure.

It should have excited her wildly, but she felt nothing other than admiration for the skills of the dominants.

She came to a halt in front of the glass window of a playroom. It was a one-way mirror, allowing the occupants of the room to be watched, yet still feel private, with the added bonus of a large mirror in which to observe themselves. A Victorian gentleman had a naughty French maid over his knee. Her ruffled panties were down at her ankles, her pert derriere turning red.

The clone of that maid's costume hung in Karen's closet. Wearing it, she would serve Matt dinner and pretend to open the wrong wine, or fail to refill his glass promptly. He'd force her to serve the rest of the meal with her uniform unbuttoned and her breasts bared.

Even as she blinked back tears, she realized her leather thong was soaking, her nipples hard against the silk lining of the corset. She found a table in a dark corner and sat down, digesting the significance of her body's reaction, in direct opposition to her aching heart. Perhaps the reason her body had been sexually frozen was that she had never allowed herself to mourn the loss of her master.

Karen had wept for Matt and the years they wouldn't have together—but *mysty* had never had a chance to grieve. Now, hidden in the shadows, mysty mourned the master she would never serve again.

She had no idea how long she had sat there when a dark shape suddenly blocked her view of the dance floor. Karen looked up to see an elegant magician in tails and a swirling, scarlet-lined cloak. He swept her a bow worthy of an Elizabethan courtier.

"I was stuck at a rehearsal and got in too late to call you last night," Jamie said. His voice wasn't Connery's Celtic purr, but it was close—a baritone with lovely dark velvet in its depths. Some women were ass women—Karen was a voice woman. "I see Matt's package arrived safely."

"How did you know?" she asked, startled.

"He talked to me before he died. It was sent to me, and I was supposed to make sure it got to you the day before your birthday—he was very definite about the date." For the first time in all the years she'd known him, Jamie seemed uncomfortable. "Do you mind if we go somewhere more private?" he asked. "I reserved the Victorian study for an hour."

She nodded, and together they climbed to the themed playrooms. One was done up like the cabin of a pirate ship, another was a medieval room with pseudo-stone walls and tapestries. There were also a sultan's bedroom, a speakeasy, a schoolroom.

Karen followed Jamie into the Victorian gentleman's study. He hung a Do Not Disturb sign on the door, and locked it. This particular playroom had a deep-brown leather couch and two wing chairs with cleverly hidden restraints built into them. From past experience, Karen knew that the tall bookshelves opened to reveal a suspension system for tying up a careless maid or restraining a naughty ward. Her cheeks flushed as she recalled some of the games she and Matt had played in here.

She chose one of the wing chairs, and Jamie took the other, drawing so close that his knees touched hers. She felt a small electric shock at the point of contact. He reached out to take her red-gloved hands between his. She had always liked his hands, long-fingered and eloquent when he gestured, with an actor's instinctive feel for the nuances of the moment. His thumb stroked her palm through the silk, and liquid heat rushed over her body in a wave.

"Matt told me what he planned to ask you," Jamie said. "He asked how I felt about it. I told him the truth. That I've always wanted you."

His forest-green eyes mirrored her sorrow. Of course—he too missed Matt. And Matt had known the sexual tension that flowed between them, yet had never said a word to her, knowing she'd only feel guilty. Now he had given them the freedom to explore their bond, something she doubted they would have had the courage to do without Matt's having created the opportunity. It reminded her of just why she had adored her husband.

Of one thing she was quite certain: She wouldn't allow Matt's gift to be wasted. Her sortie into the dungeons had made her realize that she could still feel desire. And across from her was a delicious man—dominant, handsome, sensual. "When Matt told me what he wanted us to do, he said he knew that I'd be careful with you, and that I'd abide by your decision if you didn't want to go ahead with it."

"What if I don't *want* you to be careful?" she ventured, allowing mysty to emerge. "What if I want you to be deliciously cruel and wonderfully demanding?"

For a moment, Jamie hesitated, searching her face. Then the subtle change that marked his transition into Master Jamie took over: There was something slightly arrogant, commanding, about his posture.

"I can only try." His tone was cool, as if he was amused that mysty would challenge him. "But I want to give you time to think about it, and I don't want to play with you publicly. I want your first time to be just for you."

"But I like being watched," she said with a pout. "I adore it."

He shook his head disapprovingly. "I know you're a shameless exhibitionist, mysty. But I am the master, not you. It's what I want that counts. You may choose to play by my rules, or not play at all. Those are your only choices."

He reached into a hidden pocket in his cloak and drew forth what appeared to be a long-stemmed red rose. It was a riding crop, the shaft covered in forest-green suede, the bloom made of red suede petals.

"In a few minutes," he said, "I'll leave you alone, and go home. If you accept my terms, you'll take the cab that will be waiting for you in fifteen minutes. You will come to my home, and you will kneel before me and place this in my hands and beg me to use you in the way that Master Matthew has requested."

He placed the crop in her hands, stood, and walked out, the door closing behind him with heavy finality.

Matt had been right. Jamie was the right man, maybe the only man. She didn't know what would happen afterward, but she wanted this night. She went downstairs, collected her coat, and gave the waiting taxi driver Jamie's address. Karen Darcy entered the cab. When they pulled up to Jamie's home, a large brick townhouse in the West Village, it was mysty—seductive, challenging, occasionally naughty mysty—who emerged.

He opened the door as soon as she knocked. He had changed into a piratical crimson silk shirt, a black suede vest, and leather pants that fit like a second skin. He looked dangerous—and sexy as hell.

She knelt before him. "I am mysty, Master Jamie. Master Matthew has ordered me to serve you tonight. I am to give you pleasure in any way you wish." She extended the rose-tipped crop in her satin-gloved hands, looking up from beneath her lashes.

"Did I tell you that you could look at me, girl?" he asked, his voice cold. "I'll take your master's gift, and I may well use it to teach you some manners. Look at you. You're dressed like a mistress. Did you hope to fool me into thinking you're an equal, you vain slut? Stand up."

When she had risen gracefully, and stood with her hands at her side, eyes cast down, he examined her carefully, one hand lifting her chin as if searching her face for defiance. Then he circled her, enjoying the view of his new toy. At least she hoped he was enjoying himself.

"The only thing a slave wears in this house is a collar." He reached over to the buffet table next to him and picked up a small dagger. "Turn around."

With infinite precision, he cut the lace at the back of the corset, the satin ribbon giving way easily to the razor-sharp blade. "Now take it off."

Her fingers were shaking as she struggled with the clasps. He made no move to help, simply leaned back against the buffet with his arms crossed, the crop dangling from one hand, watching her. His eyes were the color of jade, and just as stony.

At last the final metal clasp was free. She allowed the corset to drop to the floor.

"Now the panties."

That was easy. Two quick flicks, and they joined the corset.

"Bend over and slip off the boots and stockings. Turn your back to me as you do it. I want to see your ass."

She slid one boot off, then the other, then slowly rolled down the stockings, bracing herself on the table.

"Lovely." A hand gloved in leather slid over her bare cheeks, stroking, caressing, then lifted and struck hard. "But you were too slow. Obey me swiftly next time. Now stand again, but don't turn."

He lifted her hair, his fingers caressing her nape, and fastened a collar around her neck.

Soft leather and cold metal against her throat. She felt wildly vulnerable.

"You can turn and look at yourself in the mirror. Look at yourself, wearing my collar, marking you as my property. Mine. No one else's."

A delicate strip of red leather encircled her throat, its only decoration a single gold rose that dangled in the hollow of her slender neck. In the mirror she saw a woman no longer young. Her breasts were not the perfect breasts of a twenty-two-year-old centerfold. They were softer, with more droop than they'd had in her twenties.

Her waist was small, but her stomach had a roundness to it that not even a hundred crunches a day could flatten. No, she was not a girl, but a woman of fifty-two, wearing the traces of time on her body and face. Could he want her? Matt had, but he had loved her for twenty years, had seen the changes happen over time. Jamie was seeing her naked for the first time.

A gloved hand caught her chin before she could avert her eyes from the mirror. "How dare you question the value of your master's gift to me? I see it in your eyes. If I'd wanted a twenty-something, I could have had one. I wanted you. Yes, you have lines around your eyes and mouth. Those lines tell me who you are, mysty, and they please me more than you will ever know. You're sexy as hell, and you've made me hard as a rock. And for that, I'm going to give you the punishment you deserve."

His eyes met hers in the mirror, searching, questioning. "One last time, mysty. Do you trust me?"

This time there was no hesitation. "Yes, Master Jamie. I do."

"Then we'll begin." A pair of black silk scarves materialized from a drawer. He used one to tie her hands in front of her, the other as a blindfold. It astonished her how helpless the simple lack of sight made her feel, and how much more alive every inch of skin felt. He took her arm. "We're going downstairs now. I'll tell you when we've reached the bottom of the stairs."

They walked down what she assumed was a hallway, and then a door opened and he took her downstairs. The lack of sight heightened other senses: She became sharply aware of the sound of his boots on the wooden stairs, the coolness of the wood under her toes, the sandalwood and musk of his cologne, and, most keenly of all, the firm grip of his leather-gloved hand on her arm. The descent seemed endless, but finally her bare feet touched carpet, thick and plushy. The blindfold was removed.

She was in Jamie's dungeon. The walls were covered with thick crimson velvet, except for one that was a mirror. The carpet was a lush Oriental with dragons in the corners. There was a desk of heavy dark wood, with a matching chair behind it, upholstered in leather that looked as soft as silk. A pair of armoires flanked a St. Andrew's cross. A leather bench with an adjustable padded kneeler and attached restraints stood in the middle of the room, facing the mirror. There was a wooden frame for suspension and objects that looked like a leather swing and a table with stirrups.

It was a room out of her most decadent dreams. She imagined herself spread-eagled on the St. Andrew's cross, or suspended by velvet cord from the wooden frame. Where would he place her first? Would he use a whip, paddle, or riding crop to mark her as his? The anticipation was enough to make her wet.

"These are *my* breasts." Jamie reached around her to cup and fondle them, pulling at her tight nipples, igniting her. "*My* nipples." He moistened a finger and stroked them until she moaned. "*My* ass." His gloved hands pulled her against him, so that she could feel how hard he was. "*My* pussy." Leather slid down her shaved mound, exploring her moist core, sending shock waves through her—she feared she would come just like that, so quickly.

But he wouldn't permit that. "Mine," he warned her. "You won't have an orgasm until I allow you, and you'll have to beg me for that." He let her go, and her knees almost buckled, but he caught her.

He led her to the spanking bench and pushed her into position, her torso supported by the bench, her ass lifted high. He tightened the straps around her ankles and wrists. Karen could only move her head and arch her back a bit. The tension and vulnerability of her position aroused her unbearably; small thrills arced through her like static electricity. He had positioned the bench so that she could see them both in the mirror. The sight of him, fully clothed, in contrast to her nakedness, excited her.

He stroked her back with his gloved hand, the leather soft and smooth against her silky skin, enflaming her until her pussy was dripping onto the bench. Then he lifted his hand and brought it down hard, without warning, in a swat against her bottom. A flurry of swats. A caress of her back, and then a blow. Another caress, then another blow. A savage, sweet rhythm that quickly brought her to the point where she couldn't tell them apart. Leather on flesh, hurting and pleasuring with equal skill. The gloves were tossed aside, and then it was his bare hand against her naked body, sharp, hard slaps in quick succession, each one a little more forceful than the other until he found the level she could bear. Ten slaps, twenty, then he increased the frequency and the pain level, until she was short of breath, begging to be allowed to give in to climax.

"Not yet, mysty. It's too soon. You're just beginning."

His fingers found her wet, hot core, and thrust into her. His thumb flicked her clit, kept her straining on the knife-edge of a climax. Then he combined his caresses with hard, fast slaps on her reddened cheeks, distracting her from the pleasure, yet increasing it at the same time. Matt had done this to her. She hated it and loved it.

His hands left her body and he strode to the desk to get a soft deerskin flogger. He worked with that, first using blows so soft that they felt like a massage, then picking up the pace. When she was close to her limit again, he stopped and stroked her back, bottom, and thighs with gentle hands, soothing her.

"You're doing so beautifully, mysty, so beautifully," he whispered. "You're taking the pain so well. You make punishing you a gift."

mysty panted, watching him through glazed eyes as he walked casually back to the desk to select another flogger, the strain of his cock against the tight leather the only indication of his reaction. He took his time, removing his vest and folding it over the chair, allowing his shirt to gape open, revealing his chest. He picked up one whip, then put it down, handling several before choosing one.

The new flogger struck her sensitized skin, the blows stinging rather than thudding; he wielded the whip deftly, alternating blows with caresses. mysty heard herself making wordless, animal cries, nothing but a mass of need, wanting what only he could give her, the pain and pleasure mixed. She felt as if she were outside her body, yet she was acutely aware of each stinging stroke, each caress.

The blows stopped. Fur glided over her tortured, glowing skin, fur with small thorns in it, soft and harsh.

Back, ass cheeks, thighs, even her face—finally he brought it up her thighs and across her labia. It slid over her swollen clit. The silky fur and the sharp little thorns were maddeningly, achingly sexy. And then he lifted the rose-tipped crop.

He whispered in her ear, "Come for me, mysty. Do it now."

As the crop stung her sensitized derriere, the dizzying spiral of climax took her, exploding into fireworks of sensation; she knew nothing but this moment, this man, this touch. She wanted to belong completely to one man, body and soul. She had been terrified that she had lost that with Matt, but he and Jamie had given that back to her, and she felt it as keenly as she did the wild, hard contractions of her pussy. She rode the shuddering climax for a long time, an eternity, sobbing with release. Then she fell back into reality.

Hands stroked her gently—her hair, her face, her back; comforting, soothing hands, easing the transition for her. He whispered soft words into her ear. "Do you need something? Water? Shall I untie you?"

Her answer came in short pants, her voice raw. "Just—untie me."

He unfastened the straps, lifting her from the bench. He carried her to a chair, murmuring comforting phrases, bringing her back to herself. The warmth of his body through the silk shirt was immensely soothing. She felt like a child being rocked to sleep.

All she could say was, "Thank you. Thank you. Thank you."

"Shh. Not necessary. The pleasure was mine."

As she returned to full awareness, she realized that she still wanted something: She wanted to be fucked.

She wet her lips, swallowed, and said, her voice husky with lust, "I want more. I want you. I want you in my mouth and my pussy and my ass." She was pleading—a desperate, needy slave.

"Well, when you beg so sweetly, how can I refuse?" he said, laughing. "Upstairs, then."

He was stronger and more muscular than Matt, lifting her into his arms and rising with no effort. He carried her upstairs to the bedroom. He placed her on her hands and knees, her calves and ankles over the edge of the bed, and inserted a finger inside her. mysty writhed, and moaned with loss when he removed his hand.

"After I fuck you, I'm going to eat you till you beg for mercy—and then you'll suck me, because I'll be ready for you. All night long, mysty. All night long." His velvet voice was harsh with urgency.

He moved to the other side of the bed to undress, slipping out of his shirt and pants. He was built like one of the great cats, a panther perhaps, all sleek muscle and dark fur, and he padded toward her like one on the prowl. It was impossible not to notice the size of his thick, hard cock.

He pushed into her in one swift stroke. Karen cried out his name as he thrust. She pushed back against him, moaning deep in her throat. He withdrew slowly, agonizingly, then entered her again, millimeter by millimeter, and then pulled out again, repeating the process until she was begging him to fuck her, take her, use her. Only then did he increase the speed of his thrusts, alternating between hard, swift strokes and long, slow ones. Finally she couldn't hold back, and came around his cock, her muscles clenching, rippling like fingers around him, a hard, almost painful climax that left her weak and shaking.

Even then he did not stop. He moved slowly inside her, teasing her toward another climax. As her excitement built, he pumped harder, his hips setting a driving, demanding rhythm that carried them both over the edge. They came together, one of his hands clenched in her tousled hair as he knelt behind her, and he groaned with the depth of his release.

She was trying to regain her breath when he turned her on her back and put a pillow under her hips, positioning her legs off the edge of the bed so that he could suck his own salty semen mingled with the fluid from her swollen pussy. He seemed determined to wring as many climaxes out of her as her body could bear. Two more and she was too sensitive to continue. She pulled him up beside her, to cradle him in her arms.

He was still hard. She knelt over him, taking him into her mouth, her tongue licking over the slit of his cock, sucking him with hot, desperate lips. Each time her head bobbed up and down, her pussy ground against the velvet duvet, its soft fibers exciting her swollen, well-used pussy. His hand found her clit and began a teasing rhythm to match her lips on his shaft. It wasn't long before he exploded in her mouth, and she came with him, his orgasm triggering hers.

Exhaustion at last overcame lust, and they slept wrapped around each other.

Karen woke in Jamie's arms, her bottom pushed up against him, his cock pressed against the curve of her ass.

His erection was obvious. She turned on her back and found him watching her with half-closed eyes. His hair was tousled into small curls. Why, she wondered, did men wake up looking sexy, despite bed-mussed hair, while women just looked messy?

"Only one night?" mysty asked. "Was that enough?"

She knew his answer before he told her. mysty was back, and Karen would never lose her again.

JAMIE JOY GATTO

A Wardrobe of Souls

Heidi: 1959. I remember her as if she were still sitting on my front porch swing, creaking, gliding, white paint peeling. She always picked at the paint while she swung, her toes barely touching the gray concrete. Heidi, with her chipped watermelon-pink toenails; Heidi, with her ruffled gingham midriffs, arms akimbo, blonde braids sprouting colorful ribbons; Heidi, the first girl I ever kissed. We fed each other the juiciest blackberries we'd pick in May. We never fought. She wasn't my girlfriend, or so she said. We were only practicing for when we'd get a "real" date with a real boy. She'd kiss me long and sweet as we lay in bed on sleepovers, wrestling with our budding libidos on muggy summer nights, toes wriggling under the sheets. Playing footsie was OK, but our hands were too young, too afraid to explore.

Leslie: 1962. She was the first girl who ever punched me in the nose. Leslie was a spitfire hellion, hair never combed, head always cocked to one side; she taught me cuss words

I didn't yet know the meaning of. Leslie was my biggest crush in junior high, except for Jimmy Creed, the pretty, quiet boy whom every girl loved. I think they call it a "crush" because of what happens to your heart and soul after the recipient decides they never want you. Leslie was a known dyke by eighth grade. Then, she still didn't want me. I think I was too much of a pussycat for her.

Melanie: 1963. Melanie was a cousin I never kissed, but I watched her from behind a tree one day, kissing her boyfriend in the car, and I felt strangely faint. I think I forgot to breathe. I'm not sure if I imagined I was the girl or the boy. They were both so pretty, faces flushed and panting, all covered in buckets of teenage lust. Melanie wasn't a girl I wanted, Melanie was a girl I wanted to *be*. She grew up to marry a black guy, and my family shunned her. Once she had babies with him, they never spoke to her again. I haven't heard any more about Melanie, nor did I ever meet all my little cousins whom she brought into the world. I always knew she was daring in love. I modeled my teenage self after her.

Michael: 1964. He was a towheaded kid, skinny as a rail, but he had a nice, crooked smile. He was the first boy who let me touch his penis—through his pants, of course. My first-hand experience with a hard-on came after begging the skinny boy in pale-blue denim to let me feel it. We were sitting knees up, asses sunk deep in a fungus-green couch in the playroom/basement. The sound of his mom's feet shuffling above us in the kitchen while she cooked, pans clacking, kept rhythm to my soft strokes on what seemed to be his unusually large cock. All I know is, once I started to feel it, I wanted to see it, smell it, taste it. Denim still gets me wet. I instinctively knew there was more to do than just touch, though—but we were both too frightened to try anything more. A week later, he threw a rock at my head, scarring me for life. I'll wear Michael on my forehead 'til the day I die.

Alice: 1968. I don't think I can talk about her just yet. Women will take you and eat your soul. Men, they can be assholes too, but women make you bleed. They're wicked like that. Is it because men are so easy to second guess—are they really that transparent? Is that what saves me from the torment of loss with men—that I can see it coming from a mile away? Do I expect it from a man, but not from a woman? Maybe. I'll never know for sure. Women are still a mystery to me, even after all these years. Believe me, I'm a woman, and I'm not a misogynist. I'm just scared to death of other women, no matter how much I may love them. I'm not proud to admit it.

Warren: 1970. When Warren and I got married, I knew I'd found the right guy. He was just quirky enough to keep me interested, and he was always ready to fight with me if he disagreed. I can't stand wusses. I like the passionate ones, the troubled ones, the ones with history. Warren was all that and more. He was a survivor, a fighter like me, and a very good cook. My specialty was toast. On a good day, I could scramble eggs without burning them. He'd be up at dawn making eggs benedict for two. He'd cook French toast with vanilla. That was someone I could live with.

Sometimes we'd lie in bed and talk about love and life and pain as if we shared the same mind. Some days we'd fight so hard, the walls shook, the dishes broke, the dog hid under the bed. Mostly we got along. Mostly we did whatever it took to get along just fine.

Warren, I later found out, also had a penchant for pantyhose. Not me in stockings, no—he liked to wear them himself. One night we were so drunk, he told me about it, and I didn't laugh at him. I just got some stockings out of my drawer, rolled them up leg by leg, and offered to ease his trembling toes into each nylon bundle, sliding them up slowly over muscular, hairy legs. His cock was so stiff; I'd never seen him so voracious. He fucked me madly, coming more than once. He begged to eat me for hours, savoring each droplet of my come on his lips as if my pussy was his Muse. He drank from me, and I felt myself pulsing into him over and over again. I got lost in his mouth. My whole body became his lips, his mouth, his tongue. I couldn't count the orgasms; they all seemed to merge into a timeless place. Bliss. Pantyhose definitely changed our love life.

He started shaving his legs. I loved the silky feel of his legs against mine, our legs entwined in the sheets. We'd shop together for lotions and nylons, garters and stockings, adding to his wardrobe of leg accessories over time. Warren was a good man, but, as I said, Warren had a bad temper. I didn't so much mind his hitting me once in a blue moon, when he'd really lose it, but when he hit Ellie, our three-year-old, that did it. I packed us up and left. He cried. I cried. Ellie cried for him at bedtime, damn near broke my heart. He's still a good dad to her, pays her college and all, I'll give him that.

Freedom to date was a new concept, and a whole new experience. It was one thing meeting people in high school, and then easy having started classes at a coed college in the late '60s, but after seven years of marriage, I had no idea where to begin. I must say, my best dates—during that period—were a dildo named Wayne, and a shower massage named Wanda. It took me five years to meet anyone new, real, worthwhile.

Sheila: 1977. Sheila was a frail thing, wispy-haired and bleary-eyed, always sniffling from some allergy. We met in a pottery workshop, which kept my fingers busy in something other than my sex, and kept my mind on trying to build something out of nothing. I liked the feel of the slippery clay between my fingertips. I liked the smell of the classroom, and the intimacy of the art form. I liked meeting Sheila after class for a Coke in the rec hall, and finding out her frailties were only surface deep. Her passions were wrapped tightly in the fast-paced, controversial women's movement, in supporting the proposed ERA, and, I found out soon enough, in the art of perfecting the female touch.

One day at a Judy Chicago exhibit at the New Orleans Museum of Art, she hovered behind me, snaked her tiny hands around my waist, and breathed into my neck, "Your cunt must be more beautiful than even those." She nodded toward the walls bearing canvasses of huge, abstract femalia. I sighed when she put her hands into my jeans, and trembled at the possibility that someone might find us in such an intimate pose, hanging onto each other, draped in the reckless intoxication of arousal and newly born love. My heart pounded an arrhythmic meter, my knees felt impossibly transparent, unable to hold my body upright. Sheila's insistent hand found my center. She barely lingered in my coarse, tangled down, then she slipped her hand away. I nearly fainted from the release of her touch. I don't remember the bus ride home. I only knew we were together after that.

She had the strongest hands of any woman I'd ever met. Sundays when my momma had Ellie, we'd meet in her cramped apartment and smoke a bowl. She'd play some Joan Baez or Carole King, maybe Phoebe Snow. I'd lie on the floor, hugging the shag carpet as if it were the finest grassy meadow, floating away into the day, stoned while she massaged my weary body from neck to foot. The music would rush over me like a cool, feminine breeze. I would connect with a thousand voices, with all the women who'd ever lived. I'd die. When I was nothing but gelatinous ooze, meringue in a sea of flesh made buttery soft by her earnest handiwork, Sheila would roll me over, and I'd comply, my body no longer belonging to myself, but to the hands of the goddess who now ruled me, body and soul.

We'd always begin with soft kisses that grew more urgent, and finally we'd lock together, legs entwined. Cunts wet with hunger would find one another, and finish what our mouths had begun. With our legs scissored, we'd work together, and then instinctively relax, our clits demanding, our bodies taxed. We'd play a rhythm in time with the music, growing faster, clashing furiously, soon creating our own tempo. Time would hang indefinitely, then fall fast and rage into us as we snaked and coiled and rode every pleasure thread we could find in our union. Breasts in hands, and fingers in mouths, cunts in fury, licking, tasting, touching, rubbing, fire, tantrums, exploding, falling, weeping, laughter, happiness.

Ellie came to love Sheila almost as much as I did. One chilly day Ellie came home from school, snot-nosed, head low. "Jacob Wasserman says you're a lesbian, Mamma," she whined. "Is that true?"

Sheila looked at me as if to say, *I'll take care of this.* She bent down carefully, eye-level with my daughter, and offered, "Yes, Ellie, your Mamma is a lesbian, but that's not a bad thing. It only means she loves me, and I love her."

"Oh, OK," Ellie said, looking relieved. "What's a lesbian?" she asked curiously, a typical eight-year-old girl.

My heart was pounding, my brain was trying to take it all in, process the information as it was, for the *first* time, being spoken aloud. Somehow being in love with Sheila had made me become gay—but that didn't make sense to me. I just loved people; I wasn't gay, I wasn't straight, but I knew I wasn't a lesbian. I had never felt like "a lesbian." I didn't want that label, and I certainly didn't want another person telling my daughter who and what I was, even if I loved that other person deeply.

Yes, it was true that I loved Sheila, but it was also true that I'd loved Warren. I'd loved them both, passionately, intimately, even desperately. I didn't feel I could let it slide, that I could allow another person to teach my daughter something about me that simply didn't jibe with my guts, with my heart. I wasn't in denial about my relationship with Sheila. We were open and free with our affections and commitments. But I couldn't let it go, I simply had to stop her.

"I am not a lesbian, Ellie," I said firmly, almost in an exasperated tone. I didn't know what else to say. I blurted it out as if it were the biggest secret on earth, and I'd been holding it in confidence for a lifetime.

Sheila flinched. "What?" she said, her mouth slowly opening. A look of betrayal ran across her face and played along the edges of her eyes.

"Mamma is not a lesbian," I said, crouching down, taking Ellie by the shoulders and shaking her gently, assuredly.

Sheila went to the kitchen and started banging pots and pans.

That night I tried to talk to her, to tell her that my love was abundant, that I'd loved both men and women, and that I couldn't commit to the label of lesbian, but that I'd certainly commit to her love, if only she'd be with me, stay with me, maybe even for a lifetime. I pleaded: I was a person, not a name, not a label. I begged her to understand me.

Sheila wouldn't speak. She took up a tiny space in the bed, facing the wall, blending in with the linens, a lost doll consumed by blankets and sheets. I watched the moon as it soared through the night sky and I prayed to her, to the weeping face of the moon goddess. I prayed for peace. I prayed for understanding. I prayed that Sheila wouldn't leave. The moonlight filtering through the trees seemed to play with my thoughts, to keep hope alive, aloft. The moon goddess held me. I couldn't cry; I'd let the moon cry for me.

Where did I belong? With my equal love for men and for women, I was nothing but a twilight being, a ghost. I felt alone, banished by the very person who should understand me the most. I knew that night that I could never live in Sheila's lesbian world, spotted with friends who were radical feminists, who believed that men caused all the pain in the world. Sometimes I'd see that same glimmer of hatred in Sheila's eyes, too. As much as I loved her, and believed in so many of the things she did, I could not become a lesbian simply to fulfill her idea of the perfect mate. I could not lie to myself, my family, my daughter. I wasn't willing to do that, and I'm sure that, in her heart of hearts, Sheila understood. But I had seen her face withdraw from me. I had felt her love retreat. Her body lying next to mine in our conjugal bed gave off nothing but neutral, cold vibrations. Sheila, my Sheila, was gone.

Sheila left at dawn, rising and gathering her clothes and a few books. She only came back once, to pick up her records on a lone, gray Sunday when she knew my momma had Ellie. Instinctively, Ellie cried only that one night for Sheila, even though I hadn't told her Sheila had been back for a final visit. It was the last time I ever saw or spoke to the woman I now consider my ex-wife. After that, Ellie never asked for Sheila again.

Rhody: 1982. Rhody came into my life with all the tact and demureness of a camel wearing tap shoes. Rhody was big, lumbering, and gentle, with a mouth like Judy

Garland and the fashion sense of the mother of the bride. A man dressed up like a woman or a woman wearing a man's body—I wasn't sure which, 'til we fell into bed after a night of gin and tonics and too much dancing for an out-of-shape gal like me. We met at Charlene's, a dyke bar. Rhody spilled her backpack in my lap and then managed to drop her wallet through a gap in my full skirt, popping off a crucial button. With my panties flashing, white satin intermittently exposed, and both of us drunk as skunks, we danced 'til they kicked us out of the bar. Rhody's been with me ever since.

Present: 2001. Rhody says she'll always stay pre-op and simply continue her hormones, but either way, I'll love her and her huge body, and her loud mouth. Her compassion will always hold me close to her heart, her love and ample affection for my now-grown daughter will always warm my soul. With her small cock and tiny breasts, she'll always find a way to make me want her. The only thing we tend to argue about is when she steals my last pair of clean underwear.

KRISTINA WRIGHT

Buzzed

So I'm hauling ass down A1A, top down, nose sunburned, wondering where in the hell I'm going, but knowing exactly what I'm running from. Six feet four inches of solid muscle formerly known as my husband, John. I split yesterday when he put his fist in my face. It wasn't the first time, but I was determined it would be the last. Now I'd put enough distance between him and me that I could laugh about my shiner clashing with my sunburned nose.

I kept driving until Michigan was a memory. The 'vette ate up the miles and before long I'd run out of mainland and was traveling over water. Seven Mile Bridge stretched out before me like a Band-Aid over the ocean, soothing the hurt with the promise of healing sea breezes and cold bottles of beer. By the time I hit Key West, I was windblown, parched, and running on fumes.

I was home.

The dinky little island known as the Conch Republic isn't a haven for criminals and misfits anymore. Now, tourists bedecked in nautical wear by Chanel fill the seedy little bars and tacky tourist traps, pouring their dineros into a shaky island economy. The Keys have lost their surface grit—Key West more so than the rest—but it's still there, beneath the surface, like oil mixing with water. Scum always rises to the top, given enough time.

With that in mind, I skipped past the bars the tourists flocked to. Those places with their neon lights and handsome bartenders hold little appeal to a chick who at seventeen was tending bar and fending off grabby hands in the roughest joints on the island. I'd given up fluff for substance a long, long time ago, at least when it came to my taste in bars.

I cruised down Duval Street at a crawl, looking for my own personal grotto. I have a lousy sense of direction, but the soul doesn't forget. Just as the sun was dipping down to the ocean to please the crowds in Mallory Square, I pulled up in front of One-Eyed Jack's.

If Key West was home, then One-Eyed Jack's was the rec room of my youth. A seedy little dive with oyster shells underfoot, beer on tap, and a ragtag assortment of scruffy patrons who'd as soon spit in your eye as say hello. In other words, they were just like family. I missed them something fierce.

I took a deep, cleansing breath as I crossed the threshold, the aroma of cigarette smoke and stale beer as sweet and pure as a baby fresh from the bath. I claimed my old bar stool, second from the end, directly in front of the beer tap. Jack was nowhere to be seen, but there was a pretty little thing regaling two old salts with some tall tale.

They seemed more intent on getting a gander at the tits straining her tight little baby-doll T-shirt than in getting all the details of her story.

"Watcha havin', sweetie?" she called, sauntering down the bar like a long-legged egret gliding along a marsh. She batted her baby blues at me and flipped one honey-colored braid over her shoulder. Its twin hung near her waist, hugging one tit like a python seeking warmth.

"Tequila. One shot after another until I fall on my ass."

She eyed me up and down as if I was dinner and she was starving. She zeroed in on the shiner and squinted at me. "You new here?"

"Nah," I said, tapping a Camel out of the pack on the bar. It wasn't my brand, but beggars can't be choosers. "*You're* new."

She pursed her lips as if she'd been sucking lemons. "I've been here six months."

I jabbed a thumb in the direction of the plate glass window. "I was born up front under the Corona sign." It wasn't true, but it might as well have been.

Honey girl shook her head, obviously thinking I was already three sheets to the wind and full of shit. "You really think you need any more tequila, babe?"

Now, "babe" isn't exactly my favorite nickname, but it beats the hell out of some of the things John liked to call me when he went on one of his three-day benders. I raked a hand through my rat's nest of hair and simpered sweetly, "Tell you what, you take my money, pour the tequila, and leave it to me to know when I've had enough, *babe*."

She obviously knew when to back off. She filled a shot glass and slid it across the wide bar without spilling a drop. A couple of lime wedges followed. I pushed the lime to the side and tossed the shot back, feeling the burn as it eased down my empty gut. The glass was refilled almost as soon as it hit the bar. I was starting to like my honey girl.

"What's your name?" I asked while the second shot was still scorching my vocal cords.

"Georgia." She swiped at the bar with a dirty rag. "Georgia Lee."

"Sounds like a porn star," I said. The tequila was burning a path through my veins and I was starting to feel woozy. I motioned for another shot. Woozy wasn't nearly where I wanted to be. "I'm Rae. Jack's daughter."

Georgia's eyes went saucer-wide. "I didn't know Jack had a daughter. Wow."

"Yeah, well, Jack's never been the sentimental type," I said, trying to remember whether I was on my third shot of tequila or my fourth. It didn't matter. "I'm not really his daughter. Stepdaughter, actually."

I'd need a fucking flowchart to figure out exactly how I was related to Jack, but I didn't bother telling her that. Jack had been the closest thing to a father figure I'd had during those formative years of boyfriends and blowjobs, so I liked the idea of calling him Dad. It pissed him off because he was only about fifteen years older than me to begin with.

"Where is the old goat, anyway?" I asked, checking out the score for the Knicks–Heat game on the TV set above her head.

The Heat were getting their asses kicked. I grinned. Old John-boy was probably in a rage. I knew he'd bet a bundle on this game, including our mortgage money. That was partly why I was sporting a black eye roughly the size of his fist.

Georgia cast a look down the bar at the two coots drinking their Old Milwaukee. When she looked at me again, I knew. The truth hit me harder than John had. Jack had gone and died on me.

"Damn. No," I muttered into my glass. "When?"

"About three months ago. Cancer," she said, dropping her voice an octave in that way people do when they talk about death and disease. "I guess no one knew to call you."

"I guess."

She slid a small hand with cotton-candy-pink nails across the bar. One finger, then two, then her whole hand rested on my wrist. "I'm sorry," she said. "He was a neat guy."

Georgia was a cute little thing, so I didn't snarl at her like I would at anyone else who'd call Jack "neat." "Thanks. Who owns the bar now?"

She flashed a row of perfect white teeth. "I do. Jack wanted to make sure it went to someone who would appreciate it."

I nodded. I guess he hadn't thought of me. For all he knew, I was living the life of a suburban housewife. And I had, for too long. "Great."

I sat there, contemplating what to do next. It took a full minute for it to dawn on me that the only thing I could do was finish what I'd started and get rip-roaring, falling-down drunk. It seemed a fitting tribute to Jack—

not to mention an appropriate memorial service for the end of my marriage.

"I need to get out of here," I muttered to the empty shot glass in front of me. I had no idea how much time had passed, but the bar was near full to capacity and my honey girl had been joined by a longhaired dude I might have recognized from my glory days if I hadn't been bleary-eyed from the booze.

I kicked back from the bar and nearly toppled my stool. Georgia said something to the other bartender before coming around the bar. "Let me help you," she said softly, her arm wrapping around my waist. She was a petite little thing, but she was strong.

"I'm fine." I pushed her off and fell on my ass. "See, this is exactly what I wanted to happen."

She ignored my fit of giggles and helped me to my feet. She barely winced when I brought my sneaker down on her instep, but wobbled on her platform shoes. I felt bad—but she was the one insisting on playing Florence Nightingale.

She led me out of Jack's and into the crowded street. People were packed so close together I could barely breathe. I stumbled off the curb, Georgia's arm still around my waist.

She started to lead me down the street, but I pointed at the 'vette. "I've got a car."

"You're not driving."

I fished my keys out of my jeans and dangled them from my finger. "Fine, you drive."

She put me in the passenger seat and tried to open the driver's door.

"It sticks," I said. "You have to climb over."

She took it in stride and hopped over, giving me a good long look at the space between her legs. Georgia wasn't wearing panties under her little denim skirt—the curls between her legs were the same silky honey color as her braids. She slid into the seat and grinned. "I've always wanted to drive one of these."

"Damn, baby, this car's older than you," I said, closing my eyes and resting my head against the back of the seat.

She put the car into gear and pulled into traffic. "I like 'em older."

The '63 Corvette Stingray had been a gift from John, a high-school graduation present about thirty years too late. The car hadn't been much more than a gray-primed engine-less wreck when he'd towed it home behind his pickup. I'd done all the work myself, from rebuilding the 327 humming under the hood to applying the twelve-coat, sunshine-yellow paint job.

A few minutes later we pulled up in front of one of the little shacks that dotted the island. It was tucked into a cove beside half a dozen other tiny cottages. When she cut the engine, I could hear the water lapping softly against the sand. It had gotten so dark that I couldn't see much except the glimmer of the cloudy sky off the water.

"Here we are," she said brightly, her long braids swinging as she climbed out of the car.

I managed to get out of the car on my own. Walking was another thing. Before I'd stumbled more than a couple of steps, Georgia was there to hold me up.

"Thanks," I said, misery and alcohol seeping from my pores in equal doses.

"You can crash on my couch tonight. My roommate is in Miami for the weekend."

I nodded. The pebbled walk was loose in places and I stumbled more than the usual drunk. We got to the front porch, moths fluttering around our heads, but the sound of the water made me veer off.

"Hey," Georgia called.

"I'll be back in a minute."

I stumbled from the pebbled walkway to the uneven sand, bits of scrub and grass fighting to survive in the inhospitable ground. It was only about ten steps to the water's edge. I plopped down in the sand and struggled to unlace my sneakers. I got them and my thick socks off and dug my toes into the cool, damp sand. I wrapped my arms around my waist and rocked in time to the waves lapping near my toes.

I heard Georgia jingling her keys behind me—my keys, probably. I guess I should have been more concerned about her snatching my one and only possession of any value, but I couldn't work up the energy to care. She settled gracefully beside me, bare feet tucked under her. She watched me and I watched the ocean, feeling sorry for my pathetic self.

"Are you gonna be OK?" she asked. "I mean, do you have some place to go after tonight?"

I didn't want to think about tomorrow or the day after. I didn't want to think about anything at all. I nodded. "Yeah."

She didn't push. We sat there, hip to hip on the sand. It felt good. At some point, I leaned against her, my head dropping to her shoulder. She smelled like smoke and gardenias. Her braid pressed against my cheek and I wondered if I'd have a waffle-mark on my face when I got up. I kind of liked the idea of being marked by her. I shivered.

Georgia turned her head toward me. Maybe to ask how I was doing or to tell me her ass was getting wet from the water lapping so close to us, I don't know. Her head turned, her lips nearly brushing mine, and suddenly I knew what I wanted. I leaned in the fraction of an inch that separated us and put my lips against hers. It wasn't a kiss, just a meeting of mouths. I held myself there, unsure of how she would respond and whether I could handle it if she pushed me away.

She didn't push me away. Her lips softened under mine, parting slightly as she breathed into me. We kissed, slowly, sweetly, like the strangers we were, trying to learn each other's feel and taste. I slipped my tongue between her lips and she sucked on it. The sensation sent a zing of electricity to my pussy and I moaned. She did it again and I squirmed in the wet sand, hungry for her softness.

Georgia slid her hand up my waist and stroked my tit through my T-shirt. I pressed against her hand until she rolled my nipple between her fingers. I groaned, twisting toward her. Her sweet tits were way more than a handful; I wasn't complaining. I cupped and squeezed them, releasing her only long enough to tug at the buttons on her blouse. Her bra was next, popping loose to reveal the tits I'd been mauling. Dusky-pink nipples capped her luscious, tanned breasts. I raised them to my mouth, licking and sucking each sweet nipple while Georgia dug her fingers into the damp sand and groaned.

"I want to fuck you," I said, staring into her eyes and pressing her hands to my tits. "Let me fuck you."

She nodded and began to stand up.

I pulled her down on top of me. "Here. I want to fuck you here."

I think she would have argued if my hand hadn't slipped under her skirt and zeroed in on her cunt. I could feel her wetness on her thighs, pouring out of her like heat off hot asphalt. It had been more years than I cared to count since the late-night, drunken gropes with my best friend from high school, but my hands knew what they were after. When I palmed Georgia I thought she'd go off like a rocket in my hand. She clutched at my shoulders, quivering and whimpering. My middle finger made slow circles against her clit, my fingers pressed up against the tight curls on her mound.

"You're soaked," I murmured against her ear. "Does my honey girl like that?"

She nodded into my neck, her hands slipping down to squeeze and knead my tits. Her fingers tugged at the waistband of my jeans. She fumbled with the zipper, and the material bunched up snugly against my juicy cunt. I groaned and leaned back to help her, never taking my finger from her clit. She was trembling by the time she'd stripped my jeans off, then the panties that clung to my wet flesh. I jerked my shirt over my head with one hand, completely naked in the sand now, wet from the ocean and arousal.

She whimpered and buried her head between my smallish tits, sucking and biting my flesh as if she couldn't get enough of me. We were rolling around in the sand, each of us pushing and straining against the other, both of us wanting to get fucked. I didn't know what her reasons were, but I knew mine: I didn't want to be alone. I'd just lost two men in my life, and I needed her tenderness to soothe the ache. I wanted my honey girl to make me forget.

I snaked a finger inside her wet heat and she bucked against my hand. A few seconds later, I found myself flat on my back with her on top of me, one leg scissored between mine, her thigh riding high against my fevered cunt. She sank her teeth into my neck and pinched my nipples while I arched against the delicious weight of her leg. I squeezed a second finger into her cunt and she whimpered, braids smacking me in the face as she moved against me.

"I want to eat you," I said, voicing the urge almost as soon as I felt it. "Come up here."

She obliged, straddling my face like a buckaroo at the rodeo. I swiped my tongue over the wet, pouting lips of her cunt and was rewarded by her clamping her legs around my ears.

I'd never eaten pussy before; the thought of drowning in all that juice and flesh scared me at first. But when Georgia moaned and rubbed her clit against my tongue, my world was reduced to the cunt over my mouth. I was oblivious to the water and foam splashing us as the tide came in. I wanted only what was within my reach—Georgia's sweet cunt drowning me in her juices.

I planted my hands on her thighs, holding her open so that I could do the job right. My thumb glided across the small tattoo that curved over her hipbone. It was an inky shadow against her tanned skin, impossible to make out in the darkness. But I kept my thumb on it, stroking it like a worry stone while my tongue stroked her clit.

She whimpered and moaned, arching her back and ass. My mouth devoured her cunt. Her fingers found my slick opening and teased me with matching strokes until I delivered the goods and sucked her clit between my lips. Then she plunged her fingers into me—two or three, I couldn't be sure—and fucked me hard. I moaned into her cunt, hearing, seeing, and smelling nothing but her moist flesh and soft hair.

She froze, pressed against the flat of my tongue, every muscle in her thighs and stomach tensed. She was close. I knew that I had only to wiggle my tongue and she'd go over the edge. I did and she did.

She came hard and wet, groaning loudly. She kept grinding against my mouth as if she wanted me to eat her whole. I anchored her against my mouth and did my best to oblige.

Her fingers in my cunt stilled for a moment and I clamped my thighs around her hand in case she had any ideas of stopping altogether. I needn't have worried—as soon as her orgasm subsided, she was pumping my cunt again, fingers angling up high and hard, rubbing my G-spot like there was no tomorrow. She kept her cunt raised a bit from my mouth and I knew she was too sensitive to take any more. So I nuzzled her while she fucked me.

She shoved another finger into me. My cunt began to contract; I thought I would die from the feeling of fullness and need. But then I was over the edge, her fingers pumping into me as I rocked and jerked on the sand, legs spread out stiffly, water lapping up between my thighs, splashing my quivering cunt.

I couldn't stop coming. I didn't want to stop. I buried my face against her wet thigh and sobbed, rocking on her hand, letting her fill me up, filling the emptiness inside me.

When her fingers slipped out I felt empty. She stayed there, straddling my face, the ocean lapping at our bodies.

"That was.... Thanks," she whispered, her face ringed by moonlight, her braids bobbing against her chest. "I hope you liked it."

I laughed against her muff. I could get used to this. "It was my pleasure."

The moon peeked out from behind the clouds, and I got a better look at Georgia's tattoo. At first I thought it was a butterfly, its wings outstretched over her hipbone. But no, it wasn't a butterfly, the coloring was wrong. Studying it more carefully, I saw that it was a bee.

A honey bee.

The yellow-and-black stripes of the fat, fluffy bee hugged her knobby hipbone. I ran my thumb over it again as she eased off me and stretched. I was shivering now, with the tide coming in far enough for the water to cover my legs. Georgia stood over me, stretching her lithe, tanned body. I knew I needed to get up, but I just lay there, watching her, watching the bee undulate on her hip.

"Didn't that hurt?" I asked.

"What, this?" She rubbed the tattoo with her fingertips. "It stung a little."

I suddenly began laughing and crying all at once. A wave splashed over me and I choked on sea water, still sobbing.

"Rae?" Georgia asked, kneeling beside me, her braids draping over her body like damp seaweed. "Are you all right?"

I shook my head and tried to push her away, but she held on, propping me up and thumping on my back. When I stopped choking, she sat back on her heels, her pale blue eyes dark in the twilight.

"Better?" she asked softly, smoothing a hand over my damp cheek.

"Better," I agreed, turning my face into her hand, dizzy from tequila and honey. "It just stings a little."

MARY ANNE MOHANRAJ

Wild Roses

It started with a phone call. Sarah had been expecting the call, but it was still a shock. She had learned over the last few years, as friends succumbed to old age, and to one or another disease, that there were limits to how well you could prepare for death. It was usually cancer of one type or another. Cancer had gotten Daniel, too.

"He's gone."

"I'm so sorry, Ruth."

"Can I come out? Tonight?"

"Of course."

"The next flight down arrives at eight-thirty."

"I'll meet you at the airport."

Sarah put down the phone, meeting Saul's calm eyes as he walked out of the studio, wiping paint-stained hands on his pants. She bit back brief irritation at his calm. He and Daniel had never quite gotten along, though they had tried, for the sake of the women. Saul had been quietly pleased when Daniel's career had taken him to Seattle, though not so pleased when Ruth joined him there a few months later. Saul had locked himself up in his studio and painted huge dark canvases, ugly compositions in a dark palette: black, indigo, midnight blue. But Ruth had been happier with Daniel than she had ever been with them, more happily married and with children on the way. Eventually Saul had bowed to that truth.

Old history.

Sarah said, “I’ll pick her up. You go ahead and finish.”

Saul nodded, stepping forward and leaning down to kiss her forehead gently. “You OK?”

Sarah managed a smile. “I’ll be all right. Ruth didn’t sound good, though.”

“No.” He opened his arms then, and she stepped into them, heedless of drying paint. She rested her cheek against his chest, wrapped her arms around him, desperately glad that he was healthy. Some arthritis, a tendency to catch nasty colds: nothing that couldn’t be fixed by keeping him out of the studio for a few days. After this many years, she could manage that, at least, even if she had to scold like a shrew to do it. She rested in his arms a moment, breathing in his scent, cinnamon sugar under sharp layers of paint and turpentine. He kissed the top of her head, and then let her go.

“I’ll make up the bed in the guest room,” she said.

Saul nodded, turned, and walked back into the studio, quietly closing the door behind him.

Sarah waited at the Alaska Airlines gate window, her face an inch or two from the cold glass. It was raining outside, a cold hard rain, typical for Oakland in January. The baggage handlers drove their little carts back and forth, luggage covered by dark tarps. The plane had been delayed, leaving her with nothing to do but wait and remember.

The last time Sarah had made love to Daniel, they had been alone. It was the night before he'd left for Seattle, just before Ruth had announced that she was going with him—though Sarah and Saul suspected that she would go, that she would opt for a "normal" family life in the end. Deep inside Sarah had known this would be her final time alone with Daniel, and had planned for it to be tender, sweet, and slow. That had seemed appropriate for a good-bye. But instead, Sarah had found herself biting his neck, raking his back, riding him until they were both exhausted, until she was trembling with tiredness. Daniel hadn't been gentle with her either, had dug his fingers into her ass, bit her breasts. They had left marks on each other's bodies, dark and brutal and bruised. They had kissed until their lips were puffed and sore. And it was only in the morning, with the long night giving way to a gray sunrise, that their pace had slowed, that they had settled into a hollow of the bed, his hand stroking her dark hair, her fist nested in the curls on his chest. He had asked her then to come with him to Seattle. She had let silence say no for her, and he hadn't asked again. Sarah had gone to Saul the next night with Daniel's marks on her body. He had been gentle with her that night, and for some time afterward.

The passengers were walking off the plane, some into the arms of family or eager lovers. Ruth walked down, wearing a dark dress, her eyes puffy and red. She had been crying on the plane. Ruth had never cared what people thought about little things: She cried freely in public. She had occasionally tried to provoke screaming fights in parking lots and malls. She had been willing to have sex in the woods, in open fields, used to tease and persuade them all until they joined her. It was only in the big things that she was at all conventional.

They had once traveled east together, two couples in a car, perfectly unremarkable to all outward eyes. They had stopped in Wisconsin and decided to camp instead of staying in a motel. Two separate tents, and the night sky overhead. While Daniel and Saul were washing the dinner dishes in a nearby creek, Ruth had taken Sarah by the hand and led her into the woods, searching for fallen branches to build a fire. Sarah had dutifully collected wood until Ruth came up behind her, lifting her skirt, kneeling down on dirt and twigs and grass. Sarah wore no underwear in those days, at Ruth's request. So when Ruth's mouth reached for hers, Sarah had only to shift her legs further apart, to try to balance herself, a load of wood resting in her arms, eyes closed. Ruth's tongue licked under her ass, tracing the delicate line at the tops of her thighs. Her tongue slid up over Sarah's clit, then back again, sliding deep inside her. Ruth's hands held onto Sarah's hips, her fingers gently caressing the sharp protrusions of hipbones, the skin that lay over them. Sarah was usually quiet, but in the middle of the empty woods, she let herself moan. Ruth's tongue flickered over and around, licking eagerly until Sarah's thighs were trembling. Her heart was pounding, and just as she began to come, waves of pleasure rippling through her, as the wood fell from her arms, Saul was there with her, in front of her, holding her up—his mouth moving on hers, his chest pressed against her breasts, and his hands behind her, buried in Ruth's hair. Then they were all falling to the ground, Saul and Ruth and Sarah and Daniel too, a tangle of bodies, clothes discarded, forgotten, naked skin against dirt and moss and scratching twigs. Leaves and starlight overhead, and Ruth laughing in the night, laughing with loud and shameless delight. It had always been that way with her.

Ruth paused at the bottom of the walkway, eyes scanning the crowd, passing right over Sarah. It had been more than a year since they'd seen each other last. Between Christmas and New Year's, Sarah had gone up to Seattle for a few days. Saul had originally planned to come as well, but had gotten caught up in a painting and changed his mind. Sarah had gone alone into a house full of children and grandchildren, a house full of laughter. Ruth had cooked a feast, with her daughters and sons helping. The grandkids had made macaroons, and each one of them had begged a story from Auntie Sarah. Sarah had left their house a little envious; Ruth had built exactly the kind of home that she'd dreamed of. And while it wasn't the kind of home Sarah herself had ever wanted—still, it was lovely. It wasn't until the following March that the cancer had been diagnosed. Sarah had always meant to go up and see Daniel again—but she hadn't, in the end.

She stepped forward, raising a hand to Ruth. There was the blink of recognition, the momentary brightening of eyes. Ruth looked lovely despite puffed eyes, slender and fair in her button-down dress, a raincoat over one arm. Her hair had gone entirely to silver, a sleek and shining cap—like rain in moonlight. Ruth came down through the thinning crowd, pausing a few steps away. Then Sarah held out her arms, and Ruth walked into them, her eyes filling with tears. Sarah held her close, sheltering her in the fragile privacy of her arms, until the crowd had entirely dissolved away.

Saul met them at the door. He'd changed out of his paint-stained clothes. Ruth dropped her raincoat, letting it fall in a wet puddle on the floor, and threw herself forward, into his strong arms. She had calmed down in the car, had been able to talk about the last week with Daniel. He'd gotten much weaker toward the end; in the last few days, he hadn't really spoken. Sarah's chest had ached a little, with various regrets. Ruth hadn't cried for most of the ride, but now she was sobbing, great gasping sobs, catching the air in her throat and letting it out again. Saul held her, looking helplessly at Sarah over Ruth's head. Sarah shrugged, put down Ruth's bag, and bent to pick the raincoat off the wooden floor. She hung it neatly on the rack, while Saul led Ruth into the living room. Sarah waited in the hall, listening to them walk across the room and sit down on the sofa. Slowly, Ruth's sobs quieted. When it was silent, Sarah walked into the room. Ruth was nestled in Saul's arms, her eyes closed. His eyes were fixed on the doorway, and met Sarah's as she entered. She hadn't expected that, that he would be wanting her with him. She should have known better.

"Do you want some coffee, Ruth?" Sarah asked.

Ruth shook her head, not opening her eyes. "It would just keep me awake. I haven't been sleeping much this last week. I'm so tired."

"Dinner? Saul made pot roast for lunch—there's plenty left."

"No, I'm OK. Just bed, if that's all right?"

"That's fine, dear. Come on—I'll get you settled."

Ruth hugged Saul once more, and then got up from the sofa. Sarah led her into the guest bedroom, turned down the sheets, closed the drapes while Ruth pulled off her clothes and slid into bed. She had always slept nude, Sarah remembered. Sarah stood over the bed, hesitating. Ruth looked exhausted, with a tinge of gray to her skin.

"Do you want me to sit with you a bit? Just until you fall asleep?"

"No, no—I'll be OK." Ruth reached out and took Sarah's hand in hers, squeezing gently. "Thank you."

Sarah leaned over and kissed her twice—once on the cheek, once, briefly, on her lips. "Sleep, love. Sleep well." She stood up then, turned out the light, and slipped out the door, closing it behind her.

They sat at the kitchen table, cups of coffee nestled in their hands, not talking. Just being together. Sarah remembered the day when she'd first realized that she would rather be silent with Saul than be talking with anyone else. They hadn't met Ruth yet, or Daniel; they'd only known each other a few weeks. They'd just finished making love on a hot July night and were lying side by side on the bed, not touching. It was too hot to cuddle, too hot for sex, so they had ended up lying on the bed, waves of heat rolling off their bodies. Saul was quiet, just breathing, and Sarah lay there listening to his breaths, counting them, trying to synchronize them with her own.

She couldn't quite manage it, not for long. Her heart beat faster, her breath puffed in and out of her. But being there with him, breathing was a little slower and sweeter than it would normally be. Being with him, not even touching, she was happier than she'd ever been.

Sarah finished her coffee. "I'm going to go to bed," she said. "Coming?"

"I'll be there in a minute. I'll just finish the dishes."

Sarah nodded and rose from the table, leaving her coffee cup for him to clear. She straightened a few books in the living room as she walked through it, gathered his sketches from the little tables and from the floor, piling them in a neat stack. She walked into the hall, and then paused. To her right the hall led to their bedroom. Straight ahead the hallway led to the library, the studio, and then to the guest room. She almost turned right, almost went straight to bed—but instead she walked forward down the long hall, and at the end of it, heard Ruth crying. She stood there a while, listening.

When she came back to the bedroom, Saul was already in bed, waiting for her. Sarah stood in the doorway, looking at him lying half covered by the sheet, his head turned toward her. She knew what would happen if she came to bed. She could tell just by looking at him, by the way he looked at her. He would pull her close, and kiss her forehead and eyes and cheeks. He would run his hands over her soft body; he would touch her until she came, shuddering in his arms.

"Ruth's crying." It was harder than she'd expected, to say it. It had been a long time.

His eyes widened, the way they did only when he was very surprised, or sometimes during sex, when she startled him with pleasure.

"You should go to her." That was easier to say. Once the problem was set, the conclusion was obvious. Obvious to her, at any rate.

Saul swung himself slowly out of bed, pulling on a pair of pants. He didn't bother with a shirt.

"You'll be all right?" It was a question, but also a statement. He knew her that well, knew that she wouldn't have raised the issue if she wasn't sure. He trusted her for that. Still, it was good of him to check, one last time. It was one of the reasons she loved him so. She nodded, and collected a kiss as he left.

Sarah let herself out of the house, walking barefoot. It was a little cold, but not too much. The rain had stopped some time ago, and the garden was dark and green in the moonlight. She wandered down its neat paths, by its carefully tended borders. Saul took care of the vegetables; she nurtured the flowers and herbs. At this time of year, little was blooming, but the foliage was deep and rich and green. Winter was a good time for plants in Oakland; it was the summer heat that parched them dry, left them sere and barren. She carefully did not approach the east end of the house; even through closed windows and shades, she might have heard something. She also refrained from imagination, from certain memories. If she had tried, Sarah could have reconstructed what was likely happening in that bedroom; she could have remembered Ruth's sounds, her open mouth, her small breasts and arching body. Saul's face, over hers. She could have remembered, and the memory might have been sweet, or bitter, or both. But she was too old to torment herself.

She put those thoughts aside, and walked to the far west end of the garden, where the roses grew. It was the one wild patch in the garden, a garden filled with patterns, where foxglove and golden poppy and iris and daffodil, each in their season, would stand in neat rows and curves, in designs she and Saul had outlined. But the roses had been there when they'd bought the house, the summer after Ruth had left. Crimson and yellow, white and peach, orange and burgundy—the roses grew now in profusion against the western wall, trimmed back only when they threatened the rest of the garden. Wild and lovely. She had built a bench to face them, and Saul often sat on it, sketching the roses. Sarah liked to sit underneath them, surrounded by them, drowning in their sweet scent. She went there now, sitting down in the muddy ground, under the vines and thorns.

There were no roses in January, but they would bloom again soon enough. She'd be waiting for them. In the meantime, it was enough to close her eyes, feel the mud under her toes, and remember Daniel. The way he laughed, bright and full. The way he would return to a comment from a conversation hours past. The way he had touched her sometimes, so lightly, as if she were a bird. The scent of him, dark and rich, like coffee in a garden, after rain.

SUSAN ST. AUBIN

Re: Union

"The interesting people never come. You know—the ones you'd really want to see again."

They were traveling west on their way home from her fortieth high school reunion in the small valley town where she'd grown up. Ray drove while Donna rested, the black felt circles of a sleeping mask covering her eyes to protect her from the sunset they were riding into. He squinted through his sunglasses, feeling the beginning of a headache between his eyebrows.

"So tell me who wasn't there." He wondered if a dull weekend with people Donna kept complaining that she never had liked might have been a bit more exciting.

"Manuel." She rolled her head against the backrest, smiling, though he couldn't see that smile because his eyes were on the freeway, staring at the glittering cars, trying to see the road. Maybe there could have been a *real* reunion, she thought, if Manuel had been there.

"Who's Manuel? I don't remember him from your list of old boyfriends."

"Oh, he was just this kid I knew. Once he stole a typewriter from the typing class. We had a couple of those early electric ones—IBM Executives, I think they were called. You know, the ones with the long carriage? Typing on them felt like flying a small plane. Some local business donated two of them to the school, so we took turns while everyone else typed on the old manuals. Until one of the electrics disappeared. No one suspected Manuel, of course, but he was the one who took it, piece by piece. After a while it didn't work very well but we didn't know why until one day it just wasn't there. The teacher, the principal, everyone was outraged. Who could have taken it? Then a couple of days later I was over at Manuel's house and he was reassembling it in his bedroom.

"'People never see what they don't expect to see,' he said, 'and they don't believe what they don't expect to believe, so don't bother telling anyone.'

"I never told. As he pointed out, that typewriter had been donated for the students to use, and he was the student who needed it the most."

"What was a guy doing in a typing class back then? Only girls took typing at *my* school." Ray drummed his fingers on the wheel, humming *Wake Up, Little Susie* under his breath. They'd played all those old songs at the reunion. *Oh, Donna*. He couldn't get them out of his mind.

She sighed. "Yeah, right, back when girls took typing so they could have something to fall back on in case marriage or nursing or teaching didn't work out. Manuel was blind—didn't I mention that? He had to learn to type in order to write papers and take tests. Someone read him the questions, there in the typing room, some younger girl who wasn't taking whatever class he was having the test for. He was in that room a lot, either taking a test or a class, or just hanging out with the girls.

"His parents were from Mexico, very quiet people, older. I don't even know if they spoke English. They worked on farms around the area. He was an only child, or maybe the youngest one still at home.

"'Seeing people just don't see,' he told me, to explain why his parents never noticed the electric typewriter's gradual appearance in his room, or why the typing teacher didn't see that typewriter go until it was gone."

Ray listened to her breathing, faster than a resting person should be breathing. "You liked him, Donna, didn't you?"

"Liked? Not especially. He was kind of a dork. Smart, good at math, that type. But crazy. He stole cars, too." She ran her tongue over her lips and shifted in her seat: remembering Manuel was making her cunt throb. "He never got caught because he was this poor blind kid who couldn't possibly be guilty, even when he was at the wheel. The guys with him would get arrested, but not him."

"He drove?" Ray automatically slowed down.

She nodded. "He took me with him. He said he wanted to show me how to see. We went downtown and found this unlocked car on a side street, one of those huge boats with tail fins, painted three shades of green. People used to think that if they parked on a quiet street, they wouldn't have to lock their car. He started it with a gum wrapper he fitted into the ignition like a key. Took him maybe three minutes to do that, and it started right up."

"A gum wrapper? You're joking," Ray laughed.

"No, really. Foil works, if you know what you're doing, and his fingers had vision."

There was a long silence after the mention of fingers. Finally, Ray asked, "So, did you two make out in that car you took?"

Donna shifted, wiggling her hips on the seat. "Oh, maybe a few times."

"You stole cars with him more than once! And he drove them!"

"He did. 'You can tell me what's coming,' he said, "but I bet I'll know before you see it.'

"He knew the town, of course, so we drove along perfectly. He pulled me close as he drove, and slipped a hand between my legs, playing with the hem of my shorts before edging his fingers inside. No seat belts to get in the way in those days! I called out *stop* every time I saw a stop sign, but he knew where all the signs in town were. His fingers never stopped, though, and after a while I quit saying anything."

"So how many times did you come?"

"I didn't. I was too nervous, looking around for traffic, listening for it so I could see it before I could see it, you know?

"'You're learning,' Manuel said after I told him a truck was coming before it turned the corner. 'Seeing people usually take much longer to see.' He was proud, like he was teaching me something important, but I couldn't see yet what that was.

"On the highway, it was easy—he just stayed in his lane and listened. This freeway we're on now was just a two-lane highway then. He told me to shut my eyes, and we listened together: listened to the car ahead of us so we wouldn't follow too close, listened to the car behind to make sure it wasn't tailgating us. We heard cars coming toward us, then passing with a swoosh. We heard the hum of our car, the stolen car, all its parts functioning perfectly. So were mine: Manuel still had the fingers of one hand up the leg of my shorts, and I felt a zing that made me blank out for a second, but not so much that I didn't notice the car behind pull out and pass us. I could even feel the driver's eyes glance through the side window.

"'You see?' he asked, and I did, more than he realized. Actually, I'd never felt anything like that before. That was my first orgasm, there in that stolen car."

"You're kidding," said Ray. "I've been married to you for thirty-five years, but sometimes I feel like I'm just getting to know you."

Donna ignored him, and went on with her story. "Then we turned off on this winding little road, and that was hard. It was so noisy, with all the trees we were passing sounding like tall buildings we were about to run into. He knew my eyes were wide open. 'Can't see with your eyes open,' he told me, taking every curve with both hands on the wheel while I hung onto the seat.

"'Close your eyes,' he ordered, 'or you'll miss something. Damn!'

"A truck came around the corner so fast I shut my eyes and waited to die. Manuel steered the car off the road between the redwood trees and cut the engine.

"'OK, see what happens when you aren't listening? Your eyes can't help you there. That's the sort of thing you have to hear coming. We shouldn't have been talking.'"

Ray held his own hands tight on the wheel. "Whew," he breathed, wondering if their son had ever done stuff like that, was doing something dangerous right now. Twenty-four was still young enough to be crazy.

Donna pulled the sleeping mask off her eyes and, before Ray knew what was happening, slipped the elastic over his head, adjusting the felt circles across his sunglasses. He could see nothing but flashes of light at the corners of his eyes. As soon as he put one hand up to tear the mask off, she said, "Don't move. Listen. Both hands on the wheel."

He heard her rapid breathing.

"You're too close to the car ahead. Listen."

He fell back until the sound of the car in front of them faded.

"There. That's perfect," she said. "Hold that space."

He was almost panting, his hands slipping on the wheel. "We'll be busted," he said.

"No, we won't," she answered. "No one can tell you're blind. It just looks like you have sunglasses on. Now you're going to move into the far right lane, and you're going to do it by ear. Listen."

He signaled. Each car was separate: an old Volkswagen, a truck, another truck, then silence on the lane to his right. He held his breath and moved into it. She breathed out when he did.

"Perfect," she murmured. "Now, one more lane over so you're in the far right. We're taking an exit in half a mile. It's coming up." She counted under her breath, while he listened and signaled. A Honda Prelude? A Toyota? A Volvo station wagon—he was sure of the long, powerful sound of that one, like their Volvo sedan, but deeper and larger. He'd never noticed how sounds can be large rather than loud. Next came some kind of SUV, high and bulky, its engine like a truck, but smaller, more like a lion's intense purr than its roar. When he could hear nothing but the click of their own car's signal, he pulled over.

"Yes!" she breathed.

He wanted to take one hand off the wheel, pat her thigh, slip his fingers up under her skirt, but he didn't dare. He was afraid he wasn't as good as Manuel yet.

"The exit is here, now," she said, and he slowed, veering right, off the freeway. "Stop," she said. He listened, but heard no signal lights. A car passed. "Go," she said. "Straight ahead."

He listened to the road, and to her. When she sucked in her breath, he knew a curve was coming and took it. He heard the whoosh of tall trees overhead. He was sixteen again; he was Manuel.

"Is this the road you took?" he asked.

"Yes," she said. "Halfway to the coast there's a town, and a good seafood restaurant, so keep going. You can get us there."

He felt cool, but wasn't sure if this was because the trees were dense, or because the sun had slipped behind the hills. He could feel hills on either side of them, and realized the twisting road went through a valley. He had sonar now, hearing the hills, the trees, even the occasional boulder by the side of the road.

"Big rock on the left, isn't there?"

"Yes," she answered.

They rode silently, breathing together, concentrating. He heard the approach of a large truck, still a distance off.

"Lumber truck, am I right?"

"Yes," she said, "but I can't see it yet."

"Around the next bend," he said, and suddenly it was louder than he thought it should be.

They both stopped breathing as he pulled over to the side of the road, but kept moving slowly until the truck rumbled past.

She took his hand while they breathed again. "Excellent," she said.

They drove on, uphill.

"There's a drop to the right, isn't there?"

"Yes. We're climbing out of the valley now."

He heard the height of it, and hugged the center of the road. He was glad he heard nothing coming because he sensed there was no place to pull over. He listened to his engine, hearing the gears shift even though the transmission was automatic. He'd never realized there were still gears in there, even if you didn't have to shift them yourself.

"Manuel always preferred a stick," she said, as though she could hear the gears, too, and perhaps even his thoughts. "He didn't like the new cars with automatics, because he thought it was too weird to hear gears shifting when you weren't in control of them."

"I never noticed before," he said.

She smiled. He knew she smiled, he could hear that smile, a slight pop of breath as her lips opened and curved, a glide of saliva over her teeth. If he turned, bent, and slid his tongue into that smile it wouldn't matter because there was nothing he needed to see—but he was afraid he would lose control of the car.

"You could go faster," she said. "There's not much traffic. The sun's going down, turn on your lights."

"You trying to prove you can be as crazy at sixty as you can at sixteen?"

She laughed. "We're only fifty-eight, young enough to be crazy. Maybe we'll go straight when we're sixty."

He sped up a little, honking his horn each time he sensed a curve, an old mountain driving trick he'd picked up in the army. A car passed them. She sucked in her breath but nothing happened.

"God, you're good," she said. "Almost as good as Manuel. He'd be proud of us."

"What about that car he took?" Ray asked. "The boat you were telling me about."

"We were on this very road," she said. "After we almost hit that truck, we sat there a while." She chuckled. "Well, we didn't just sit. We fooled around. He pulled my shorts off, and my panties, and fingered me, played me like an instrument until I came again. He knew parts of my body I didn't know about. My clit, my cunt—I'd never touched myself before. I was a good Catholic girl. Maybe not so good because I talked about sex all the time with my girlfriends, and I used to kiss guys and let them feel my tits, but never anything below the waist, not anything like this!

"Then I unzipped him and put my hand around his cock, and held it while I took a good look at it because I'd never seen one before. I'd just felt them as something hard bumping against my hip when I kissed a guy. Manuel wasn't circumcised—Mexicans often aren't. As he got harder, the tip of his cock sort of poked out of that fold of foreskin like a little head emerging, as though something had been mysteriously growing inside him. I thought all guys were like that, so when I saw my first cut dick later, I was shocked. Most men really have no idea what they've lost, and neither do most women.

"Then, I don't know why I did this, I put my mouth down there and licked that little cock face, sucked it until he came, all creamy and salty when I swallowed it. God, I felt so sinful! I don't know why I did that, or how I knew what to do. I don't think I'd ever even heard of such a thing before. Sex must be mostly instinct, I swear to God. Maybe he pushed my head down a little, maybe that's what gave me the cue. I was listening to his body like he'd taught me how to listen to the road. But I really did it, and he really stole that car and drove it! It was all so wonderfully perverted! He told me we didn't need to confess anything, ever. He said priests were the ones who were truly blind, and I believed him, then and now."

"Well, I always knew you weren't such a good Catholic girl. I could see that as soon as I met you." Ray's cock grew hard. "What'd you do with the car?" He could still hear the road, which was straighter now, and he could no longer feel the drop on one side. They were going downhill.

"He drove it back and parked it right where we found it," she continued. "He took the gum wrapper out of the ignition and left the doors unlocked—everything was just the way it was. He never actually *stole* cars, he only borrowed them. No one ever knew after we walked away." She sighed. "I guess he was my boyfriend after that, for the rest of the summer and several more cars. He taught me how to drive, too, but I always kept my eyes open. A typical high school romance, except maybe for the cars."

"Ah-ha! Now you admit it," he joked, still driving blind, his sonar alert to every object. He felt an open space, clear of trees.

"Turn left," she said, laughing at him when he signaled. "No one's coming."

He pulled into the open space, stopping when he felt a building near.

"Well," she said. "It looks like they're closed. About a year closed, I'd say."

"You didn't see that coming?" He shut the lights off. "The past doesn't last forever, you know."

"No, but sometimes you can meet it again. That's what class reunions usually fail to do. You go back there and you're all just older, unless you learn how to see what's important." Tenderly she took off the eye mask, then his sunglasses. He blinked into a very dark, moonless night. A large old house took shape in front of them.

"This used to be a great place," she said. "Most people around just came for the bar, but the seafood was wonderful. The specialty was barbequed oysters. They did a good business at one time."

He unfastened his seatbelt, then hers. "Want to fool around?" he asked, trying to sound like Manuel, with a kid's urgent desire casually disguised. "We can always find some place to eat later, back on the main highway, if you're still hungry when I get done with you."

When she smiled he could still hear her lips part with his newly sensitive ears before he saw her teeth in the darkness. He leaned toward her, tasting that smile. He wanted to take her innocence all over again.

"My senses are miraculously increasing with age," he said.

"I told you, it just takes practice," she answered. "Back seat?"

The best route for the no longer limber was to get out the front and enter through the back doors. She brought her purse with her because she was prepared, the way women have always had to be. Did he bring condoms? Never. She did, even now, long after fertility was gone, and not just to satisfy her fantasy of meeting a new lover, either. She liked condoms because they were neater—she wouldn't have to go dripping into some strange restaurant and need to ask for the restroom right away. He didn't mind them—in fact he liked the firmness of the encasing sheath, like a girdle holding his cock tight, making it feel firmer. But he never thought to pack them.

She sucked his cock until it was hard and wet, then slipped on the rubber. She took a tube of lubricant out of her purse, slathering some of it over him, while he felt under her skirt and pulled her panties off. How did they manage such gymnastics in the back seat of a Volvo sedan? Like any exercise, sex keeps the muscles flexible, the bones strong. She took a small plastic bottle from her purse and slipped the tip into her cunt to squirt a creamy lube inside because she no longer got as wet from excitement alone as she had when she was younger. She'd imagined a sex life free of devices and spermicides after menopause, only to find out nothing's free—she still had to carry a purse full of stuff for sex. She even had a small vibrator that fit neatly into the palm of her hand to help increase the blood flow to her clit, but that was packed away in her suitcase in the trunk, and anyway she didn't need it this time because she was still quivering from the road.

Ray lounged back on the seat with his eyes closed while Donna sat herself on his lap, guiding his cock inside.

"Did you do *this* with Manuel?" he whispered.

"Not all the way," she answered, with a light slap to his cheek. "We didn't *fuck* in high school. Did you?"

He remained silent, smiling. "Well, some of us did," he said, and she playfully slapped him again while starting to move up and down, slowly, until he groaned and put his hand on her hips to move her faster.

Then he stopped, holding her, feeling her face with fingers that seemed to have more nerve endings than they used to. He brushed them across her closed eyes, feeling the tickle of her eyelashes. They couldn't joke, there in the back seat of the car, about not having done this since high school, because they had. When the kids were young, the car in the garage had been their private bordello, quiet, removed from the rest of the house. Who would have guessed what they were up to in there on a Sunday morning or a Tuesday evening? They still liked to pull over at rest stops at night to join the active, lithe bodies in other cars, like group sex with each couple in its separate vehicle as if they were still on the freeway, moving through their own time to their own rhythm while staying in order, side by side.

Here they were alone, moving to the wind through the trees, the occasional hoot of an owl, a rustle in the bushes that was probably raccoons, still searching for the restaurant garbage that had fed them for generations. He was amazed at how sharp his hearing still was. He realized that after all these years together, each time they had sex was like a reunion, the memories of past encounters enriching the present. His ears seemed to reach into the past, hearing old songs, old voices, and cries of pleasure.

She thought of Manuel, remembering the taste of him. Sperm was what they used to call it, those good girls who worried when some of it got on their dresses while they were necking. "Yuck," they'd say, while she'd kept quiet, licking her lips.

She wondered where Manuel was now. A kid like that could go either way—he could be the CEO of some corporation, or doing time in a federal pen. She imagined two Manuels, one dressed in a three-piece suit, sitting behind a desk of highly polished wood, the other lifting weights in an exercise yard. The same smart, inventive, rebellious spirit lived in each of them, but she liked the image of a beefed-up Manuel lifting the barbell high above his head, muscles glistening with sweat. She put her hand between her legs and pushed her clit against him. This was the real reunion, right now, the past and present mingled, with both Ray and Manuel. She was going to come, coming close. When she had finished, Ray lifted her off, saying, "How about a protein snack to tide you over?"

She knelt on the seat beside him, her eyes closed while her lips, like magnets, found his cock instantly. Slowly, gently, she pulled the sheath off with her mouth. The suction almost made him come, but he managed to slip into her mouth first and pump a few times before flooding into her.

She swallowed and said something, though it was hard to tell what with her mouth full of him. "Manny," was maybe what she said. She was calling him Manny! Ray felt as though the three of them were united. He was back in her past, erect again, hard as a sixteen-year-old, sliding his cock in and out while her lips grabbed at him and they both moaned in amazement. Then he got on top and entered her, his fingers finding her clit by feel. He rubbed his thumb across, seeing every ridge and fold through his fingertips, as he had for years. Who needs eyes? As she came, her feet kicked the door.

When he finished, he collapsed on top of her. "A perfect union," he murmured in her ear.

"Reunion," she reminded him as they disentangled themselves and sat up, carefully stretching the knots out of their limbs.

"Let's try driving back," she said. "Now that you've learned the road, it'll be easy."

"You're the boss," he replied, as they opened their back doors.

In the front seat again, she slipped her eye mask over his head while he opened the glove compartment to put his sunglasses away. He wouldn't need them at night.

DEBRA HYDE

Riding the Face Train

The rhythm of the PATH train riding its tracks felt the same now as it had during Doreen's childhood. Back then, so long ago, she believed they had named the train PATH because it always took her from the drab New Jersey suburbs to the magic of New York City. With a child's wonder she would watch houses give way to apartment buildings, which in turn would bow and back away before the imposing skyscrapers that defined the city skyline. Whenever the big buildings appeared, she knew magic was close at hand. Once, PATH had led to such wonders as the Macy's Thanksgiving Day Parade, FAO Schwarz, and the skating rink at Rockefeller Center.

Later, when she'd outgrown childhood, PATH had brought her to N.Y.U. and the nightlife of the city. There, Doreen had outgrown her innocence. She found her way to Plato's Retreat where the air pulsed with sexual abandon as bodies tangled in sweaty undulation. She found her way to the nasty old Hellfire where she could spur a horde of dick-clutching men into a circle-jerk frenzy simply by whipping someone—anyone—willing to suffer a taste of her flogger.

Even then, the PATH train had led to magic.

But now, Doreen was older and wiser, and she wondered if any magic could still exist for her. The decades of sexual abandon had given way to AIDS and careful regard, years during which she turned her back on the city for the tenured life of her much older husband. Clive had claimed her, citing as the perfect measure of a wife her genius between the pages of ancient European literature and her prowess between the sheets of their bed. So she settled into adjunct teaching and occasional translations, while Clive dealt with the frustrations of an academic career. She hadn't missed the city because, quite frankly, academia had its own sexual underground; she never lacked for the feel of a cane blazing across her ass, or hands relishing her body.

But things had changed drastically in the last few years. Doreen needed to see if the city would restore at least some of what she had lost.

She wondered if personal restoration was possible as she looked up at the approaching skyline. It no longer smoldered, but stood stoic and somber, diminished by the lack of its tallest majesties. Wounded, the city no longer shouted its greatness. It seemed to have passed from a brilliant middle age into a sudden, unexpected deterioration.

Just like Clive.

Doreen sighed as the train found the tunnel and dipped into blackness.

You know you're getting old when you can't stand the lighting or the music, Doreen told herself as she entered the basement party space and found herself assaulted by riot grrl music and unflattering lighting that would deepen every wrinkle on her face. But the instant she saw the sway of bodies—some clothed and dancing seductively, some naked and involved at various play stations—she vowed to forget about it.

Bodies were, after all, why she had come to this space in midtown Manhattan. Doreen wanted to see bodies, to touch bodies, to make her own body come alive after so much neglect. She felt like one of those forgotten European gardens, the kind that once sprouted flowers from bulbs, trained ivy to spread but not climb, and organized itself in an esthetic beauty. Old and forgotten, a garden chokes itself and loses its identity.

Secret garden, perfumed garden. How ironic, Doreen thought, *that "garden" can also mean "cunt." How ironic that the same thing happens to both when neglected.*

Doreen watched two young women slip away from the dance floor to a couch. There, in dim light, they kissed and groped each other in mutual heat until one slipped her hand between the other's legs. Instantly, top and bottom were established; Doreen decided that the first one to the cunt wins. The bottom girl, capitulating to the hand that worked her, leaned back and spread her legs wide. She pulled her shirt up to reveal firm, youthful breasts and ran her hands over them, motions that enticed the top girl to go to town on her.

Doreen could've watched them get each other off—hell, the twitch that throbbed between her legs practically begged her to—but she felt a hot and determined awareness growing inside her. At first, she didn't recognize it, but when she turned away from the couple and scanned the room, she realized that her prowling instinct had been reawakened.

And prowling meant working the party. Most of the crowd was young, under thirty-five. Most had pert bodies, not yet sagging with age, nor yet wise and world-weary. Were there even any older butches around, she wondered? Doreen felt old, out of place, and acutely aware that too much time had passed since her last outing.

She hadn't meant to let so much time lapse, but Clive's descent had been sudden and unexpected. One day he was tinkering in retirement with some archivist work, then the next he forgot how to enter data into his project database. From the moment the plaque began to deaden his brain, Doreen dedicated herself to keeping Clive's life as recognizable to him as possible. She kept him on a routine, helped him repeat tasks too new to earn a place in long-term memory, called up old songs, poems, and dialogues lodged far too deeply in his mind to ever forget.

In the process, Doreen's own needs had been forgotten. Eventually, their lovemaking stopped because he had become too childlike to understand adult intimacies. Eventually, his care became so demanding that she stopped fantasizing about sex with others. In the weeks before she admitted that Clive needed the constant care of a nursing home, she had even stopped masturbating.

But now Clive had round-the-clock care and Doreen was free to renew herself. Long ago, she had promised herself lots of women in her old age and, that time now at hand, she had chosen this party to rediscover herself—only to find herself feeling like a chicken hawk.

All around her swirled girls so queer that she knew she looked like their mothers' generation of bisexual. Yet their heat, their energy were as joyously blissful as they were erotic, and Doreen couldn't help but smile. Off in a corner, a slender femme of a girl, hands tied over her head to the wall, took a bull dyke's flogger on her tits and between her legs. Doreen knew from the girl's sounds that she could soon come. Elsewhere, harder action ensued: A woman got tag-teamed by a fist up her pussy and a silicone dick down her throat. Watching women play hard renewed Doreen's faith in humankind—but she needed a more personal faith restored to her as well.

She wandered and spied more bodies tangled together in the nooks and crannies of the club. Moans reached her ears and her eyes darted to see the motions of mouths on nipples, of heads lowering themselves to clits. Seductions surrounded her. More than once, the cry of a sudden orgasm rose above the din.

She moved like a ghost among this young crowd, a crowd so preoccupied with youth and beauty that, as the women undulated and writhed in their own energy, they didn't notice her. Rendered invisible, she began to doubt that she could score here, even anonymously.

And then she spotted an opportunity to do just that: A woman was lying face up on a wide table, naked except for a blindfold and panties. Her round breasts rose from her rib cage, firm and full, nipples rich-brown and hard. Short black hair spiked out from the blindfold, and a tattoo snaked out from her panties and along her butt cheek, disappearing under her back. Its red-tipped scales hinted at a Chinese dragon. Doreen wondered if it went all the way up her back.

Atop the woman, things were beginning to happen. A second woman dropped her leather shorts, climbed on top of the waiting woman, and hovered cunt first over the woman's face. Then she lowered herself.

A muffled moan of delight rose from the bottom woman, and her hands flew up to clasp the top woman's buttocks. Immediately, the bottom woman went to work—and no one would mistake the mutual grinding of mouth to cunt as anything other than a great tongue at work.

Almost immediately four women formed a line at the table. A fifth, a stout butch, joined them. They all watched the top work the bottom's mouth with rapt attention. A sixth woman joined them.

Doreen.

They stared at her as she stepped into line, a range of reaction written across their faces: amazement, curiosity, even a touch of embarrassment. She smiled briefly at them, then turned her attention to the game at hand.

Doreen knew a face train when she saw one. And she knew the mechanics of the game: Wait your turn, climb on board, ride until you come, get off, and give the next person in line her turn. Don't get chummy with the face. Acknowledge her as "good tongue" and little else. After all, she's in it for the objectification.

Doreen herself had been a train hole in days gone by, among both men and women: people who fucked her every hole, sometimes two at once, with cocks and fingers and dildos. One woman had even fucked her ass with a strap-on while a man face-fucked her. Together, they used her and compared her holes, assessing how good it felt and what a piece of meat she was. Around the trio, men had jerked off and several shots of come had hit Doreen, making her moan. When she finally rose hours later, she was spent, sore, and completely high on objectification. Just like the woman now before her would eventually be.

The first woman rode the face in hard, determined humping and, as she grunted through an orgasm, the bottom lifted her head slightly, as if to swallow the orgasm pulsing over her.

The top climbed down and grabbed her shorts. As she dressed and stepped away, someone—a gatekeeper, Doreen decided—wiped the bottom's face. She nodded to the next woman, who climbed aboard.

Something about the way the next woman swung herself onto the face reminded Doreen of fucking Clive. Which led to her memory of the last time they had fucked. She had straddled him, taken his hard cock into her, and rode him. She told him how hard he felt inside her, how she liked to clamp her insides around him, how she liked to come squeezing his dick. They had worked themselves into a slick sweat, and Doreen came twice. She urged Clive to come, to shoot his spunk inside her. "Come on! Give it to me!" she ordered, driving each word home by slamming up and down on him. But Clive didn't come and, just as Doreen saw the befuddled look wash across his face, just as she realized he had forgotten the point of sex, she came a third time.

Guilt had overwhelmed her, and she'd quickly climbed off him and took him in her arms. They didn't speak; he didn't ask any questions and she didn't apologize. They had lain there, he in a mental fog, she aching with remorse.

That day, Doreen's sex life died. As if to remind her that time was not on anyone's side, two days later her first hot flash seized her.

But now, several years later, she stood watching a lithe bitch of a top demand more and more tongue. The woman could really dominate; Doreen wished herself twenty-five years younger. Who, after all, would want to screw someone old enough to be her mother?

Thank God for anonymous sex, Doreen thought. As she watched the parade line dwindle ahead of her, she stopped thinking about her lot in life and focused on what was yet to come. She watched with increasing attention as each woman climbed on board, as the face took another cunt and worked it to satisfaction. Her cunt tightened in anticipation. Her nipples hardened. Her body was awakening.

It was her turn.

Doreen climbed on, lifting her skirt just enough to see the face below her. The woman was older for this crowd, probably well into her thirties. Her skin had already slouched slightly, a few wrinkles etched across her face. Doreen smiled, endeared by this discovery.

She knew better than to betray her feelings to the face. She lowered her skirt so that it buried the face underneath it, and then lowered herself onto her target.

The first touch of the tongue to her cunt was electric. Doreen shivered, thrilled by the living touch of another human presence.

Then, the tongue moved. Gloriously, it moved. It ran up and down her labia, tripping across several labia rings along the way. It ranged over her slit as if mapping the terrain between Doreen's legs. It licked and lapped, caressing her lips as it made its way to her clit. The angle, however, was far from superb and the face could barely keep its tongue there.

"Forget that," Doreen ordered. "Stick your tongue inside me, Face. I'll take care of my own clit."

The woman moaned. None of the other women had called the face by name, and few had ordered her around. But Doreen would.

"You better make your tongue good and stiff for me. I want to fuck it until I come."

Doreen felt the tongue try to push in, but she was dry. The tongue dutifully worked itself around the perimeter, bringing with it saliva and salvation. She loved the feel of the tongue so much that she didn't care whether her body was putting out any juice of its own. In fact, as the tongue pushed inside her, held itself rigid, and waited for her to fuck it, she completely forgot that she was past her prime. She lost herself in the primal experience of sex. She put her own finger over the skirt, touching her clit, and said, "Time to fuck, Face."

Doreen rocked up and down and worked her clit in a matching rhythm. She closed her eyes and felt everything: the tip of the tongue, its length, the cadence of its movement inside her, her clit's hard nub singing with pleasure, the walls of her cunt responding. She felt the bottom woman's periodic moans vibrate around her labia and echo up inside her.

As her breath quickened, other parts of her body came alive and begged for attention. Her tits ached, nipples so hard they seemed to scream for someone to pinch them. Her asshole pulsed and pouted, crying that if cunt got a tongue, it needed a finger. Even her mouth, which huffed and puffed as she fucked, longed for something to suck—a tit, a cock, a cunt, a clit—it didn't matter which.

Her entire body wanted contact. Eyes still closed, finger still working, Doreen wallowed in the sensations. The tongue, sensing her body's cries, started wiggling around inside her, caressing every billowed surface it could reach. Doreen shuddered. Her clit throbbed. It was only a matter of time.

She imagined a fist in the bottom woman's cunt, working the opposite end of this anonymous encounter. She imagined the squirming, heated response as the woman got pumped from below while Doreen worked it from above. She imagined the woman coming, a scream rising up from her throat and into her cunt.

The fantasy pushed Doreen into orgasm. The pinnacle seized her, then contractions pushed outward and grabbed the tongue, squeezing it in wave after wave of explosive release. As the sensations cascaded away, she felt a warm, honeyed thickness leave her and, when the woman below moaned in delighted surprise, Doreen realized she had ejaculated. She was amazed her body could still do this. And thankful.

Spent, Doreen ceased rocking on the tongue. When she caught her breath and her senses, she got down, taking her skirt with her, without so much as a thank-you to the woman.

To the surprise of the women around her, she got back in line. The butch who had earlier preceded her even joined her. "Going for seconds," she said matter-of-factly.

"Yeah, it's not often you come across a good bit of face like that," Doreen answered.

"I live with that face," the butch said. For a split second, Doreen worried that she'd issued fighting words, but then the butch added, "I know what she *really* likes." Her eyes were wicked and inviting—and creased with wrinkles of experience.

Before she knew it, the butch invited Doreen to caboose the face train exactly how she had imagined it—she on top while the woman got fisted, facing the butch so that she could watch. "Let's show these party princesses how it's really done," the butch said, sticking a well-lubed finger into her partner's hole.

When it was over, Doreen made her way home. The PATH train had brought her to magic yet again and, more important, her body still sang with magic. It was a completely satisfying ending to what had begun as an uncertain journey.

As Doreen watched the weary city fade from sight, she thought about what tomorrow would bring. She'd spend the morning sleeping off the night. She'd spend the afternoon archiving her husband's library, readying it for donation to the university. Clive was, after all, nearing the end of the eight-year average that Alzheimer's gave most people.

In the evening, she'd visit him and take him out to dinner. She would help him revisit as many old memories as possible. She would marvel at his ability to read a menu aloud, yet minutes later fail to remember that he had even held one in his hands.

Later, if the staff would allow them some privacy, she would put Clive to bed. She'd lie down beside him and draw the covers up around them. She would kiss him on the cheek and cuddle him in her arms.

And if Clive reached down between his legs to hold his penis while he fell asleep, she would reach down there and hold it with him. *I can,* she thought, *give him that much tenderness. That much human touch I can provide him.*

Because no one, she decided, as the train clacked along in the wee hours of the night, should go without.

JEAN ROBERTA

A Dowager's Hump

I came home from work on a day cold enough to freeze a witch's tit, to use a vulgar old cliché. As I walked into my welcoming house, warmth hit me like a burst of hormones. The phone was ringing.

"Margaret?" begged the voice on the other end. "I kicked him out. I hope you can forgive me."

This melodrama from my ex-sister-in-law matched the extremes of temperature in a Canadian winter. "Pfft," I told her. "It was overdue. You'd better come over. Otherwise you won't eat—or you'll binge."

Sarah was pitifully grateful, and she arrived at my door before I had had enough time to confer with myself. Emerging from her parka, she looked sodden. She shook her brown hair like a cocker spaniel.

"Have a drink to warm up," I told her, "then we'll go out for dinner."

Childlike, she sat on my sofa, sipping a scotch-and-seven as if it could restore lost hope. I had catered to her taste: old scotch ruined by the adolescent fizz of Seven-Up. A good hostess, like a cruel ancient god, gives her supplicants what they think they want.

I noticed that Sarah's breasts were fuller than they had been; she must have gained weight. I knew that she must consider this a disaster. We both sighed.

"I mean," she was complaining, "I can see why he fools around. Men have this biological need to find younger women as long as they can. It's just in them, no matter what they promise. But what's left for us?"

I glanced ironically at the framed print hanging next to my bookcase, a sepia-toned photo of Emmeline Pankhurst giving a speech on women's rights, watched admiringly by her grown daughters. Sarah missed the reference.

"I'm thirty-five," she complained. "I have to face it."

"So you do," I agreed. Then she remembered that the digits in my age were hers in reverse and was embarrassed. "Not that we're too old for some things," she assured me, politely ignoring the near-generation gap between us, "but we can't pick up guys the way we used to."

I was wearing my favorite royal-blue knit dress with the pantyhose that are supposed to stimulate my legs. I considered whether most male patrons of meat-market bars would like the way the dress skimmed my breasts and hips. I asked myself whether Sarah would sputter with envy if I explained that I stay slim by eating only when hungry and by traveling on foot whenever possible. But I realized that better food for thought was on the table.

"Do you want another man so soon, girl?" I asked her. Better to wallow in scotch-and-seven, I thought.

Now she looked deeply distressed. "I don't want to end up like..." she blurted. "You haven't been with a man since David died, have you?" Cancer, my only successful rival, had taken my husband ten years before.

"Not often," I agreed. "The ones I meet usually lack depth, so I don't keep them long. They're appetizers. But I wouldn't underestimate the value of a good fuck."

Sarah stared, obviously wondering whether the combination of alcohol and gassy bubbles had affected her hearing.

I smiled. "I don't need their money anymore," I explained. "Sometimes they need mine. I believe in noblesse oblige, of course, and I don't mind helping them, but when they assume I'm a fool, the romance is over."

I could see that my thinly veiled advice was whizzing past Sarah's ears like pub darts missing their target. I reached for her empty glass, took it to the kitchen, and refilled it.

On my way back to the living room, I caught a glimpse of myself in the hall mirror. I liked the salt-and-pepper effect of the silver sprinkled through my trademark haircut, a kind of blue-black helmet. Sparks of light in the darkness, I thought.

"I'll make us a fire," I told Sarah, placing little logs in the grate of the fireplace. I focused on my task, sensing that she would feel more comfortable if she could avoid looking me in the eyes.

"I just...I mean...," she stuttered, on the verge of weeping into her drink. "I want someone I can relate to, you know? I'm not looking for some stud." The fire crackled and popped like background music. "Margaret, doesn't it bother you that all we older single women are living longer than ever before, but our chances of remarrying are running out?"

I laughed out loud. "Honey," I answered, "I am bothered by many things, most of them caused by men in power. But not that."

"Mike is the only guy who was ever really attracted to me," she mumbled. "Um, sexually."

"I doubt it," I informed her, knowing that most of what I had to tell her would fall on deaf ears. "You probably wouldn't recognize attraction unless a crew of shipwrecked sailors took turns ravishing you. Would that convince you?"

Sarah stared at me, cross-eyed with confusion.

I took the drink out of her hand and held her by the shoulders. "Sarah," I asked patiently, "you don't want to eat yet, do you?"

"No," she apologized. "I'm not hungry."

"Not for food," I grinned. "To start with, my brother Michael is a child, case closed. You need to understand that. I know whereof I speak. Children can be delightful company, but no sensible adult would rely on one. What are you really hungry for, little sister?" I pulled her up and held her against me, breast to breast. I could feel her body vibrating. "Tell me," I prompted.

"You smell good," she ventured. This was her version of talking dirty.

"Do you want to bury your nose in my armpits?" I teased. "Or my neck? Learn the bouquet of the ripe fruit between my thighs? You can ask, baby."

"Margaret," she sighed. "You always...I never...."

"I know," I chuckled. I pressed my lips to hers, parted her teeth with my tongue, and stroked the lonely cave of her mouth.

She pulled away, breathing hard. "I'm not like that," she protested.

"I'm not asking for a commitment, Sarah," I reminded her. "You're a free woman." I tried to control my sarcasm. "Eating peaches doesn't prevent you from eating sausages, if that's your choice." I looked into her troubled gray-green eyes. "If you don't want me, I'll back off."

Sarah seemed to be waiting for the second course. I petted her silky, disheveled hair.

"I want to bond with someone real, I guess." She sighed. Her eyes were tearfully bright. I was tempted to slap her just to watch the tears overflow and run charmingly down her face. "I must have chosen the wrong family," she mused.

I recoiled. She had beaten me to the slap. I waited for her to leave my house. She waited for my response. We watched each other for several minutes until the silence tickled me into a snort of laughter.

"What's real to you, baby?" I asked. "If you want promises, you're asking for sleazy predictions. If you expect unselfish devotion, are you capable of giving it? The one thing we all know about the future is it hasn't come yet. We don't know what it holds. We only know what we want at this moment." Sarah was obviously trying to think up a retort. "If you want to leave my house," I pointed out, "you could have done it already."

Sarah brushed the hair out of her face, appearing more flirtatious than she probably intended. "You're always there when I need you," she explained by way of apology. "I wouldn't want to ruin our friendship with sex." Her breasts rose and fell under her forest-green sweater.

"Ah," I responded. "You want emotional comfort *and* sexual relief, even though neither satisfies you enough by itself. And you're afraid to get them both from the same source. You don't want to think of yourself as spoiled goods in the men's marketplace, so you'd rather be alone with a cheesecake than accept me as a last resort. Am I right?"

Sarah wouldn't look me in the eyes, but she moved her face closer, as if hoping for a kiss. I quickly stepped sideways to take aim, then slapped her butt. I hoped her corduroy pants wouldn't muffle the effect. "Am I right?" I repeated.

Her surprise and ambivalence were interesting to watch. "Margaret," she begged, "please don't let me down."

I wrapped my arms around her. I nibbled one of her earlobes, which made her squirm. I held her steady as I kissed my way down her warm neck and slid my hands under her sweater to find the sweaty skin of a panting midriff. My hands progressed to a hard pair of breasts squeezed into a cotton bra that created a deep gorge between them. Sarah moaned.

"Very nice, honey," I assured her. "You don't have to apologize to anyone except your poor despised body. She deserves better."

I found a confined nipple and tweaked it to a point. With my other hand, I tugged at her sweater. "Take them off."

Like an obedient child, Sarah pulled her sweater over her head and tossed it aside. She unhooked her bra and threw it after the sweater. She was blushing like a wannabe stripper auditioning for a jaded nightclub manager.

"Poor, naughty girl," I clucked. I held her breasts in both my hands as if they were melons, and ran my thumbs over and around her hard nipples. "Do you need a real spanking, over my knee? Would that improve your attitude?"

"Yes," she whispered. "But I want you to fuck me first. Please."

"You're learning to express yourself," I laughed.

I pulled one of her berry-like nipples into my mouth and sucked rhythmically, flicking it with my pointed tongue.

"Ah!" she panted, as if she were unfamiliar with such attention. I switched to the other breast, holding onto the first.

I unbuckled her belt. She quickly unzipped her pants and pulled them down, exposing a triangle of curly brown hair. In the firelight, a central line of hair shone wetly. Her pale flesh looked as smooth and solid as marble.

Sarah sat down on the sofa, then stretched out full-length. She spread her legs and fingered her hairy slit casually, but with purpose. Pink folds appeared as she grinned boldly up at me.

"You'll get your wish," I promised. "I have just the thing." I pulled a large black candle down from the mantel, caressing its curves. It was the black queen from an oversized collection of candles shaped like chess pieces.

Sarah moved her hips against the mulberry brocade upholstery. "Greedy," I chided her.

"I always wanted you, Margaret," she gushed.

"Hot air," I answered. "A mouth full of smoke. But never mind." I guided the head of the candle into her wetness and gently twisted it from side to side. It entered her in spurts as she opened to accept it. I pushed and withdrew until I felt resistance at the bottom of her filled cunt. I worked up an accelerating rhythm like the heartbeat of a runner.

Sarah moaned loudly, pushing against me with determination. Her eyes were closed, but she held my shoulders, seemingly afraid that I would suddenly stop or vanish into thin air. "Can you come, honey?" I probed.

"I don't know," she wailed, possessed by need and helpless to guarantee its fulfillment. I fastened my mouth on the swollen button just above her stretched opening, and sucked until I felt spasms.

Sarah's inner muscles were still clutching the candle when the phone rang like a gatecrasher at a private party. I slid a hand under one of her ass cheeks and squeezed.

"Stay," I warned her. "They'll leave a message."

My brother's voice invaded my home. "You there, Sarah?" he demanded. "Margaret, you have nothing to do with this. Sarah, we can work this out, but you had no right to change the locks on my own house. You'll be in deep shit if you don't pick up the phone." Sarah jerked as if she had been branded. Once again, Michael had sabotaged her pleasure.

I picked up the receiver before she could reach it. "Michael," I told him, "your manners could hardly be worse. I was seducing your wife and I expect her to return the favor. I'm sure you can find a place to stay for the night. We can discuss your marriage and your place of residence tomorrow after work."

Sarah scrambled off the sofa to discover Michael's location displayed on my phone. She read the name "P. Green," followed by a number, and she yelped in outrage. She pulled the receiver from my hand. "You're there!" she shrieked. "You're calling from her place!" I heard indistinct words as Michael defended himself.

I took back the receiver. "Michael," I interrupted him. "Since you've shattered my privacy with this unnecessary drama, we will all meet at Confucius Chop Suey in half an hour to negotiate. Bring Philomena or Primavera with you."

"Prima," he retorted. "That's what she's called."

"I expect to see you."

"Yep," he snarled. I hung up, smiling grimly. I knew that Michael wouldn't defy me outright.

My naked Venus on the sofa looked at me in distress. "A summit meeting and an indigestible meal," I informed her. "I'd be honored if you would accept my invitation."

"I don't want to talk to him," she sulked. The fire had died to a sullen glow. I noticed the sheen cast on my nylon-clad legs by the dim light, and ran a hand up my right calf for the comfort of it.

"You have to," I told her gently, pinching one of her nipples. "For your sins. We all need to clear the air." I helped her to dress, touching her possessively to remind her that she too now had a lover.

We arrived first. The main dining room was almost deserted, and we were seated in a booth under a large photo of the last Dowager Empress of China. She seemed to be surveying her domain impassively from under an elaborate headdress. I've always liked the word *dowager* to describe a widow of note, though I've wondered what activity could be defined as *dowaging*.

We were drinking wine when Michael arrived with his girl, who looked no older than my twenty-five-year-old daughter Katie. Sarah stared pointedly at the wasp-like black-and-yellow stripes on the sweater that hugged Prima's high breasts, and the black leather skirt that barely covered her crotch.

"Sarah...Margaret," my brother acknowledged tersely. He was flushed and smelled excessively of cologne, as if he expected it to give him a sexy air of confidence. The hair at his receding hairline had been gelled in wild strands over his forehead. "I have to get into my house," he whined.

"Not tonight," I told him.

"*Your* house?" screeched Sarah.

"Sarah," I warned her, "the property issues will be settled in court."

"That's not necessary," said Michael.

"You never told me you were an old married man until your wife caught you," Prima said accusingly. "I don't want to be the excuse for your divorce."

"Very sensible, Prima," I told her. "Do you want to keep on seeing him if everyone here agrees to a general amnesty and promises not to call you names?"

She considered my question for a minute. "No," she spat. "I'm sick of this. It's not my problem." Michael clutched her arm, but she shook him off.

"I hope you won't leave us just yet," I said. "You're refreshingly honest." She smiled.

Ken, alias Chan, grandson of the restaurant owner, came to take our order. He had been Katie's classmate in high school, and he still asked about her with dazzled fondness. I suspected that he had enjoyed nursing a broken heart after she moved away to attend university.

We agreed to order a dinner for four to avoid disagreements about specific dishes. I jumped into a tense lull in the conversation. "Sarah, do you want to negotiate a reconciliation with Michael?"

"No," she sneered. "He'll never change. I don't need a man."

"You said you wanted children," he reminded her.

"I only need sperm for that," she gloated. "They keep it frozen." Prima guffawed.

"Great," snarled my brother, "I knew you were...."

"Michael and Sarah," I interjected. "You'll need to consult lawyers about the division of your property. Until then, Sarah, I advise you to collect everything of his that's portable, and give it to him."

"He's not staying with me," Prima announced. "I can't keep him *or* his stuff in my apartment."

"Prima," he snapped, half threatening, half begging.

"It appears you have no place to lay your head, Michael," I remarked. "It's not unusual in cases like this." He looked at me, and I saw the bad boy of years past, the creative brat who was always trying to spark a reaction in others. "You could stay with me for a few days until you find a temporary nest of your own," I offered, "but you'd have to follow my rules." My brother's eyes gleamed beneath lowered lids. He didn't object.

I reached for Sarah's hand to reassure her. "He won't cause any trouble," I predicted. She looked uncomfortable, but she squeezed back.

The general perversity of desire never ceases to amaze me. Michael exuded the secret relief of a man facing the guillotine, which in this case would be a celibate retreat in my home, where I would be openly exchanging pleasure with one of the women he had betrayed. If not both.

But Michael had the sense to know that incest has never appealed to me as one of the forbidden routes to ecstasy. In our case, familiarity has bred a certain contempt, at least in me. I wondered whether fantasies of the impossible had taken hold in his imagination. If so, I thought, he still has the mental limitations of youth. I find the world as it is to be full of interesting possibilities.

Ken brought our fortune cookies, as if to clarify the outcome of this gathering. He lingered to chat quietly with Prima. Self-assured white girls with dramatic tastes were clearly his idols of choice. Prima wrote her phone number on a matchbook, and everyone at the table noticed Ken's delight.

Michael reached for the bill as if it were a shredded codpiece, some last remnant of traditional manhood. I resolved to leave a generous tip.

A few practical arrangements still needed to be worked out. "Michael," I asked, "do you need to pick up any personal items for the next few days from Prima's place or Sarah's?"

"I'll put them in the street," offered the mistress.

"Get them from her," sneered the wife.

"Women," I said sharply, "the more he can take now, the less you'll have to haggle over later. Think about it."

Finally it was agreed that we would all (minus Ken, who seemed to regret being on duty) travel as a jolly caravan in two cars to Prima's, where she would remain after giving up Michael's shaving gear, then on to Sarah's, where he would pick up several changes of clothes, and finally to my place, where he would be installed in the special guest bedroom which—unbeknownst to him—could be locked from the outside. Despite a lingering bitterness in the air, this scavenger hunt prompted snickers all around.

When Sarah, Michael, and I entered my house, I told him to take his belongings to the end bedroom on the second floor. He looked wistfully at Sarah, who glared at him.

"No," I told him. "It wouldn't be a good thing now, even if you both wanted it. You need more perspective on yourselves and each other, and only time can give you that."

"Jerk off into a jar, Mike," gloated Sarah.

Before he could respond to her advice, I did. "That's one option," I pointed out. "There are books and magazines in the room that could stimulate your mind. You'll also find other things you'll need: a pitcher and basin, a chamber pot, a small fridge with food, a hot plate, a mirror for self-contemplation."

"I'm not going to stay that long," he said. "I wouldn't be here at all if I wanted to get tough about the bullshit with the locks."

"Gracious of you to accept my invitation under such conditions," I said. "Close the door after you."

The door closed, and I secured it. Sarah looked at me. I looked at her. I asked myself whether near-incest with an in-law appealed to me when accompanied by another form of kinship or another broken taboo. *Nah,* I answered myself, *I just like the person I want Sarah to be.* And as one of my dearest friends likes to say, sex is sex.

"Beautiful woman," I said, "now we have all the time and space we need. We can plan an adventure that will satisfy us both. If you want a man to join us, that can be arranged." I traced her lips until she nibbled my fingers. "I know one who can fuck all day and all night," I said. "I haven't reached the end of his endurance. Are you curious? It almost compensates for his limited intelligence. You can't know what wretched excess is like until you try it."

Sarah looked like a child who suspects an adult of lying to her. "Not tonight," she said, laughing. "You're enough for now." She wrapped her arms around me, pushed me against the wall, and pressed her breasts against mine. Her eagerness made her adorable to me.

I eased just far enough out of her grasp to pull my dress over my head. I shimmied my way out of everything below my waist while she reached around to unhook my bra. I stepped out of my shoes and stood shamelessly in my bare skin.

Sarah tentatively cupped my breasts as if searching for invisible wires. "You look so young."

"For such an old hag?" I teased, showing my teeth. "I have perverse ways of renewing myself, like bathing in the blood of virgins whenever possible."

"Turn around." Sarah guided me by a shoulder.

"My ass," I announced, showing it to her. "Not as good as my front side, I'm afraid. It's harder to maintain."

Sarah squeezed each of my lower cheeks. "Margaret," she confessed, "I just want to bite you."

"That's the idea, honey. We're all cannibals and life is a feast."

She kissed that favorite spot of vampires just under my ear, inhaling the scent of my neck. She pulled me close with a hand on each of my butt cheeks. Her hunger for me was intoxicating. "Now you see, Sarah," I cooed into her soft hair. "Do you want the floor or my bed?"

She pulled me down to the carpeted floor in the hallway, pushed me onto my back, and lay on me, sucking my breath with hot lips. I laughed quietly deep in my lungs—I suspected that her demanding kiss was a way of shutting me up. I wasn't offended.

Sarah kissed her way past my collarbone, pausing at each nipple. She worked her way to my belly, which appeared flat in my current position. Her tongue measured the depth of my navel before traveling on to the grassy well between my thighs. "Oh, Margaret," she moaned. "You never told me."

"About this? About Michael? About men or women, or being old or being young? Baby, you never asked."

She used two fingers to spread my outer lips. I opened my legs wide to make it easier for her. She found my aroused clit and rubbed it experimentally. She seized it carefully in her teeth, provoking spasms in my little button that were like brief electrical shocks.

She pushed two fingers into me and began to pump

as she explored my inner folds with her fingertips. She might have been amazed that my pussy was so much like hers, or so different. I couldn't be sure. Perhaps, I thought, her epiphanies are none of my business.

I focused on letting pleasure flow into my wet core and the surrounding flesh; I chose not to focus too precisely, though. Before long, I was coming, making little noises that bordered on squeals. Sarah was flushed and proud.

As we lay breathing in rhythm, we heard a persistent squeak from Michael's room, as if someone were trying to take a door off its hinges without the proper tools. "Uh," muttered Sarah, forcing herself to remain still.

"Never mind, honey," I assured her. "Confinement can work wonders." She laughed until I caught it from her, and we lay shaking in each other's arms.

I did not feel at all like a good woman who deserves the gratitude of her loved ones. On the other hand, I felt very far away from a lonely old age.

DAWN O'HARA

Dicks, Digits, Dildos

Penises. Vibrators, dildos, tongues, even pens in my hungry youth. Fingers—mine, men's, rubber-gloved doctors', and one fumbling young girl's before boys occurred to me. Spermicides, sponges, diaphragms, condoms, lubricants. Seven-day yeast infection treatments—they didn't used to have the quick and tidy fixes they do now. Acidophilus tablets, vinegar douches, progesterone creams. Chocolate syrup. Tampons I could never tolerate: They just never felt as good as in those horseback-riding ads. Two miscarriages. Thermometers when we were still trying for kids. A quack regime of herbal vagi-packs during my holistic phase. Four-hundred ninety-two periods. Sixty-seven speculums. Forty-three pap smears. One cryosurgery. One hysterosalpingogram, as difficult to tolerate as it is to pronounce. Two biopsies. Eleven ultrasound wands. And this particular cock, my husband's, 4,682 times. I'm sure I've left some things out. At my age I have a hard time keeping track of what's trespassed between my legs.

You'd think all this would have earned me some loyalty. After seeing it through so much—the ups and downs of a lifetime, so to speak—my vagina picks a hell of a time to betray me. It's our thirty-first anniversary. And we've never had an anniversary without nooky. But I'm dry as a dead insect stuck in the lampshade. Parking lot closed for business, neon sign flashing, parking arm down, tires will be slashed if you enter the wrong way.

There I am, spread-legged while my husband hunts around in his softening state like a worm lost at the edge of a leaf. Not that he was rock-hard to begin with. Instantaneous erections only happen in the mornings, now.

Never mind the lubricant. I feel fragile, that I will rip and tear if he succeeds in his coaxing entry—like my grandmother's transparent skin, bruised by a whispered touch. Even my husband's soft cock feels angry against my desert tenderness.

You'd think there would be nothing left to shame me. This man has seen my flesh jiggle in every possible sexual position over the course of thirty years. I'm twenty pounds heavier than on our wedding day, when I foolishly starved myself into a dress I couldn't fit into two days later. Once, in the emergency room, he stood behind the doctor as the speculum was tightened. "The cervix," the doctor announced with a flourish of his gloved hand, as if he had created its hidden wink. "Wow," was all my husband said.

I have been inadequate in producing the requisite children. Deficient in jeans size, cooking skills, apologies, and in-law relations. I got over all that and concentrated on blowjobs and yoga stretches instead. You think my husband minded unmatched towel sets and shopping without coupons?

But feeling sexually inadequate after all these years, when the lack of children gave us space for sexuality that so many couples don't have? When is my body going to cut me a break?

Fourteen years ago, reaching for the box of tissues to wipe up (he, always solicitous, tucks a tissue between my legs before he tends to himself), our hearts still pounding, my husband looked at the clock. "It takes us half an hour now. Used to be twelve minutes." Oh, we laughed at that one. But there's nothing funny about not being able to do *it* at all.

My vagina is a hand-puppet with nothing to say. I am the mouth of a rolled-up sock, crusty and used, discovered with mothballs under the bed. No O'Keeffe flower, but a cracked lobster claw. The Star Trek alert sirens go off all around us: *Frigid vagina alert! Menopause approaching at warp speed!* I beam myself out of the room, after first meditating on dinner choices and considering the feng shui ramifications of our bed placement and wall color. Intense concentration has earned me many orgasms in the past, but I don't want to think about what's happening down there, my husband the spelunker rooting around for the opening of a collapsed cave. Think I'll get him one of those head lamps for Christmas. At the moment I wish ole Columbus would give up, abandon the exploration as a lost cause so that I can return to my flower bulbs.

He knows I've vacated the continent. I've got the same look as the one I wear when I'm naked on the scale. As on the first day of my period, when I don't want him to watch me dress, feeling like I've tripled in body size. Not a hostile look, like when he crawls into bed with cigar farts or enters halfway through a five-hankie TV movie and snorts at the obvious stupidity of the characters. It's the "Stay Off My Planet" look.

"Never mind," he says, rolling off me. "I have an idea. Something new."

After one-third of a century together, what else can be tried? Creative positions have gotten trickier with the need for glucosamine supplements. I could tell you what we've done on every stick of furniture in the house, but lately we stick to the basic bedroom standbys.

He fumbles around in the special dresser drawer, his thwarted pecker dangling below his belly flab. I admire his ease. Orgasms never elude him. Unexpectedly flaccid states don't disturb him. His confidence remains firmly rooted in his slightly above-average cock size (he's measured), and nothing seems to shake it. Not weight gain, hair loss, or below-average height. Even when he wore a dress a couple of times, his penis was *present* in his attitude. He never tires of my watching him, no matter which end of a diet he's on.

But now he turns away from me. "I got us a present," he says.

This current dilemma hasn't blindsided us out of the blue. My body's been working its way up to emergency drought levels for months, but I've ignored the signals and haven't practiced water rationing. I have procrastinated the doctor's visit, dreading the prognosis and resultant pills—but it now appears that *he's* been taking some preventative measures.

"I thought we said no presents this year." After three decades together, we buy for ourselves when the mood suits us. No more dropping months-long hints that the other one never gets.

"No, *you* said no presents this year."

There is a great deal of rustling going on. He's dropped down to the floor, so that I can't see him over the side of the bed. I even hear him giggle. A fifty-four-year-old man, giggling! I giggle in response. We're a pair that way, like pizza and acid reflux.

He stands and faces me. "Tah-dah!"

He has strapped a miniature dildo to his leg. A little Bacchus sprouting from Zeus's thigh. It is lifelike in shape and color, as if his cock has reproduced, a tiny silicone replica of the real thing.

He climbs onto the bed next to me. "Come on. There's more holes here than just one."

"You're gonna fuck my ear?" Fifties kids, we still love the thrill of foul language. Not during sex, but as part of our banter. "Wanna fuck?" we say. Or, with his midwestern lack of verbs, "I need fucked."

"No. Your nostril. Now open wide."

I flare my nostrils, one of the few small-muscle movements I can manage. He can wiggle his nose like a rabbit, but when I try it, my whole face contorts.

He wags Bacchus in my face. I swat him away, laughing.

I know what his intentions are. And he's incorrect. This isn't something new. Although I rarely let a chance go by to point out that he's wrong, since it's maddeningly infrequent, I keep my mouth shut. But we *have* tried anal sex before. Years ago. Before the twelve-minute era came to an end. We tried it only once, just for kicks during my Dickens phase, when I learned that at that time anal sex was the preferred method of "birth control." The literary experiment didn't work out, and we never attempted the back door method again. I never saw the need while my other hole was cooperating.

He lies beside me, his hand on my chest. My breasts have always fit perfectly into his palms. "I got a really small one, just for you," he says. "I remember that the last time it hurt."

So, he *does* remember.

"Come on." He nudges me to roll over. I sigh and roll my eyes, but comply. He rubs oil between his hands and massages my back. He sits back on his haunches, and Bacchus tickles my left buttock.

"Watch the armpits!" You'd think after spending more than half a life with me he'd have memorized the ticklish spots, which encompass most of my body, and tread a fine line with my erogenous zones.

"Yeah, dummy," Bacchus pipes up in a high-pitched, nasal tone. Inanimate objects in our house have developed voices over the years, usually in falsetto, facilitating our highly evolved and effective means of dysfunctional communication. It is best during an argument to have a third party to blame, especially when the object has no vocal cords and cannot defend itself. We attribute the long-term success of our marriage to this system, though the African violet resents taking the heat for eating the last cookie, or for certain foul odors permeating the room.

"Sorry."

He skims his hands up and down my spine, across my tush. I begin to relax. I'm warm and expansive. I am an O'Keeffe blossom under the New Mexico sun, splashed on the bed in purple and pink hues.

He spreads me, and I let him. I know that my ripe and rippled derriere will never make a magazine photo spread, but I also know that these cheeks look good to him. He slips inside, a centimeter at a time. It's not difficult at all this time, like the last time we tried it in the prehistoric age of our careless youth. Maybe it's because of Bacchus's minute size, or the lubricant, or our ability to work together, or that my lifelong lover has learned patience and self-denial. Whatever the reasons, I moan. I let him enjoy pleasuring me while he receives no physical gratification in return, only the sensation of giving. His real cock dangles and knocks against my lower back as he moves, right above my birthmark. His leg hair prickles my bum.

He can't tell what my vadge is up to, but I'm well aware of the state of his cock. It rapidly returns to its instant fossilized state of youth. He stabs my birthmark now with each gentle thrust inside me. My vagina stretches, yawns, and blinks, discovering that her coveted spot in the hierarchy has been usurped. Worse, the instigator is not even a member of the immediate household, but a Lilliputian godhead. Jealous, she puts up a fuss, causing a commotion between my legs. She even resorts to calling in the reserves, and my clitoris joins the clamor.

"I think Bacchus needs some air," I say over my shoulder.

My husband—this lifelong friend and lover who knows me better than anyone and yet doesn't know me at all—rolls off and lies beside me. He gazes at me, not expecting anything, though his Big and Little Dippers demand otherwise. He plays with my hair. For years he looked forward to its turning gray, saying with a wink that he wanted to sleep with an older woman. I know that in his rich inner life I've often been the siren schoolmarm seducing his helpless virginity, so I've never wrestled with hair dyes, despite the random streaks through the still-shiny black.

Then I'm on top of him, our puzzle pieces connect, and my body swallows him in one easy gulp.

Bacchus taps my rump, as if to say, *Hey, did you forget about me?* But he doesn't say a word.

LUCINDA EBERSOLE

The Art of Losing

I saw it happen. She had just stepped off the curb to cross the street to her apartment, which is only four blocks from my apartment, but mine is on Third Avenue, not Park. A taxi rushing for a fare knocked her down. He wasn't even from America, and he didn't even know her—just thought it was any old lady you might run down. She is the greatest actress that I have ever seen. The slightest movement of her hand can bring tears to my eyes, and some idiot who knows nothing of theater runs her down.

I held her hand as we waited for the ambulance. Caressed the finger that bears the stain of writing with a fountain pen. We are both left-handed. I believe I have seen you, she says, and I nod. She doesn't know my name, but we both shop in all the right places. I give her my card with the number written in black ink on the back. As they lift her into the ambulance, someone in the crowd says she must be eighty by now. She is seventy-four, forty years to the day older than I am. I know we have the same birthday, because someone once sent me a birthday card with a list of famous people who shared my birthday, and she and I were both born on March 3rd. We are Pisces. Many actors are Pisces.

Once, in the liquor store on Park Avenue, I was buying a single bottle of champagne for my birthday and she noticed. Krug is her favorite champagne too, but she buys it in cases. It is my birthday, I said. It is *my* birthday, she said. And we laughed. The wrinkles around her eyes seemed to multiply, engulfing her face. The fine lines around her mouth betray the fact that she once smoked, but she stopped after the cancer, she told the *New Yorker*.

The card that I gave her when they put her in the ambulance was engraved at the same stationer she uses. Their window is filled with samples of their work. Her stationery is a pale blue. Engraved. I wouldn't have thought that of her. White or ecru. She may have been Lady Macbeth or Medea on the stage, but offstage she is poised and conservative. She still writes with a fountain pen. Mont Blanc. I have the same pen, with a fine point. I do not know what point she uses, but my guess is fine. She has delicate hands that seem to move in slow motion. I have paid special attention to her hands in all of her movies. Sometimes, I will watch a movie on the VCR and freeze the frame on her hands. I could watch them, immobile for hours.

The *New York Times* says the next day that she is crippled, but it is untrue. The woman in the household boutique has spoken to her. She was badly shaken and the doctor wants her to use a wheelchair for a while. She is spending a lot of time in bed and so she has ordered new sets of Porthault sheets. She gets the plain ones. The ones that cost $1,500 a set. Simple, white linen. I chat with the woman at the store and buy an elegant silver frame; there is a picture of her in it. A picture from the '50s, when her hair was dark and windswept.

Our favorite used bookshop is closed because of illness. We buy a great deal of poetry. Once, when we were there together, she pulled down a copy of *The Complete Poems of Elizabeth Bishop*. The first complete poems of Elizabeth Bishop in the blue and yellow and white dust jacket, not the later complete poems with the watercolor on the front. She pulled down the volume marked $100 and said to no one, Elizabeth would be quite amused. I said to no one, I think of her every time I open my box of Crane's stationery. We both know that Elizabeth Bishop and Louise Crane were lovers.

Now that she is no longer mobile, she will be needing a secretary to help her out. I am waiting for her to remember the card with my name engraved on the white Crane's paper. I know that she will call me because we are the same. She will run her finger over my engraved name and flip the card over to find my number in a fine black ink.

She will call me and beg me to be her secretary. She will say she has lost the ability to walk, she has lost all hope, and I will say the art of losing isn't hard to master. I will make her laugh. We will discuss the fact that in the last few years of her life, Elizabeth Bishop took young lovers and made them secretaries. They were to call her Miss Bishop in public. But what did they call her in private? Those early afternoons, when the vodka bottle was close to full and she could still navigate the bed? When she forced open their knees, when she thought of Lota, when they made her tremble, did they still call her Miss Bishop?

When I am her secretary, we will have Krug every afternoon. She will sit in her wheelchair by her bed and peel an orange, the tender rind giving way under the pressure of her long fingers. I will set the Baccarat flutes on her nightstand and fetch the cold bottle. As I unwind the wire encasing the cork, I will remember the danger of the pressure of the cork. I'll get a tea towel, I say. Never mind, she will say, as she slides her hands oily with oranges under my black sweater, peeling it from my body. She will hold it out to me on the finger stained with ink. I will open the champagne, the cork exploding into my cashmere heart.

After several glasses of Krug as the humming of the Baccarat grows silent, I will rest my knees on the outermost corners of the wheelchair, leaning into her, arms supporting my weight as her orange fingers slide inside me, one after one until they are gone. I will whisper in her ear, I can make you this wet, and she will laugh a low, deep laugh. After a time, I will lay her on the bed, on the Porthault linen, and promise her that it is like riding a bicycle.

I will run my tongue inside her. She will tousle my hair and tell me that she hasn't been wet in years. Not since she was sixty-seven and receiving a presidential medal because everyone thought that the cancer would take her. She will tell me the truth about the story that has always been rumor. How she excused herself from the dinner party at the Kennedy Center to go to the ladies room. How the actress who thought that she would play Evita in the movie, and who wore her platinum hair slicked back so that the director would think she looked the part, offered her some cocaine. She will tell me of the numbness and the bliss as Evita knelt on the tile floor. She will tell me that three days later, as the anesthetic for the operation took effect, she thought not of death but of the *petite mort.* She will tell me that she never thought of implants or prostheses. The scar made her an Amazon.

It's no use, she will say, as my fingers caress her. She will tell me of the time that Eva Le Gallienne courted her. The play ran for 126 days. Each day she received a single yellow rose from Le Gallienne. On the night the play closed, she walked home, twirling the rose. She heard footsteps following her. Saw the man in the wing tips and fedora. A wrong turn placed her in an alley with the man beside her. Before she could scream, Eva Le Gallienne tipped her hat and offered up a final yellow rose. Beside the dumpster overflowing with rotten bananas, Le Gallienne went down on her. To this day, she will tell me, she is fond of rotten bananas.

You are so very persistent, she will say as my tongue moves up and down. Once I was Juliet. We rehearsed for two weeks before we found out that the actor who was cast as Mercutio was a woman. Each night the clicking of the foils as she fought to her death made me wet. After taking the poison from Friar Laurence as I waited for Romeo, Mercutio would take me. Her tongue made the same click as her foil.

And she will come in my mouth hard and fast, coating the back of my throat like Mercutio's, like Eva Le

Gallienne's, and even like Evita's. I will crawl up beside her on the wet Porthault sheets and lay my head on her shoulder. She will reward me with a single slice of orange. I will bite into it and the juice will run down my cheek and onto her chest where it will follow the fault line of the scar that made her an Amazon warrior. It will happen. It will happen when she runs her finger across my engraved name, when she smells the acid of the Mont Blanc ink, when she remembers the single bottle of Krug for my birthday, her birthday. She will know that we are the same fishes, and she will swim after me deeper and deeper into the effervescent water, losing herself in me because the art of losing isn't hard to master.

About the Authors

JOLI AGNEW's work has appeared in *Amoret, Gay Black Female Magazine*, Hoterotica.com, *KUMA*, LadiesWeb.net, *Prometheus,* and *suspect thoughts.* As Jenesi Ash she writes erotica as well, and was published in the first *Best Women's Erotica.*

SALLY BELLEROSE received a Creative Writing Fellowship in Prose from the National Endowment for the Arts to write a novel, *The Girls Club*. Her work has been published in numerous anthologies and literary journals. Her prose was chosen as finalist for the Thomas Wolfe Fiction Prize in 1998, the James Jones First Novel Fellowship in 1999, and the Bellwether Prize in Support of a Literature of Social Change in 2000. She is working on a novel titled *Legs Cheyenne.*

BERTICE BERRY is the author of two novels, *Redemption Song* and *The Haunting of Hip Hop,* and four works of nonfiction. She holds a Ph.D. in sociology, is a former stand-up comedian, and lives in Southern California where she is raising her sister's three children. Her fiction appears in *Best Black Women's Erotica* (Cleis Press). She is working on her third novel.

LUCINDA EBERSOLE is the author of the novel *Death in Equality* and the editor of *Mondo Barbie.*

LAURA FEDERICO is a freelance journalist, web writer, copywriter, nightclub publicist, and fiction writer. Her erotic fiction has appeared in *Virgin Territory, Bad Attitude, Doing It for Daddy,* and *Best of On Our Backs.* She is a regular contributor to *Girlfriends* magazine and *San Francisco Spectrum.*

GILLIAN FITZGERALD has had her fantasy stories included in *Dragon, S&F,* and several anthologies, including *Year's Best.* Her erotic tales have appeared in *Australian Women's Forum* and *Prometheus.* Formerly a teacher and librarian, she is now a full-time writer, residing in Maine with her husband and four cats.

JAMIE JOY GATTO is a bisexual activist in New Orleans. She is editor-in-chief of MindCaviar (www.mindcaviar.com). Her erotic work is included in *Best Bisexual Erotica 1* and 2, *Best SM Erotica*, *Guilty Pleasures*, and dozens of other anthologies. She has authored *Sex Noir* (Circlet 2002), *Suddenly Sexy: Erotic Flash Fiction* (Brilliant Smut Press 2001), and a chapbook of prose and poetry, *Unveiling Venus*.

RACHEL HEATH has been published in *A Movement of Eros: 25 Years of Lesbian Erotica, On Our Backs, The Spanke Shoppe, Stand Corrected Jr.,* and *Bad Attitude.* She enjoys lying in bed, listening to the radio, and reading—among other things.

DEBRA HYDE awaits the new home menopausal testing kit so that she can see just how peri-menopausal she is. Hot flashes haven't stopped her from writing erotic fiction, the most recent of which appears in *Body Check* (Alyson Publications), *Herotica 7* (forthcoming from Down There Press), and *Erotic Travel Tales* (Cleis Press).

EMMA KAUFMANN slaved away until recently in London's art world by day and observed its fetish subculture—the inspiration for many of her short stories—by night. Strange and unexpected circumstances led to a move to Baltimore where she now lives. For more about her novels and short stories go to www.emmakaufmann.net.

HELEN E. H. MADDEN is a writer and graphic artist living in Virginia. Her creations include *Xena Warrior Milkmaid* (www.warriormilkmaid.com) and other cartoons for the Web. When she's not working on websites or writing erotic fiction, she can often be found researching her stories with her loving husband, Michael.

PAIGE MATTHEWS decided in middle age to retire not only her pussy, but also her typing fingers, people she doesn't like, and doing anything she doesn't *want* to do. As a result, she has few friends and no lovers and is about to become homeless. She is, however, extremely happy.

JOANNE MILLER has written and published nonfiction and fiction since 1990, and was a runner-up for the Raymond Carver Short Story Award in 2000. She is working on her second novel and is always on time.

MARY ANNE MOHANRAJ (www.mamohanraj.com) is the author of *Torn Shapes of Desire*, editor of *Aqua Erotica*, and consulting editor for *Herotica 7,* and has been published in a multitude of anthologies and magazines. She founded the erotic webzine Clean Sheets (www.cleansheets.com) and is editor-in-chief for another webzine, Strange Horizons (www.strangehorizons.com). She is editing *Bodies of Water*, a waterproof book, forthcoming in summer 2002, and is a doctoral student in Fiction/Literature at the University of Utah.

DAWN O'HARA's closet is stuffed with dirty stories, but she maintains that her only real perversion is writing them down. Her work is included in *Shameless: An Intimate Erotica* anthology. Her alternate personalities, of which there are many, have been published in *Calyx* journal and on *MindCaviar.com*. Contact her at dawno_hara@hotmail.com.

JEAN ROBERTA is a woman of a certain age who teaches first-year English classes to new recruits in a Canadian prairie university and embarrasses her friends and relatives by writing erotica. Her stories have appeared in various anthologies, magazines, and e-zines.

TERESA NOELLE ROBERTS is a fiction writer, poet, and Middle Eastern dancer. Her works have most recently appeared in *Stars Inside Her* (Circlet Press) and *Such a Pretty Face* (Meisha Merlin Press), as well as in other anthologies and literary magazines. She is involved with the Society for Creative Anachronism.

SUSAN ST. AUBIN, proving that life begins at 40, published her first erotic story in *Yellow Silk* in 1984. Since then, her work has appeared in the *Herotica* series, *Best American Erotica* (1995 and 2000), *Best Women's Erotica* (2000 and 2002), *Best Lesbian Erotica* (2001), and several other periodicals and anthologies.

LANA GAIL TAYLOR's stories have appeared in *Playgirl* and in *Best Bisexual Women's Erotica* and *Bedroom Eyes: Lesbians in the Boudoir*. Her erotic stories have also appeared in *Dare for Women* and *Brilliant Smut*. She lives in Colorado with her son, a cat, and piles and piles of books.

DOROTHY B. TYLER, retired from more jobs than her three children ever believe, lives and works in obscurity in Michigan. She has been a lawyer, a waitress, an Air Force officer, a high school teacher, and a nude model—and those are just the jobs she *brags* about. Her first novel, *Memories of a Mother,* should be available by early 2002. She is testing the waters for yet another career change.

JANE UNDERWOOD is a teacher, writer, and editor who has been publishing poetry, prose, articles, and essays for more than thirty years. Her erotica has appeared in several periodicals and anthologies. She is also the founder and director of the Writing Salon, a school of creative writing in San Francisco (www.writingsalons.com).

ERIN CRESSSIDA WILSON is a critically acclaimed and internationally produced playwright and screenwriter. She has been honored by the National Endowment for the Arts, the Rockefeller Foundation, and the California Arts Council. Her plays are published by Smith & Kraus. She is coauthor of *The Erotica Project* (Cleis Press).

KRISTINA WRIGHT is a full-time writer and an award-winning romance novelist. Her erotic fiction has appeared in *Best Women's Erotica 2000, Sweet Life: Erotic Fantasies for Couples, Best Lesbian Erotica 2002,* and *Good Vibrations* magazine, among others. She lives in Virginia with her husband, surrounded by pets and books.

About the Editor

MARCY SHEINER is editor of the *Best Women's Erotica* series and *The Oy of Sex: Jewish Women's Erotica* (Cleis Press). She is editor of *Herotica 4, 5, 6,* and *7* (Plume; Down There Press). Her stories and essays have appeared in many anthologies and publications. She is also the author of *Sex for the Clueless* (Kensington Press) and *Perfectly Normal*, a memoir of raising a child with a disability, available at iUniverse.com. Her website is www.marcysheiner.tripod.com.